Acclaim for

"Melissa Ferguson is a sparkling new voice in contemporary rom-com. Though her novel tackles meaningful struggles—social work, child abandonment, adoption—it's also fresh, flirty, and laugh-out-loud funny. Ferguson is going to win fans with this one!"

—Lauren Denton, bestselling author of *The Hideaway* and *Glory Road*, on *The Dating Charade*

"*The Dating Charade* will keep you smiling the entire read. Ferguson not only delights us with new love, with all its attendant mishaps and misunderstandings, but she takes us deeper in the hearts and minds of vulnerable children as Cassie and Jett work out their families—then their dating lives. An absolute treat!"

—Katherine Reay, bestselling author of *The Printed Letter Bookshop*

"*The Dating Charade* is hilarious and heartwarming with characters you truly care about, super fun plot twists and turns, snappy prose, and a sweet romance you're rooting for. Anyone who has children in their lives will particularly relate to Ferguson's laugh-out-loud take on the wild ride that is parenting. I thoroughly enjoyed this story!"

—Rachel Linden, bestselling author of *The Enlightenment of Bees*

"A heartwarming charmer."

—Sheila Roberts, *USA TODAY* bestselling author of the Moonlight Harbor series, on *The Dating Charade*

"A jolt of energy featuring one of the most unique romantic hooks I have ever read. Personality and zest shine through Ferguson's evident enjoyment at crafting high jinks and misadventures as two people slowly make way for love in the midst of major life upheaval. A marvelous treaty on unexpected grace and its life-changing chaos, Cassie and Jett find beautiful vulnerability in redefining what it means to live happily-ever-after."

—RACHEL MCMILLAN, AUTHOR OF THE THREE QUARTER TIME SERIES, ON *THE DATING CHARADE*

"Ferguson delivers a stellar debut. *The Dating Charade* is a fun, romantic albeit challenging look at just what it takes to fall in love and be a family. You'll think of these characters long after the final page."

—RACHEL HAUCK, *NEW YORK TIMES* BESTSELLING AUTHOR OF *THE WEDDING DRESS*

The Dating Charade

The Dating Charade

a novel

MELISSA FERGUSON

THOMAS NELSON
Since 1798

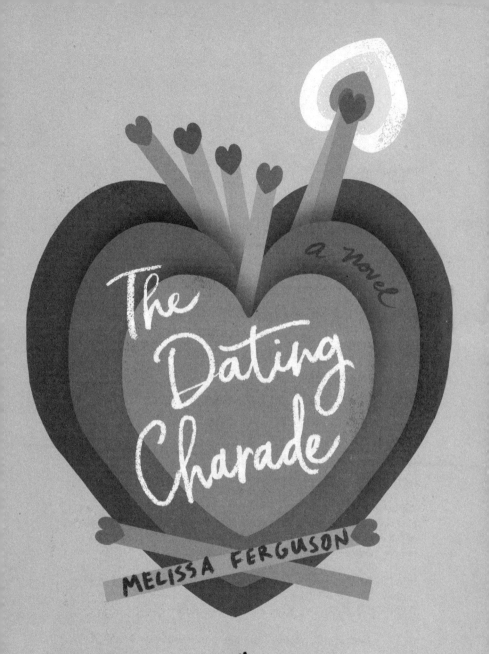

The Dating Charade

Published in Nashville, Tennessee, by Thomas Nelson. Thomas Nelson is a registered trademark of HarperCollins Christian Publishing, Inc.

Published in association with Hartline Literary Agency, Pittsburgh, PA 15235.

Author photos by Taylor Meo Photography.

Thomas Nelson titles may be purchased in bulk for educational, business, fund-raising, or sales promotional use. For information, please e-mail SpecialMarkets@ThomasNelson.com.

Publisher's Note: This novel is a work of fiction. Names, characters, places, and incidents are either products of the author's imagination or used fictitiously. All characters are fictional, and any similarity to people living or dead is purely coincidental.

ISBN 978-0-7852-3100-4 (trade paper)
ISBN 978-0-7852-3101-1 (e-book)
ISBN 978-0-7852-3102-8 (downloadable audio)

Library of Congress Cataloging-in-Publication Data

CIP data is available upon request.

Printed in the United States of America

20 21 22 23 LSC 10 9 8 7 6 5 4 3

To my husband and three little minions,
Isaiah, Joy, and Gracie,
for the wealth of real-life stories

Cassie

If one was going to dip one's toes into the murky, pestilential waters of online dating, an escape plan was critical.

Fake emergencies worked on occasion. You know, the gasp as you take a "phone call" and dash out the door to an imaginary emergency with an imaginary friend. But in general, Cassie found the method too cliché and utterly devoid of, well, imagination. Besides, whenever she needed to make a hasty exit, her dates usually saw through such tricks.

It'd taken months to create the perfect escape plan. Months of trial and error, of late nights scribbling elaborate routes under lamplight, of miniscule alterations schemed up with her most devious of friends.

But here, watching the stingrays circling the scuba diver in the aquarium glass behind her date, she knew she'd finally done it. Her plan was positively, utterly airtight.

"Married, you ask?" He cocked his head to one side as though the question actually required mental searching. His thin lips pressed together, resembling the fish floating behind his head.

"Yes. Are you married?" Cassie's eyes ticked to the culprit: the ring finger on his left hand. The tan line was minimal, almost nonexistent. His nails were clean, and in Cassie's mind nothing good ever came from a man with immaculate hands. And yet even if her eyes had wronged her on those matters, there was no getting around the slight indention where a band would be and the slightest puff of the skin between ring area and knuckle.

Two minutes. After a year of online dating, she'd developed the ability to spot a rat in under two minutes. That deserved some sort of recognition.

His hand swiftly dropped from the glass just as hers lifted to discreetly tap it twice.

Escape plan in motion.

"Technically . . . yes. But it's more complicated than you think." He laughed good-naturedly as he scratched the back of his head with his pristine hand.

She didn't smile in return.

His smile slipped down with his arm. "Surely you didn't expect me to drop something like this in the first five minutes, Cassandra—"

"Cassie."

"I was going to tell you. But I just couldn't live with

myself if I scared you off right away. Not someone—" He paused momentously, two fingers drawn to his lips. "—like you."

Ah, there it was. The date had moved into stage 2: overly sentimental compliments wrapped in false humility.

Cassie shifted her jacket to her other arm. Right. Here it came. "Because of our energy."

"*Yes*." He bobbed his head like the baby Groot sitting on her desk at work. "It's kinetic. The way I've been able to open up to you these past few weeks . . ."

Six days. Via e-mail. On topics as deep and moving as the Yorkshire terrier in his profile picture.

Cassie pinched her face into a quiet, patient smile, letting the man go on with his excuses.

She knew she appeared complacent standing beside the floor-to-ceiling glass of Ripley's Aquarium of the Smokies, her gaze on him and yet attentive to her periphery. Echoes of excitement bounced around them as a massive blacktip reef shark slid across the wall. Children in dripping overcoats and galoshes stood on toes and pointed. Since the start of Thanksgiving break, the aquarium had been more crowded than ever.

But crowded was good. Crowded was ideal. The aquarium's ample noontime distractions were key factors in why she always chose her best friend's workplace to meet, greet, and ultimately sprint as fast as she could away from men. A restaurant? Facing your foe at a candlelit table for two? Fleeing from there mid-date would be the real challenge.

She slid her eyes to the glass, relieved to see Bree, her best friend, her quintessential partner in crime, kicking her fins their way. Parting a group of yellowtail fish, Bree halted directly behind her date.

His back touched the glass as he faced Cassie completely. “Why don’t we get out of here and find someplace quiet to talk? I know of a great little lunch place that just opened up on Newman—”

The sudden bang on the glass jolted him, halting his monologue. Startled, he turned around to find the scuba diver, all six foot two of her, shaking a gloved fist at him.

She banged again. Every face in the room turned from the glowing ultramarine tank to him.

“Do you know her?” Cassie raised an eyebrow as she took a step back.

“I’ve—I’ve never seen her before in my life.” He squinted, clearly trying to see beyond the long floating braid, mask, mouthpiece, and BCD vest to the woman underneath.

Bree banged a third time.

Then, at last, she began the incomprehensible—and, it should be noted, utterly meaningless—show of charades. To the innocent onlooker, it looked positively seething.

“You sure? Old girlfriend, perhaps? Did your wife take up diving?”

“No, I . . .” His eyes were glued to the glass, his neck reddening to match his thin polyester collar.

But Cassie was already melting into the crowd of onlookers, sharks, and spotted eagle rays. Her eyes never left his now babbling form as she moved backward like a chessboard knight, slipping around parents and kids and disappearing before he’d even realize she’d gone. At the private, staff-only door, she gave Bree a salute and slipped through it.

Married.

Both her smile and energy melted as she shut the door and leaned against it. For a brief moment she let the slime of the date slip off her, imagining it oozing down her mulberry velvet skirt and knee-high boots to the water drain in the middle of the floor.

Married.

To be honest, she'd really hoped for good things with this one. He was educated, good looking. His pictures avoided posing with toilets in the background. His interests followed the same strain as hers: running, cooking, festive gatherings with friends. He even claimed to volunteer with the residential kids at Wears Valley Ranch. She'd been particularly interested in talking with him about that one.

But what had happened? Where was she now? Back in her trusty panic room beside a rack of wetsuits, cleaning tanks, and a bucket of squeegees.

Cassie let herself indulge in one more minute of pity partying before kicking off the wall and heading for the exit door. Gold and persimmon maple leaves danced around her boots as she stepped around the backside of the building to her car. She dropped her purse into the passenger seat and, with the engine humming, sorted through her choices for the suddenly free hour. It didn't take long before she shifted her car into Reverse.

Back to work it was.

Eight minutes and twenty-three seconds later, she pulled into her parking spot with its rusted sign: *Crazy Boss Parks Here: All Other Cars Will Be Sold on the Black Market.* (Sure, she probably shouldn't have kept the sign the Haven girls gave her a handful of years ago—encouraging delinquent behavior and all that. Still, it made her smile.)

Two large pots of orange mums sat on either side of the otherwise dull entrance to Girls Haven. It was a typical government building: all sharp brick corners and long-paned windows. The cobwebs adorning said windows were about as permanent as the emotionless beige paint on the inside walls—and not for Cassie's lack of trying. She'd vacuumed the webs from her office window at least five hundred times in the seven years she'd been director at the center for disadvantaged girls. As punishment for unruly moments, girls had been guided to her office window with a vacuum and bleach bottle more times than she could count. And yet somehow the webs always grew back overnight, wafting in the breeze as if laughing each morning at her return.

"What're you doing back already, Miss C?" Star's Chucks rhythmically slapped the brick wall she sat on, her feet swinging as she watched Cassie ascend the concrete steps. "Don't tell me. You got another flake."

"Oh, quite the contrary," Cassie replied, reaching the top step. "I'd say he was *quite* keen. Maybe by our third date he would've had all three of us out for dinner—him, me, *and* his wife."

"Hey, at least you would've made it to a third date." Star laughed, then dropped off the wall. Pausing, she looked Cassie up and down, then rested her fist resolutely on her hip with all the sass a fourteen-year-old could give. "You know what, Miss C? You're too picky."

Cassie gave a blunt laugh. "Is that so?"

"And I think it's about time you let us girls have a shot at finding you a man." The wind picked up, making the beads at the end of her dreadlocked ponytail clatter together. "Because let's admit it: you're cute, but you're not getting any younger."

"Cute but not getting any younger. How did you know *exactly* what I needed to hear today?" Cassie smiled, her eyes catching a glimpse of the rows of fire trucks parked across the street.

At least once a month someone asked if she was married. Had kids. Once she was asked if she had grandkids. She was just thirty-three. But anyone age twenty-five or older was the same to these girls—lumped into a giant bag labeled "ancient."

"Nice 'do." Cassie took in Star's new locks. A silvery blue string weaved through it, all the way down to the bare, bony shoulders Star was sporting in thirty-degree weather. "You do it last night?"

"Yeah."

Cassie looked closer, and her smile faded as her antenna rose.

Star stepped back, slipping the craftily spun lock through her fingers.

It looked good. Too good. "You do it yourself?"

Star's eyes darted to Cassie's boots, then the mums, before finally resting on the basketball hoop on the aged concrete pad beside the building. "No."

Cassie crossed her arms. Waited.

Seven years on the job at Girls Haven, and she was a master of the teenage standoff. People from nonprofits around the nation sought her advice and expertise on the teenage standoff. She practically led conference workshops on the teenage standoff.

Finally, as though the words had been extracted by pliers, Star spoke. "Ershanna did it."

Cassie's lips pursed. The times Star let anyone experiment with her hair were few and far between. Whenever she showed up with something worth keeping, you could bet a dime it was because Ershanna had taken her in. And the only time the nineteen-year-old, barely-an-adult-herself neighbor took Star and her sisters in was because something bad had happened at home.

"Why didn't you call me?" It was difficult to execute a perfectly even, calm tone.

"Because it wasn't a big deal." Star leaned against the brick, her eyes on the parents toting their kids across the Dollar General parking lot. A taut banner hung between two fire engines: *Touch a Truck, 12–2 p.m.* "Nothing worth calling about."

"Then *why* were you at Ershanna's? Because we both know it wasn't to do homework."

Star wrapped her arms tightly around her chest.

Cassie shrugged, tucking her arms around her own chest, protecting her fingers as they pressed between the layers of thickly quilted down. "Fine. I can wait out here all day. And, Crazy Girl in a Tank Top, let's remember I'm the one who dressed for winter."

Star shifted her weight from one hip to another. Seemed to fight a shiver with another frostbitten breeze. "Antony just came back. I didn't want to get into it, so—" She shrugged. "I left."

At that, both Cassie's breath and fight fled. The last gift Star and her sisters should be getting for the holidays was a crusty, sporadically violent, drug-abusive stepdad back in their living room. Cassie would know; she'd been around for the sorry details the last time he landed in jail. "Last I checked, he wasn't allowed to be in the same three-hundred-foot radius as you. Or your sisters."

Star laughed without smiling. "Yeah, well, last I checked, he wasn't much into playing by the rules."

"Let me make some calls. You can stay with me tonight—"

"No, don't do that," Star said quickly. "He said he's moving on this week. We're staying with Ershanna until he goes." Star paused, then pointed a finger at her. "I'm calling confidentiality on this, Miss C. You can't tell. You'd only make it worse."

"I think we should—"

Star glared.

"But—"

Star glared harder.

Cassie clenched her jaw. "*Fine.*"

Star nodded and put her finger back into her jeans pocket as though holstering it. Then she involuntarily quaked in the cold.

Cassie put an arm around the girl's shoulder. "But I *do* want to hear that he's gone by Sunday, all right? I'm going to be blowing up your phone the next few days until you confirm that."

"Yeah. I know. I already blocked your number." Star gave a mild smile beneath Cassie's downy wing, and together they spun toward the double doors.

A blast of hot air greeted them from the radiator. The entrance hall was empty, only a few voices coming from the game room. It wasn't surprising. Girls Haven always emptied out during the holidays. Those who showed up did so because they either had no other option or were loyal to the Haven. Star, the special case, came for both.

Together they walked down the hall. It smelled of bleach and microwaved popcorn. To be fair, it *always* smelled of bleach and microwaved popcorn.

"So? What'd'ya say?" At the last second Star slipped past Cassie into her office and dropped into Cassie's rolling chair. She spun it in a circle before putting her hands on the keyboard.

Cassie slung her purse onto the hook behind the door. "What do I say to what? You being in my seat? Move."

A gleeful scream echoed down the hall, and a second later a girl grabbed the door frame like a life raft before two others popped up behind her. Whatever game they'd been playing was swiftly abandoned, the girls lured in by the sight and sound of fresh gossip.

"What are ya doin'?" A suspicious tone lilted Bailey's voice as she pushed her hair from her eyes and strolled in.

"We're setting Miss C up on hotornot.com," Star replied.

Cassie raised her voice. "It's *not* hotornot.com," she said, nudging Star out of her chair.

Still, in a matter of seconds the girls crouched around Cassie and the computer, breathing the same twelve inches of air despite the two hundred square feet of unoccupied, perfectly good office space. Through the window, flakes started to dust the road as a song played from one of the girl's phones. Cassie couldn't hear the words but recognized the unsavory tune enough to double tap an icon on her desktop. Sinatra's "You Make Me Feel So Young" filled the room.

All four girls moaned.

Cam spoke, the song from her phone still playing somewhere within her cheetah-print jeggings. "This song definitely *doesn't* make me feel so young. I feel a hundred and five listening to this cra—"

"Crazy awesome mix, Miss C," Star said. She threw two thumbs up. "It's downright inspirational."

Cassie rolled her eyes. Clearly Star was more interested in spending the next hour searching for suitors than listening to another of Cassie's soapboxes on self-respect and teen pregnancy.

"Knock-knock." Bree's words matched the rapping on the open door. Her fire-red hair fell to her waist in a wet braid, the weave so thick one could've trusted it to rappel down a burning building. She held up two gas-station coffees. "I came as fast as I could. Left a trail of gear all the way to my car." She handed the coffee to Cam, who handed it to Bailey, who bypassed Star and gave it directly to Cassie.

Bree pushed a couple of stacks of papers aside and took a seat on Cassie's desk.

Cassie huffed and waved a hand around the room. "All right, guys. There are, like, five other chairs here if you haven't noticed."

Nobody moved.

"So, what happened with the guy?" Bree said. "Besides, of course, trying to get me fired after you left."

Cassie's brows shot up, both shoulders and knees pinched

together from being compressed between the group and wall. "He talked with Louis?"

Bree gave a flippant wave. "Oh, you know how he is. Louis fiddled with his whistle while your guy rambled on. But then your guy turned on me and started to get in *my* face about it, and you should've seen Louis. Went all Hulk on the guy. I ended up pulling him back and calming *him* down." She smiled as if at a fond memory. "Good ol' Louis."

Cassie grimaced. Bree's supervisor, Louis, was *not* the kind of man who'd spent his prime years scuba diving in Bermuda and off the coast of Peru, in much more adventurous places than Ripley's Aquarium. He was *not* the type who'd purposefully shaved his head to achieve a Bruce Willis look. No, Louis, poor Louis, was a kindly middle-aged man ten years Bree's senior. He was fond of whistles—some would say oddly so. He liked the twelve African black-footed penguins that made their residence there. Rumor had it he sang to them with squid-and-fish cake on their birthdays. Last, but certainly not least, Louis was head over off-brand Keds for the woman with enough spice to flavor a ten-gallon pot of chili.

Bree.

Louis's happiness was a crucial piece of the perfect escape plan.

"Don't worry, Cass. I took him to the café to cool off. He practically passed out when I let him pay for my chili cheese fries." Bree picked up one of the many misplaced fidget spinners from Cassie's desk and began spinning.

Cassie stared at her cup for one long moment, then looked to Bree, the girls, the computer.

It was time to call it.

"Well, on the bright side, I don't think we have to worry about this happening again. I think I just had my last blind date."

Bree halted the spinning spinner. "That bad?"

"Somewhere between the guy who shoplifted the stuffed dolphin and the one who ate through a pack of gum in five minutes and stuck every piece on the walls—"

Bree's eyes widened. "No, Cass. Not Gum Man."

"He was married." Cassie set her cup down on the only available inch of table space in front of her. "The charming youth volunteer who stated loyalty was the biggest characteristic he was looking for . . . was married." She shrugged. "So, I'm done. I think we can all agree I gave online dating more than a decent shot."

Star and the others looked to Bree, who gave them a resolute, don't-worry-I-got-this nod. "Let me see for myself. I'm hearing you, Cass, but let's take a look before we try to cut the one cord that's been sending men your way—mad as a March hare or otherwise."

Cassie pushed the keyboard her way. "Be my guest. Username is 'Cass0312.'"

Bree started typing.

"Password is 'mrjeeves.' No caps."

Bree's fingers typed the letters and then froze. She removed one hand from the keyboard and pinched the bridge of her nose. "Cass. Please don't tell me you created a password out of your cat. Please tell me I misheard you."

But sure enough, the pop-up disappeared, and a dozen male faces filled the screen. Cassie pushed herself up and slid over the desk, mulberry skirt and all. If she was going to be humiliated, she might as well get a little distance. While the girls scrolled, she moved to the window, taking her coffee cup with her. Across the street a fireman in full gear stood with his back to one of the trucks, talking to a group of kids.

"This guy seems nice."

Cassie flicked her head back to see Star pointing to a message titled "READY FOR LOVE WITH SOMEONE LIKE YOU."

"It's spam."

Star read aloud anyway:

> HEY LADY,
>
> READ ABOUT YOU LAST NIGHT. CAN'T STOP THNKNG ABOUT YOU. WANDERING IF THERE KOULD BE SOMETHING SPECIAL ABOUT US, SPARKS TURNING TO FIRE. MSGE ME BACK. CAN'T WAIT.

Cassie returned her attention to the fireman, now holding up his ax in demonstration. "Told you."

Star pointed to the screen. "What about that one? He likes cats too."

"Yes," Bree began in an instructive voice, "but let us all remember there is a line between having a cat and wearing a cat on your head in your profile picture. Not a big line." Bree threw Cassie a hard look. "But still, a line. And the goal here is to keep our girl from wandering entirely over to the other side."

Five more minutes with no leads, and the girls began to sink back in their chairs.

"You can say it: there's no hope." Cassie took a sip of her lukewarm coffee. Across the street, the fireman was now lifting a toddler into the driver's side of the fire truck, the child looking as though he was on the best rollercoaster of his life.

At least she'd have Bree to depend on the rest of her life. Bree, the free-spirited tropical fish without a care in the world. Bree never worried when she didn't have a boyfriend. In fact, whenever she did have one, she tended to forget him.

Cassie flicked a new cobweb off the windowsill.

"What is this?" Bree pointed to the line halfway down her profile. "What do you mean you *don't* want kids?"

Ah. Bree had found it.

Star unscrewed the cap of the large jar of pretzels on Cassie's desk and dug a hand in. "You don't like kids? Miss C, hate to break it to you, but you got the wrong job."

"No, of course I want kids. I just can't have them. Physically, I mean." Cassie smiled, her tone upbeat though she kept her eyes on the world outside. "A few years ago, I was in an accident. As it turns out, sometimes you make things worse when you try to fix them."

She trained her eyes on the firefighter settling another kid into the driver's seat, trying hard not to think about the scar tissue presently sitting like a bowling ball in her uterus or the lines across her stomach from the surgeries she'd endured in attempts to repair it.

A loud honk erupted from the fire truck, and the fireman laughed while pulling the toddler's hand away from an overhead cord. Cassie allowed herself a whisper of a smile.

"By that she means she should've sued the socks off the doctor. Then she could've bought herself a husband and we wouldn't be having this conversation." Bree paused, giving the memory the moment of silence it deserved. After all, she, too, had been there amid everything Cassie lost those years ago. She'd watched Cassie learn the hard way that not all scars were physical.

Suddenly, Bree stood and dropped her hold on the mouse and, along with it, the moment. She waved an accusing hand at the computer. "Well, that's your problem, Cass. You're attracting jerks because you put yourself in the jerk category. All the nice guys are on the other side. You need to get out of the 'I love traveling, gourmet food, and myself' world and move into the 'Athletic man seeking companion to whisper sweet nothings to as he coaches beloved children's little league.' Now, of course you know *I* don't want to be tied down to little life suckers, baking pies in floral aprons, but *you*, now . . ."

Several of the girls shot her a dirty look. Bree pressed her hand to her chest and amended herself. "*Unless* they came out fourteen and potty-trained, of course. But babe, aprons and kids are *all* you. All you have to do is change your preference in your bio."

"Were it that simple, I would jump on the opportunity. But I had to check one way or the other: do or don't want children. And I have no intention of leading someone into the wrong impression on a first date. Wanting kids is a big deal. Monumental."

"And you *do* want kids."

"And 'by adoption' wasn't one of the options, was it?" Cassie shot Bree a meaningful look, the kind that warned her friend she was putting her hand too close to the fire. The kind that said, "*Yes, but from personal experience, you and I both know that I know exactly what it feels like to be dropped—brutally—right when the man you thought was your soul mate finds out you can't have biological kids. I won't dare go that route again.*"

"You know who I need?" Cassie turned her head again and this time pointed to the window. The firefighter was now lifting what must've been the fifteenth toddler into the driver's seat. "That guy. Right there."

They all watched him put a helmet on the little girl. The girl giggled as the protective gear wobbled on her petite head.

"*That* kind of guy wouldn't be caught dead on a dating site. That guy, I just know, is making someone the luckiest girl in the world."

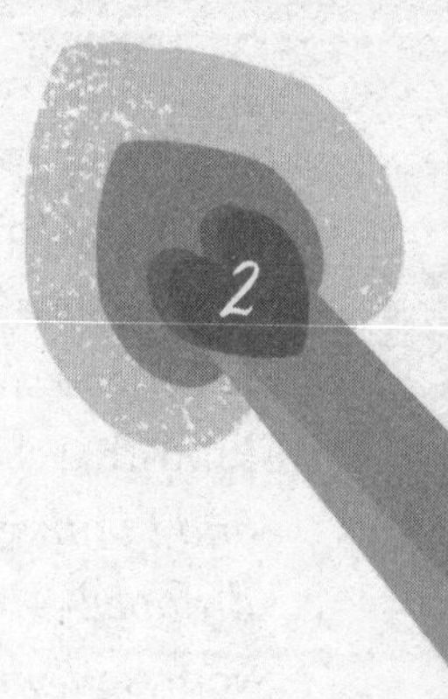

Jett

The alarm rang through the building. Jett paused, chin tilted slightly upward as he held onto the blade.

"Medic 2–10, Ladder 2–0–2, med 1 response . . . 525 Skyline Drive. Female . . ." The dispatcher's words came so quickly through the speakers that to anyone other than a firefighter it would've sounded like a foreign language.

His shoulders eased as the dispatcher rambled off the rest of the situation and address. He even managed to calmly set the knife down, scoop the halfway chopped onion onto a plate, and toss the unopened package of chuck roast back into the commercial-sized steel refrigerator.

No fire today, just Donna Gene needing her weekly visit.

"Bentley!" A man twice his age stepped out from a bathroom, soap suds covering half his chin. He pointed a razor at Jett. "Give your lady friend your schedule. Tell her not to call on days you're up for dinner duty."

Jett smiled. The bushy mustache above Captain Ferraro's half-shaved chin, however, didn't so much as quiver. "Yes, sir." Jett straightened his shoulders. "I'll tell her, sir."

Jogging beneath the pulsing blue lights through the stark hall, down the stairs, and into the bay, he met Sunny squatted beside Medic 2–10, lacing up his boots. They were dressed in identical paramedic uniforms: navy-blue buttoned polos with fire-rescue patches, navy pants, black boots, black belt. The badges gave off a silvery shine, reflecting the morning light coming from the sixty-paned fire-station doors that held the four engines neatly inside.

Jett twisted the key of the gleaming Medic 2–10, and it began to hum.

Sunny hopped in the passenger seat beside him and hung his elbow out the window. A moment later, he slapped the door twice and yelled to the two men jogging into the bay. "Let's go, ladies. Clock's a runnin'."

Jarod and Kevin gave Sunny looks that said well and clear they were not impressed. But then, Jett and Sunny weren't the ones shrugging on Kevlar for what they all knew was a bust call.

"I like you, Bentley," Jarod said, hopping into his boots and pulling up his suspenders. "You've been a good addition these past few months. But that doesn't mean I'm not starting to think up ways to get you kicked over to Station 3. If you don't get those two to stop—"

"Then what? You'll complain to Captain that you're missing out on beauty sleep when you're supposed to be on toilet duty?" Jett patted the wheel. "C'mon. They're just two lonely old ladies on a mountaintop looking for something to occupy the time."

"Yeah?" Kevin slung his jacket around himself. "I have a neighbor who's eighty-five. You know what she does for fun? Cross-stitches pillows. Drives a camper out to Utah. Goes to rock concerts with her grandkids. Won in her age group last year for the Turkey Trot 5K. Makes these little star-shaped cookies around the holidays filled with jelly—"

"Should I feel concerned by the depth of these details?" Jett's voice rose as the station doors lifted.

"Does yoga on a little back patio surrounded by sunflowers she grows in her garden—"

"I'm definitely uncomfortable."

Kevin yanked open the door to Ladder 2–0–2 beside him. "Notice nothing in that list included calling the fire department."

The engine roared to life, drowning out any more disturbing details Kevin might've been planning to add. Jett closed his window.

Amid the muted noise, Sunny pulled out a Hot Pocket stowed somewhere inside his jacket. "My meemaw likes to catch raccoons sneaking in her chicken coop. She spray-paints their tails and drops them off ten miles past the river, just to see them track their way back." He shrugged and bit into his Hot Pocket. Through his mouthful he added, "Everyone's got a hobby."

The trucks filled the narrow streets as they made their way through Gatlinburg, sirens reverberating off stores and churches. Soon they were surrounded by a landscape of rock and pine. Higher and higher into the mountains they went, and just when it seemed the asphalt had run out, the battered and tilted road sign for Skyline Drive peeked its head out from behind thick, wild bushes.

The airbrakes on Ladder 2–0–2 gave a squeal at the sign, and the massive engine plopped down in the middle of the all-but-abandoned road. Kevin leaned his head out the window. "Go meet your sweetheart, Bentley. Send for us if, miracle of miracles, you actually need our help."

Gravel sputtered beneath back tires as Jett pressed his boot firmly to the floor and powered the much smaller emergency vehicle up the drive. Tree limb after tree limb snapped at the sides of Medic 2–10 until the one-bedroom house came into view, smoke curling upward from its humble chimney. Frail, eighty-four-year-old Mrs. Edna "Edie" Kolak, the one and only neighbor to Donna Gene in a five-mile radius, tightened her robe about herself as she stood from the rickety lawn chair on the front porch. Jett pulled into the driveway, and Edie grabbed the siding as she began to step off the porch.

Cold air blasted into his lungs as he opened the door.

Despite the mere twelve minutes it took to get to 525 Skyline Drive, he always felt like he was suddenly a hundred miles from downtown Gatlinburg. The air was crisper in these elevated parts, and what was a light dusting in the town below accumulated to well over three inches here, confirmed with a quick glance at the snow overlaying the old, forgotten array of lawn art in concrete shapes of rabbits and angels.

He slid on blue latex gloves.

Like a hesitant ice skater, Edie tested her unsteady slipper on the grass. "Oh, Law', I am glad you are here."

"Now, just get back up on the porch there, Mrs. Kolak. Let us come to you." Jett slung the blaze-orange medic pack over his shoulder.

Edie obediently stepped back and waited. She rubbed at her gnarled, arthritic knuckles, fear powerful in her expression. "I know we weren't supposed to call, and we've been doing so good until lately, but—"

A loud moan came from behind the screen door. A long moan. A moan so long it was a wonder the woman hadn't run out of breath.

"It's no trouble at all." He smiled down at all four foot nine inches of the woman as he took hold of her frail elbow. "Now, why don't we get out of the cold and see what's going on?"

Edie all too willingly let herself be guided inside. Jett could gamble on the exact location—to the foot, really—where Donna Gene had taken a tumble. But even if he'd somehow blocked his memories of the last twenty-two times he'd been inside the house, he would still need no directions. They could simply follow the long, continuous moans interrupted only by millisecond breaths.

He led the way through the small, confined living room. On the large television covering the window, a woman yelled hysterically at a man, and the audience unanimously began to boo.

Donna's backside was the first thing that came into view as he turned into the kitchen.

"Ohh, Jetty boy. You found me." Donna held out a

plump arm, reaching toward him as though he would pull her out of her grave.

Jett pressed his hands to his knees and squatted down to her level. The woman stared back from beneath the square card table. Somehow the three-hundred-and-fifty-pound, eighty-two-year-old woman always managed to fall off her chair and land on the yellowed linoleum, and she always twisted and turned until she'd firmly wedged herself beneath the table legs, caught like a mouse in a trap. "For the life of me, Donna Gene, I don't know how you do it."

"You think you can help her? You think she'll be all right?" Edie's voice warbled as she clasped her hands together at her chest. The elderly woman had been watching the paramedics pull her friend up from the kitchen floor at least once a week for over five months now, and yet every time, she genuinely seemed to believe Donna Gene was on the precipice of death.

"She'll be just fine." Jett smiled, stood, and began the routine. He picked up a pair of small crystal salt and pepper shakers from the table and moved them to the counter. Something smelled foul, but his glance around the room suggested too many contributors to locate the item at fault. A bucket of grease sat next to the range, along with a frying pan containing chicken pieces well over a day—or even three days—old. His boot slid the overflowing trash can a couple feet away, along with another bulging trash bag on the floor. The trash bag pushed into the litter box, forcing him to wonder: when was the last time he'd seen a cat in the house?

Sunny began fighting a defiant window.

"You boys are trying to kill us! It's all but ten degrees!"

Edie pulled her robe tightly around her thin neck and fumbled in her cardigan pocket for her hand sanitizer. She sprayed it over her face to, as she often reminded them, "ward off the germs of outside air."

Sunny began his well-worn spiel as Jett emptied the containers on the table above Donna Gene's head. A deep southern accent always magically appeared whenever he talked to elderly ladies. "Oh, Mrs. Kolak, you know how I get when up in these parts. It's just like in the mountains of Colorado, so high up I can't get 'nough air in my lungs to keep me from passing flat out like one o' them faintin' goats. I need the fresh air to keep on keepin' on." He flapped his button-up a few times as he drank in a few breaths from the open window. "And you *do* want us helping your friend here, don't you?"

Edie resumed her trusty clutched-hands-at-chest position. "Oh. Most certainly."

The table cleared, Jett grabbed both sides of the table and carefully began to pull. He met little resistance as he lifted and released the prisoner beneath. Together, he and Sunny unraveled the sheet from his pack, and in less than two minutes Donna Gene was cautiously lifted and settled back into her trusty living-room recliner.

The second her legs touched the burgundy fabric, she opened her mouth, continuing a conversation as if seven days hadn't spanned their last meeting. "Now, as I was saying, Jetty boy, a solid specimen like yourself is wasting your days without someone nice to warm your toes with." She lifted the remote and, with eyes glued to Jett, turned the volume down. "Frankly, your fear of rejection concerns me."

Uh-oh. When Donna Gene used such highfalutin words as "fear of rejection," he knew exactly where this conversation was going.

Sunny grinned and headed toward the door.

Donna Gene eyed Edie, who was slowly making her way to the couch. "It concerns us both. Makes us wonder if it has something to do with childhood trauma."

Childhood trauma. Their phrase of choice.

The amount of Dr. Bob they watched in the span of twenty-four hours had done unusual things to Donna Gene and Edie, one of which was turn them into self-pronounced psychologists diagnosing anyone within a two-mile radius. As nobody actually lived within a two-mile radius, all their enthusiastic energy fixated on one of their favorites. Him. So far he was dealing with PTSD, middle child syndrome (he was, in fact, the oldest of two), dependent personality disorder, OCD, an overactive thyroid, and couvade syndrome—which he hoped meant something different to them than the usual definition. Otherwise he'd developed the pregnancy symptoms of an imaginary wife.

Lowering his tablet and medical questions, he gave an acquiescing sigh. "Now, Donna Gene, where on earth would I find time to coax a woman into picking me out of a crowd? If I did, I wouldn't have the time to visit you."

"Oh, stop." Donna's cheeks lifted as she waved a hand at him. "I'm serious, now. You're a fine young man. Are you sure there's not something holding you back from all the blushing brides out there?" She laced her fingers together over the remote as though it were an encyclopedia. This was her office. "Are you dealing with some inner angst?"

A clicking sound came from behind him. He turned to see Edie nodding on the couch as she scribbled something on a paper. "Because we have theories."

"I have no doubt." Jett slid the tablet back into his backpack. "Well, all I can say is to the best of my knowledge, I'm not suppressing childhood trauma. But mark my words, if I remember that I am, I'll let you two know first thing."

This evidently soothed the old ladies, because Edie began nodding again, scribbling something while she mumbled, "Receptive to help."

"Do that, Jetty boy. Because we talk about it often and, for the life of us, find your case baffling."

"I can only say I'm glad you're on the case, because it's equally baffling to me as well." Jett zipped up his backpack and took a step toward Sunny standing by the door. "We'll be seeing ourselves out now. You two have a nice Thanksgiving."

Both faces fell. "So soon?"

"Afraid so. I've got a roast to cook. Can't leave the guys hungry."

Both of them waved as Sunny opened the screen door. Donna Gene tapped her temple with her remote. "We'll be drilling the old lemons, Jetty boy. Don't you worry."

The TV volume kicked back up to deafening level as they stepped out into open air. Pine icicles clicked together as a breeze swept through the surrounding trees. Everything about the world just outside their door was as opposite as could be from the inside: silent, clean, still. And yet, a part—a very, very small part—of Jett could see why these women let the raucous television shows fill their ears with sound.

If they sat in silence up here too long, chances were they'd start to feel just how lonely they really were.

"You know what you could do—" Sunny started as he climbed back into the cab of their vehicle.

"No." Jett turned on the ignition, knowing exactly where Sunny was going. He backed out and turned around. The road made a steep decline.

"Seriously, man. Just a couple months ago I went on a date with a gorgeous brunette—or was it blonde?" Sunny leaned back, resting his hands behind his head. "Met at the aquarium. She actually shared my affinity for shark culture—"

"No."

"Lost her halfway through, though." His eyebrows knit together. "I should message her . . ."

Jett shook his head, staring straight ahead. "Date however you want, Sunny, but I couldn't stand thinking women were out there swiping left and right over my picture. Judging me on the type of food I like. Deciding who I am from a paragraph."

"Fine, man." Sunny propped his feet on the dash. "But good luck trying to meet someone in our neck of the woods. You're not exactly in Atlanta anymore."

"I haven't got a lot of time on my hands anyway right now."

Sunny laughed and raised one brow. "You do realize we share an apartment. And a job. I know *exactly* how much time you have on your hands. Enough time to wear out that pull-up bar for no good reason." He rubbed his belly, now rolling like jelly beneath his shirt. "Me, on the other hand, I don't waste my time. Slim pickings in this town work in my favor. Which is why, if you just tried out the app—"

"No," Jett replied, his firm tone stating this conversation was over.

Sunny turned his gaze out the window, mumbling several more points to the glass during the rest of the ride.

Jett ignored him. But as much as he pretended not to care, there were moments it bothered him. Unlike many of his buddies, he wasn't coming up on a decade-long anniversary and struggling to find something decent for his wife. He didn't get to complain about having to stop by the grocery store on the way home because the wife was in the middle of making chili and had forgotten the diced tomatoes. He never had the opportunity to warrant a wife's wrath by suggesting she just "do without."

Now, to be fair, that also meant he didn't clean up dried macaroni glued to the carpet of the minivan on Saturdays or dress up in matching family outfits for spring photos. When the married guys crawled into work because they'd stayed up all night holding kids who'd thrown up from 2:00 to 6:00 a.m., his act of benevolence was offering a cup of coffee.

No, he had neither interest nor the need to fill his life with those things—those small human beings. Never had. But as for the other, the chance to find the woman whom, as Dr. Donna so aptly put, he could "warm his toes with"—well, that was another matter. And sometimes, more and more of late, he'd felt the nudge to do something about it.

Dr. Donna was better at this than he realized.

Jett thought about it as he wiped down the kitchen after

dinner and made his way toward his small, private room. He twisted the combination dial on the locker closest to the wall.

Missy Jenkins. Her name drifted like a song note across the forefront of his mind as the locker popped open. Had it really been that long, *that* long, since he'd been out to dinner with a woman?

Sure, there was Sarah, his neighbor across the hall. She fed him a casual meal every now and again. But that usually began with them running into each other in the shared hall and her mentioning the idea with as much expectancy and desire as she would have in asking Sunny or any one of their neighbors. They usually sat on her sofa with plates of spaghetti and chatted in between plays of the UT game. He always left with no hint beyond having strengthened their neighborly bond. And frankly, that was just fine with him.

But Missy, the woman who'd moved off to Seattle and taken his heart with her . . . Could it really be coming up on two years?

He caught his face in the small mirror hanging in the back of the locker and immediately frowned. Touching his temple, he tried to decipher if the hair poking out was white or simply his imagination.

He swung the locker closed. He needed to get it together.

In the stillness of his room he lay on his back, picked up his phone. It glowed in the otherwise dark space. Even as he typed the words in the app store and hit the download button, he felt the heat on his neck, the shame in even considering the terribly desperate option. He twisted his neck to double-check the lock on his room door. The mere act of looking into one of these sites depleted the level of his manhood.

This was just testing the waters, he reminded himself as he swiftly created a username and logged in, scrolling down the page as dozens of faces popped up. He would just take a look around, see if this was a real possibility for expanding his connections . . .

The alarm sounded, but this time it was both outside *and* in. Because there, illuminated in the red light flashing above his bed, was the profile picture of Cassie Everson. Fifteen years had changed the cut of her hair, had altered her muscular frame of high school years to something softer, more feminine. But that unmistakable smile was still all hers, thin lips tilted up as if she was on the cusp of laughter. Hazel eyes twinkled with that same down-to-earth confidence he'd seen on the court all those years before but had never managed to turn his way. She'd been a senior, after all, while he'd been but a lowly freshman.

And yet here they were, single, fifteen years later. His boyhood dreams come true.

"Well, I'll be," he murmured as he jumped out of bed, siren wailing.

Cassie Everson.

The one and only.

Cassie

"Jeeves, I'm home."

Cassie's keys clanked inside the tidy, porcelain bowl beside the front door as she proceeded to slip off her coat. Jeeves took his time greeting her—the selfish thing—determined to watch a cardinal bouncing lightly across her front yard instead. Only at the sound of his food clattering into the ornate and entirely-too-expensive-to-be-a-cat-bowl dish did he drop off the window ledge. He gave an appreciative rub against the side of her leg and dug in.

Her phone *ding*ed as she picked up his water bowl.

The notifications from her dating app always gave a lighthearted ping whenever she received a message from an interested hunter. When she'd started the dating app a year ago, she'd optimistically called them *suitors*. As time went on and she got more and more acquainted with their characters, they'd dropped down to *men* and then *humans*, shortly after *scum bags*, and finally rested comfortably at *hunters*. Still, that *ding* was addicting and so chipper nobody could resist its siren call. Surely whoever'd invented that *ding* was a billionaire.

Unconsciously she fell into the familiar habit of checking the app, no less certain of her plans to terminate the profile tonight, while setting the fountain bowl in the sink and turning on the water. As it began to fill, she read the message.

Dear Cassie.

Not Kassie, not Casey, and not Hey, Smokin' Hot Lady. So far so good.

I've never been on this site before.

Ah. The classic "I've never been on this site before, was in fact heading to the monastery to swear off hope of love forever . . . until I saw you" line. Her hand lowered an inch toward the counter.

But when I was scrolling through I saw you—

She put the phone on the counter and turned off the running faucet.

No more. Suddenly, finally, she knew without a doubt

she couldn't handle one more excruciating message. She picked up her phone again and deleted the app without a moment's pause.

At last.

Freed.

"Jeeves, if you ever go out searching for a Mrs., make sure to skip the sweet talking." She raked her hands through her hair. "And you have to stop talking to your cat, Cassie," she added, then bit her lip. "And yourself."

The house was quiet. She felt the day drag her toward the freezer, leading her to pull out the small, prepackaged box of frozen tikka masala. Three minutes and twenty-five seconds later, Cassie tucked her feet under her as she sat on the glider by the window in her modest living room. Jeeves jumped onto his sill beside her.

Some nights she turned on the television or a Pandora station just so she couldn't hear her own breath, but tonight she couldn't even muster that. Tonight, without her mother or Bree or teens to distract her and love on her and harass her and ultimately give her the strength to feel like it wasn't so bad after all, she just wanted to grieve. Just tonight. Just for a few absurd, self-wallowing minutes alone.

It felt silly to mourn the loss of something that never had been in the first place, but if she had to name the feeling, that was the word she would use. *Mourning.*

She was all too aware that people faced harder problems every day. She knew she had every reason to be thankful: An incredible pair of parents who were healthy and supportive and lived only a handful of miles away. A wonderful older sister, a sturdy brother-in-law, and two fantastic nieces and a nephew to dote on. Supportive friends, and a job she loved. She was financially stable and, apart from the accident and its aftermath, in tip-top shape. She was truly, *truly* grateful.

But tonight she looked at her white-slipcovered couch and matching loveseat and couldn't help but notice how clean, and how empty, they were. When she went over to her sister's place, Emily was usually scrubbing something her nieces and nephew had gotten into: the walls from bright purple marker, the carpet from apple juice, the couch from where one niece had smeared her peanut-butter-and-jelly lips across it like a paper towel. In those moments Emily tended to carry a frantic edge in her tone, her eyes always roving around corners as if waiting for the next crisis—crash, tear, or stain.

Right then, there was nothing Cassie wouldn't give for a long streak of red crayon across her perfectly white couch.

She sighed and rubbed her weary eyes before looking out the window. From the four-bedroom house and five acres inherited from her grandparents, only two other brick residences rested within seeing distance, propped along their own hills of pasture. Smoke lifted from the Smiths', where no doubt Mr. Smith was spending the hours busily pushing the children aside as he added wood to the fire. He was a man who loved his fires.

A few stubborn leaves clung to the branches of the large maple on her front lawn. One, especially stubborn in maintaining its rich auburn hue, finally gave in and let itself drift slowly to the awaiting pile. Cassie rose and took with her the empty plastic bowl.

Time was up.

She conceded to background music and spent the next two hours in miscellaneous odds and ends, dusting the already dust-free coffee table, taking a broom across her kitchen floor. She was halfway through spraying down the toilet when her phone rang, the *Jaws* theme song notifying her it was Bree.

She cradled the phone to her ear as she kept working. "Hey, Bree. What's up?"

"I'm about to do something, and I want to make absolutely sure you are going to remember how much you love me when this is all over. Do you think you can do that?"

"It depends." Cassie picked up the scrubber. "Will I be publicly humiliated?"

"Nope."

"Will I appreciate whatever you are about to do?"

"Yep."

Cassie began scrubbing. "Will you tell me what you are planning?"

"Not in a million years."

Cassie pursed her lips. This type of conversation was hardly surprising; Bree occasionally threw Cassie into situations "for her own good" and so they had something to talk about—besides a life of cleaning toilet bowls—when they were ninety years old together.

"Fine. I trust you. But don't mess with my Thanksgiving. I'm going to be over at Mom's all day."

Cassie could practically hear Bree's mischievous lips creeping upward in a smile. "You won't regret this. Well,

I take that back. There's a small possibility you might, but what's life without risk?"

"Wait. How much of a risk are we talking here—"

The line, however, went dead before Cassie could finish her question.

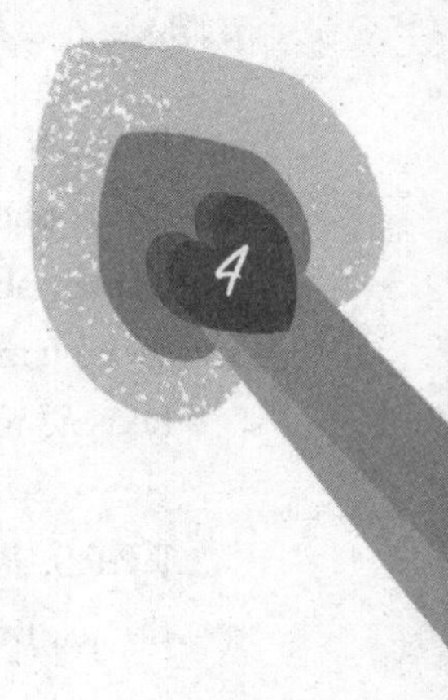

Jett

Dear Jett,

Of course I remember you. How could I not, if you know what I mean? *wink wink*

How's tomorrow night sound, 6:30 p.m.? Meet me at Girls Haven. I'll be waiting outside. I'm up for anything you want to do. Surprise me.

Cheers!

Cassie

P.S. Skip the messages and text me at 865.345.6473 from now on. I think we can both agree this online dating site is for the birds.

P.P.S. If you have any of the following conditions—agateophobia, pluviophobia, thaasophobia, Russophobia, pupaphobia, are married and seeking an affair, alcoholic seeking more alcohol, a kleptomaniac, rude, or boring—text me immediately. Deal's off.

P.P.P.S. I'm a sucker for old-fashioned chivalrous-men things. Bring flowers.

Jett read the message for the third time before tucking it into his pocket and pulling out his debit card. His eyes skimmed the row of colorful bundles before landing on an arrangement of white alstroemerias and Douglas firs mixed with pinecones and red berries, held together by a large, red satin bow. "That one," he said and handed the man his card.

As he stepped back into his car, he couldn't help feeling compelled to check the message yet again. Strange. Exceedingly strange. But despite getting commanded by his date to bring flowers *to* his date, the infraction wasn't about to slow him down a minute. Perhaps she'd turn out to be crazy. It was quite possible the woman she was up close was a far cry from the perception he'd had half a lifetime ago. Even then, the extent to which he "knew" her was the daily crossing of paths in crowded halls between the bells of 1:00 and 1:05 p.m. He "knew" how she felt each day as he watched her mood show on her face, her joy as she laughed with another teammate over some shared story, the frustration when the halls were busier than usual and the bell was about to sound, the playfulness—oh, the pain he'd felt from February on through her graduation—as she clung to Peter Eckstut, wearing his football jacket and school letters. But the time he enjoyed seeing her most was on the court.

Back then, that girl could shoot.

Jett realized he was grinning as he turned his truck around the corner and saw her standing, as promised, on the sidewalk. As he pulled to a stop in front of her, a flurry of nonsensical, boyish fears dropped in and took up residence in his chest.

Aside from the frown on her face, she hadn't changed one bit. A thin black jacket wrapped tightly around her, Cassie Everson stood—clearly freezing—on the sidewalk. Though he, too, wore a nice pair of jeans matching his black, button-down oxford shirt, she had underdressed him by a mile. The pink collar of a polo peeked out from above her jacket, and her orange-and-green Nikes met at the bottom of her skinny jeans. Her hair—or rather what he could see of it from the ponytail—looked darker than the picture, and more than a few strands were out of place, as though she had put it up hours ago and forgotten about it in the chaos of the day. She hoisted a large work bag full of binders over her shoulder.

In sum, the only item matching the level of attention he'd given to the evening was a simple pair of diamond studs twinkling behind wayward wisps of hair.

"Cassie?" Jett stepped out of his truck and, feeling more than a little silly, brought the bouquet of flowers with him. "It's been a long time."

"You've gotta be kidding me."

He and his bouquet froze on the curb.

Cassie squeezed her eyes shut. When she opened them

again, and it was clear he hadn't disappeared like a bad dream, she put out a forced hand.

"Hi, there. I'm Cassie."

Slowly, he shook hers. "I know. I just said your name."

She flew past his reply. "Look, I'm really, *really*, sorry to do this to you, but whatever you were told about tonight or—" her eyes flicked to the bouquet as though he was holding a python "—were planning isn't going to work out after all. I've been standing out here for twenty minutes waiting on a friend. But apparently—" her eyes darkened, the same look he imagined on murderers just before they pounced "—that friend got the bright idea to send someone else instead. I'm sorry."

"Oh. I see."

"Honestly, I don't think I could put my best foot forward after the day I've had. Consider yourself lucky to be off the hook."

She managed a weary smile, but her eyes seemed wary, as though half expecting him to fly off the handle at the news. And why not? It was certainly a punch in his gut to have the date he'd spent two hours cleaning his car for, put on uncomfortable clothes for, and bought absurdly overpriced flowers for barely take a glance at him before informing him she'd rather spend the evening alone than at a free dinner in exchange for conversation. Frustration, to whatever degree, was the normal reaction. *However.* This wasn't any old date who was attempting to turn him down.

Jett paused, carefully putting together the facts. "So, let me just clarify here. You never wrote me a message. We never corresponded in any way."

Cassie nodded.

"And I could venture a guess that this 'friend' of yours stole your identity and messaged on your behalf."

Her jaw clenched as she nodded again.

"And you don't actually remember me from high school?"

Her brows raised curiously for a moment, her eyes seeming to trace him before coming up short.

"Huh." He eyed the sidewalk thoughtfully. Stuck a hand in his pocket. Considered his options. Then, at last, he held out the bouquet. "In that case, I believe your friend ordered these."

Cassie put up her hands. "Oh, no. I couldn't."

"Don't worry about it. I already have three bouquets at home." He smiled, but her expression didn't register the joke. He shook the flowers a little. "Please. I insist."

He continued to hold out the bouquet, and finally—regretfully, it seemed—she took it. When she did, he dipped his head, his smile not watered down in the least. "Well, Ms. Everson, I sincerely wish you a relaxing evening and a nice holiday tomorrow with your loved ones."

He glanced around his surroundings, the slimming stream of cars, the lack of pedestrians on the sidewalk, the dark and empty building behind her. It connected to a string of boxy apartment buildings he knew only too well from work. Some of the stories he came away with made his skin crawl.

"Mind if I at least walk you to your car? I assume it's in the back."

Cassie's once-set jaw, growing softer and softer as the conversation went on, snapped tight again. She pushed the stems of the bouquet carefully into her work bag. "No. Thank you."

Clearly she wanted two free hands to ward off her attacker.

As if he hadn't descended enough from the status of "chivalrous date" to "stranger worthy of immediate rejection" tonight, he'd now dropped another peg to "potential assaulter."

Terrific. This night was going swimmingly.

"That's a kind offer," she added, though her hands noticeably played with her keys—keys with a rather large can of pepper spray attached. "But I do this all the time."

And before he could say another word she was walking toward the side of the building. She called out, "Thanks—and sorry again—for the flowers."

Jett waited behind his steering wheel until her headlights lit up the short drive to the street and an old green Subaru rolled by. She pressed her face into a smile and gave a brief, tight wave before her tires squealed onto Profit Drive. The woman couldn't drive away fast enough.

Tilting the mirror down, he looked at himself. He was clean shaven, his hair cut short. His mild blue eyes looked back at him with the dim dissatisfaction he felt. Nothing about him looked like a serial killer. In fact, nothing about him looked like he should be shot down—for a first date at least.

Great, now Donna Gene was giving him an ego.

But perhaps that was it, though. He had the distinct sense Cassie had not turned *him* down tonight but *all* men in general. In one way that was encouraging, in another it proved to be a whole other challenge.

As he drove back to the apartment he considered his options. First, and most obvious, he could take Cassie at her word and leave her alone. The most simple and straightforward solution. One he let himself consider the span of one red stoplight.

Option two: pursue the heck out of her. Charm her socks off. Now that would be hard to do. The woman obviously had a chip on her shoulder. Dramatic pursuits, like attaching a walkie-talkie to a box of chocolates delivered to her workplace, would be a gamble.

Option three: casually pursue her. Find out where she did life and just so happen to run into her there. The grocery store. The fancy-ladies-and-millennial-men coffee shop. On the greenway, perhaps, as she walked her dog. But he had the distinct feeling she would take his innocent research into her whereabouts as a sign of stalking, and that handy pepper spray of hers would come out again.

Which brought him back to option one, where he didn't want to go.

So how, then? How could he convince a woman—a very specific woman—to go out on one date? She was *on* a dating website. Unless her friend had signed her up entirely, she was actually in search of a relationship.

The predicament was beyond his ability to solve alone.

Jett ruminated on the issue in front of his complex. He barely registered his neighbor's door opening as he pulled out his keys.

"Look at you, Jett. Went somewhere fancy?"

He turned. Sarah stood in her doorway, a bundle of mail in her hand.

For the moment, he pushed the puzzle aside. "Expected to, but plans fell through."

"Oh, really?" Sporting pink slippers, she stepped an inch out the door. "That's too bad." She checked her watch. "Dinner, I'm guessing?"

"Dinner theater, actually."

Her brows rose considerably. "I didn't peg you as a dinner-theater guy."

"I'm not." Jett reached into his wallet and pulled out two tickets. "You want them? They told me at the box office *My Fair Lady* was the 'hit of the season.'"

Sarah laughed lightly and took the tickets, reviewing them. "Sixty-five bucks a seat? You can't let these go to waste."

"Do me a favor. Use them so they won't. You still have a good thirty minutes to get there."

She paused, bit her lip as she looked at them. "I'd be happy to, but I don't know of anyone I could snag in such short notice. Definitely not tonight, with Thanksgiving tomorrow. We're quite the loners, aren't we?" She smiled up at him, then pushed the tickets his way with one hand as she flapped her letters with the other. "Ah, well. Off to the mailbox. Sorry things didn't work out tonight."

He took the tickets and she passed by him. It was indeed painful to let one hundred and thirty hard-earned dollars slip through his fingers. And despite his complete and total disinterest in watching an ensemble decked in makeup dance on stage, there was still the matter of two fine dinners going to waste—according to the online menu, two New York strips in a spicy coffee rub with baked potatoes drowned in sour cream and chives, strawberry cheesecake, endless coffee. As it was, he would be lucky to find a couple slices of leftover pizza in the refrigerator.

Sarah turned the corner and went down the stairs. After a moment's thought, Jett walked over to the railing and called down as she slipped her mail into the box. "Hey, Sarah. I changed my mind. I'm up for steak if you are."

In only seconds, Sarah blew by him, calling out as she dashed in her apartment, "Give me two minutes."

"Sure."

As he waited, he drew out his phone, the Cassie quandary returning like a briefly paused game. The fact was he was not in the position to solve the puzzle alone. He needed someone closer to help him. Much closer—so close, perhaps, they were able to steal Cassie's identity and still walk away friends. If he was going to do this, he needed to have an inside man—or in this case, woman—so he could execute this perfectly.

"Almost ready! Just getting on my boots." Sarah's muffled voice called out just beyond the door as Jett began to type.

To Cassie's imposter: let's talk.

Cassie

The room was littered with scraps of wrapping paper and snips of gold and red ribbon. More ribbon twirled slowly as it dangled from the low ceiling where several of the girls had taken advantage of the holiday and taped yards and yards of the stuff throughout the room. The door to the game room, and every other door in the building, was covered in cheerful wrapping paper: reindeer in little red sweaters with presents on their backs, snow-covered Christmas trees, nutcrackers, and long, festive trains. A wooden ornament hung over the wrapping on Cassie's door depicting baby Jesus in a manger. Christmas music played loudly—and being December 1, quite proudly—over the speakers.

Every possible chair in the place was in use.

"We're going to need more shoeboxes over here, Keely." Cassie spoke as she hurriedly opened another bulk box of donated deodorants and set them beside one of the girls' chairs.

This was the biggest event of the season for the girls, and today was the culmination of all their hard work. It had been months since Girls Leadership Club, a subset of Girls Haven, had made the unanimous goal to collect supplies and assemble Christmas shoeboxes for that year. And they had worked tirelessly. Several Mondays Cassie had chauffeured them throughout town, letting them take the wheel as they charged like the businesswomen they were destined to become into stores and organizations, giving their well-prepared speeches (and poster-board diagrams). And what an incredible turnout. United, they had managed to gather enough supplies for a whopping total of 346 boxes to send to those in less fortunate circumstances overseas.

The pride in Cassie's eyes was so thick she practically needed glasses.

"Van's full. Where should I put these?" Star stood behind Cassie, an armful of colorfully wrapped boxes stacked to her chin.

"Just start making a pile by the door. This is going to take multiple trips."

"I'm running out of soap," one of the girls called out from her station. The girl dropped a bar of soap into a box and pushed it in front of Bailey's area.

Like little elves in a Ford factory, they had two extremely efficient assembly lines going. Four girls wrapped the boxes as quickly as their Scotch Tape fingers would allow, two girls ran completed stacks of boxes to the van, and the rest dropped their designated items into the boxes before pushing them along the line: a toothbrush, comb, deodorant, toy, coloring book, pencils, stickers, woodwind recorder (their pride point, for which the girls had received over four hundred donations), a Girls Haven shirt, underwear, and a sturdy three-pack of socks.

Cassie moved down the hall to her office, where cardboard boxes took up nearly every square inch of floor space. She squeezed inside and began rummaging for the soap. As she did, her eyes trailed over the blooms on her bouquet, and for the zillionth time what should have been a feeling of pleasure at seeing the festive display was overcome by a deep sense of regret.

Why on earth had she not given that guy a chance?

Sure, Cassie had never been good at spontaneous things. Despite what her currently cluttered office might say, her personality leaned on the side of precision and organization, and with those qualities naturally came a resistance to such messy and potentially chaotic things as meet-a-guy-on-a-sidewalk-at-night dates. Too much could have gone wrong. In fact, too much that day had already gone wrong.

Rachel, one of the DCS staff, had come by unannounced that afternoon, leading her to scramble for replacement staff so she could take the private meeting in her office. She was familiar with the questions, but discovering that Cam had been moved with her mother to a women and children's shelter for protection was shocking and heart wearying. Cam—cheetah-print-wearing, sassy Cam—had been tagging along with Star at Girls Haven for over a year and never said a word about the abuse she'd been facing, sexually or physically. It was Cassie's *job* to protect and empower these girls, and yet for all the training and all the careful watching, she hadn't had a clue. She ached over that fact.

So, there Cassie had stood outside, waiting on Bree to pick her up, holding it together until she could slide inside the car with her friend and share every emotion—including the guilt—that simmered. She'd known Cam was resistant to getting too close at the Haven. Why hadn't Cassie taken her resistance as a silent cry for help? Why had she let the busyness of the business—the programs, the reports, even the Christmas-box program—occupy more attention? And if she was really honest with herself, why had she gone with the flow and focused her attention on the other girls, like Star, like Bailey, who wanted to be loved? The ones who were *easy* to love. The ones who rewarded Cassie's time and attention with responses of affection. But Cam? If she had only pushed harder past her exterior walls, spent more time making Cam a priority . . .

Her nondate couldn't have stepped out of his truck, holding a bouquet of flowers, at a worse moment.

Her mood had lifted with the sun the following morning, enough that she brought the bouquet to work to be a cheerful companion. And through eleven long days, the relentless, apparently immortal, bouquet had kept its bloom. Eleven long days remembering the conversation with Jett Bentley, his purposeful stride, his nervous smile. Eleven long days kicking herself for not giving him a shot.

She'd logged back onto her hijacked account and read his message, thoroughly this time, feeling that weasel of regret stir in her stomach the deeper into his message she got. He mentioned he'd gone to school with her, and sure enough, when she'd pulled out her old yearbook, there he was. The contrast between her senior picture and his freshman one was seismic in proportion. Her in pearls, cap, and gown, her confident seventeen-year-old smile ready to take on the world. Him a tall, skinny boy with a long, thin neck and bowl-cut hair, bearing small resemblance to the man he had grown into. He awkwardly held a basketball on his hip on the JV basketball page. And that's when his face had flashed across her memory—a face in the stands out of the corner of her eye as she dribbled the ball down the court, a face as she squeezed through the halls on the way to class. To some degree, she really believed she could remember him. But then, at one point in her life she had also convinced herself she could fly.

Even so, his wobbly, freshman smile—just six pages from her own—soothed her and set him apart from the rest.

Still, she couldn't bring herself to message him again. After what both she and Bree had put him through, she knew the last message he'd ever want to receive was from her.

Lesson learned. If she wrote a how-to manual for dating, this would be a bullet point: *be prepared in season and out of season to get into cars with good-looking strangers so long as they provide flowers. And you have pepper spray.*

It would be a bestseller.

"Keely says she's out of toothbrushes." Star spoke to Cassie from the hall, her arms loaded with yet another stack of boxes. "I'm going to start putting these by the bathroom."

"No, don't do that," Cassie replied. She'd forever rue the

day she told the team they didn't need to come in to work for this. "Here, can you take these back to Finn and find the toothbrushes? I'm going to run a load over to the church."

As Cassie handed Star a box of soap, she heard a sound mingling with, and soon overpowering, the voracious chatter, heavy wrapping, and Christmas jingles floating from the game room. The sirens grew louder, and Cassie starting striding down the hall. Star left her box and followed behind. Cassie picked up speed when red flashes blinked through the windows, the roaring of sirens hitting peak volume.

She pushed open the double doors.

What in the world?

"Ho-ho-ho!" Santa bellowed as he wiggled his large body out of the fire truck. Evidently Santa was a fireman as well, because peeking from under the large red coat and golden buttons were firefighter suspenders. He grabbed his helmet, evidently thought better of it, then reached for the Santa hat and stuffed it on his head before grabbing a large black trash bag from the back door. Classy.

With jolly confidence he walked down the sidewalk with a sort of half stride, half Irish jig, straight to Cassie as a group of girls grew behind her. When he reached the bottom of the stairs, he drew out a crumpled piece of paper and stretched it out as though about to read an imperial speech. He began talking, but the sirens overpowered his words.

Cassie furrowed her brows. Several of the girls behind her covered their ears.

Santa stopped and flapped his hand at the truck. The sirens stopped.

"As I was saying," he began again, "Meeeeeeerrrrryyyy

Christmas to the lovely ladies of Girls Haven! Ho-ho-ho!" The bell on the top of his head jingled as he used his free hand to grab his belly. When the bell fell over his face, he stopped and adjusted it. "A little elf told me about all of the work you have been doing for little girls and little boys around the world. And on a Saturday too! You work harder than we do!" He grabbed at his belly again. "Ho-ho-ho!"

A chuckle escaped from a couple of girls, and Cassie turned, halfway in disbelief, to see several of them smiling.

Normally, a guy like this wouldn't last ten seconds with this crowd.

But then, normally, people didn't roll in wearing Santa suits in fire trucks.

"And we," Santa continued loudly, "at the North Pole decided to take a trip down to Gatlinburg, Tennessee, on our official fire engine. A few of my men here have volunteered to help you girls out with the delivery. That is if your fearless leader approves?"

Cassie looked closer at the dear, old Santa before them, trying to peer beyond the white beard and thick hat to the face underneath. That voice . . . Those eyes . . . She vaguely recalled that same voice in the aquarium, those same sunny, clueless brown eyes. *Sunny*. Number 24. Not the worst guy she'd been on a date with. Not the best of the bad lot, either.

If he recognized her, he didn't show it. Which meant he didn't remember her. Based on her aquarium experience, she didn't think he had the intellectual capabilities *not* to show it.

Cassie saw the girls' eyes drift to her. "Delivery. Sure. That'd be . . . great."

"Excellent." Sunny-turned-Santa clapped his oversized black gloves. "Liberty Church is what my little elf tells me?"

Cassie's surprise grew even more as she nodded. Who had put the fire department up to this? She hadn't e-mailed Jim at the paper, hadn't requested crews come in to see how successful the Leadership Club had been. But the girls had gone into just about every organization in town over the past two months, and there was no denying about half of the people in this mega city of 4,097 had heard of what was going on. Still, to know about helping with delivery? To know about such details . . .

"We'll get right to it, then." He fumbled with the knot on the trash bag. After a minute of struggling and saying a few words under his breath, he finally threw his gloves on the ground. "But first," he continued, ripping the bag open and standing ceremoniously again, "do you know what I do every Christmas season before even thinking about putting any toys into my sleigh? I give each of my hardworking elves a *very* special present. And I'd venture to say that you girls have been *very* elfish lately. So—" He went back to the crumbled paper. "—would Rayne please step forward?"

Rayne's eyes widened as she heard her name and stepped timidly out from the cluster.

Cassie crossed her arms, cracking a grin as she watched the crazy, gleeful man hand out presents to each of the twenty-two girls. *Twenty-two* presents. Her cheeks began to burn, both from the frigid air and the continuous smile, as she watched the girls rip open their gifts.

Whoever had been in charge had nailed it. Each and every one of them received a coffeeshop gift card. Cheap but shimmering lip balm smelling of cotton candy. Fuzzy socks. As Cassie watched Star pull a silver frame out of her bag, Santa spoke up, and Cassie realized he had his phone uplifted.

"Now, if you don't mind, squeeze together for a photo, and my elf will make sure you each get a copy for your pretty frames."

The girls only too eagerly agreed, several having already popped on the lip balm for shining smiles. And after some pleading, Santa himself jumped in the photo.

Three of Santa's firemen helpers followed the starry-eyed girls inside, and as Cassie took up the rear, she felt a glove on her shoulder.

"Of course, Santa wouldn't forget you."

He winked, and left Cassie with a simple white envelope, following the group inside.

Cassie slit it open. She unfolded the papers, revealing the document stapled together. The header read: *Complete Background Check: Timothy Jett Bentley.*

Jett

"It was just too cliché to bring flowers, then. You had to throw in a fire truck."

"Well, Miss Everson, if you recall, I did try flowers. The first time."

"Touché." Cassie managed to wince and grin simultaneously as she pushed up to the front of the ticket line. Condensation dripped from the tower of windows filling the front of Ripley's Aquarium, heat from the bustling activity inside melting whatever frost tried to envelop them.

A sweet and almost eerie melody came through the speakers, of strings and keyboard interrupted at random intervals by a whale's call.

She opened her purse.

"Allow me." Jett lifted a credit card from his wallet and slid it toward Mrs. Leake, who sat there with a slight and telling smile across her lips. Had Bree not prepped him for every detail of the date Cassie had picked for them—including the involvement of Mrs. Leake, Bree's own mother—he would've been suspicious then and there. Instead, he let the self-satisfaction simmer while the women started the show.

"No need," Cassie countered, and bypassing her own wallet, she dug in her purse. She set two glass jars in front of his card.

The woman's brows lifted as she picked up the one closest. The jar was filled with white chocolate, with three black buttons glued down the length, red string wound around the neck, and the sweet *Merry Christmas* message on the tag tied with baker's string.

Mrs. Leake clucked as she admired it. "Well, isn't that just adorable. Is that a snowman, Cassie?"

Cassie seemed to fight off a proud smile. "It is. The girls and I made sixty yesterday at the Haven. Will you pass this one along to Jeremy when you get the chance? He looks like he could use the sugar rush."

Jeremy, sitting at the ticket counter beside Bree's mother, was sweating in the thirty-degree weather as he printed a strand of tickets for a family of twelve—all while three of the children hung off his counter, a paper airplane flew dangerously close to his head, and the hand of an infant squatting on top of the counter inched slowly toward the scissors.

"I'll be sure to," Mrs. Leake said, then handed a ticket to Cassie.

Jett stepped forward. "Well, ma'am, it looks like I've forgotten my snowman jar at home. Do you still take debit?"

Mrs. Leake's smile grew as she paused, her eyes scanning him top to bottom. Clearly, she had been briefed.

She pushed his card away and pressed the button. The ticket began printing.

"Save your money, honey. With any luck you'll be needing it for a second date soon." She gave Cassie a wink and handed him his ticket.

He dipped his head. "I'll do my very best, ma'am." With a jaunty grin toward Cassie, Jett opened the door and motioned for her to step through. "Shall we?"

Cassie's cheeks started to pink, the light blush turning a shade darker as Mrs. Leake added loudly, "And young man? I believe the stingray exhibit is being cleaned this hour. You'd do best to skip right past it, avoiding it altogether."

Jett grinned. "Cassie, did you hear that? Let's be sure to stay far away from the stingrays."

"Yes. *Thank you*, Mrs. Leake." Cassie began to reach for his elbow as though to tug him out of earshot, then quickly pulled her hand back. Instead, she snagged a map off the round rack. As he watched her stand there, quietly scanning the pages as if it was her first time in the loud aquarium, Jett calmly took off his thin down jacket and laid it over one arm.

"Looks like the smaller fish are going to be this way," she began.

"Mmm." Jett nodded.

"And the sharks should be over there." She pointed somewhere behind her.

"Can't miss those."

"And the penguin playhouse . . ."

Jett watched her finger sliding over the open brochure as if on ice skates. So, this was how Cassie Everson acted when she was nervous. He couldn't recall her ever looking anything besides confident and oblivious to him through the black-and-white reels of his pubescent years. It was a nice feeling, knowing that *he* was making her nervous. That *he* was making her feel anything at all.

For a brief moment, he considered mentioning the loud yellow arrow to their right pointing them in the one and only direction.

But no, it was too much fun watching Cassie Everson scan her map. Too enjoyable seeing the little hints of care she put into this meeting, despite how nonchalant she was trying to be. The lightest shimmer of gold eyeshadow—made extra visible in how she was looking down and, more to the point, not *at* him. A white cable-knit sweater over dark-stained jeans. The twinkle of a silver chain with a single pearl, matching the simplicity of pearl studs on her ears. No tennis shoes this time, but a pair of Toms bearing, most festively, the design of thirty or so little nutcrackers throughout. All in all, she was stunning.

He settled against the wall.

A middle-aged woman stood supervising around a shallow, oblong area of water to their left, the sign "Touch A Ray Bay" written in clear letters above her. A dozen kids and their families leaned over, hands in the water as stingrays surfaced and swept by. "Remember, kids," she trilled merrily, wiggling her fingers in demonstration, "When sharks go by, fingers toward the sky!"

A parent hastily grabbed his daughter's fingers as a fin swept past.

Huh. Seemed like an insurance oversight right there.

"I guess we should go, then." Cassie continued to hold the map out in front of her like a platter.

He grinned. "I guess we should."

Stiffly, Cassie began to move, and Jett let her lead the way. She stopped politely at the tank of piranhas, watching them with the same quiet intensity as a private stroll through a renaissance art tour. They moved on to a cluster of seahorses with curlicued tails wrapped around *Caulerpa* microalgae. Metallic-blue poison dart frogs, Japanese spider crabs the approximate size and stature of Gollum. A cerulean wall of jellyfish using jet propulsion to inch along their way. Snippets of conversation started and ended with the topic of water life and displays in front of them, the "Did you know . . ." followed by Cassie reading the signs beside clown triggerfish and regal blue tang. They ventured off topic long enough for her to ask him about his work and then to explain about hers in turn, but little beyond that.

He had to admit, she was really, *really* bad at this.

At last the hall split, and the option came to divert away from the stingray bay and into the penguin playhouse. Cassie beelined for the bay.

Well, at least he knew where he stood.

She stopped at the glass.

"So, Jett." For the first time in ten minutes she looked straight into his eyes. It was almost startling. "I've learned from the background check about you passing drug tests and your previous employment. But you're going to have to forgive me for bringing up the little issue of incarceration. Crossing it out and writing 'nothing serious' on the background check doesn't quite cut it."

She tilted her head slightly with an encouraging nod, like a mother readying to hear a child's confession.

A stingray sailed past beside her, but her eyes stayed on his.

So, the inquisition had begun.

Bree had prepared him for this. After she herself had unloaded more questions than it took to get into the fire service, Bree had let him in on the details of the great Stingray Bay Inquisition. So earnest was Bree's expectation of tonight, he had no doubt the diver waving heartily in the background was his undercover accomplice, the overenthusiastic best friend of Cassie herself.

His eyes flickered back to Cassie.

"I did spend twenty minutes in jail. Once."

"And may I ask why?"

He tried, but couldn't hold back a grin. "Evading an officer. More specifically, getting a KOM on Strava. I'm, uh, king of the mountain."

She elucidated each word. "You are king of the mountain. I see."

She carefully folded up the map and set it inside her purse. With her hands newly freed, she crossed them in front of each other and took a step toward the glass.

Wow.

Bree had warned him of her trigger finger, but clearly he had seriously underestimated the situation. He spoke quickly. "I was biking down a segment of the parkway one day—"

"What kind of bike?"

"Road bike, and an officer caught me going pretty fast—"

"How fast?"

Here, his face and tone always had difficulty showing any remorse. "Clocked me at fifty-two."

"Fifty-two miles an hour? On a road bike?" A crack began to sliver across her forehead, revealing the merest glimmer of intrigue. "I didn't know that was possible."

She was impressed. Not fretting that he was reckless, not breaking into an emotional, womanly monologue about how dangerous road biking was, how one slick rock could've made his bike skid off and fly him into the trees. She wasn't going to tell him about how that one sister's-cousin's-boyfriend's-brother read in the paper once that some guy fell off his bike in Alaska and was immediately paralyzed from the neck down. Either she didn't care about him enough to worry about his safety or—and what he felt more assured of—the littlest flicker of the real Cassie was coming out. The strong one. The competitive one.

Gaining confidence, he switched his jacket from one hand to another. "To be honest, I think I got a couple miles higher than that, but that's what got put onto my ticket."

She grinned openly now. "For racing on a road bike? I can't believe they actually ticket for that."

"Well, when the person you dethroned from the KOM is the officer who chased you down the mountain, they sometimes take it personally."

She laughed then, the hazel in her eyes sparkling nearly as much as the glitter shadow above it. "And nothing else I should be aware of?"

"I'm still getting grilled? I sent you a background check. You know my credit score!"

She tipped her chin up. "Not as high as my 788, but you can't be too picky these days."

"Oh, good." He inched a step toward her. "Then I can explain the alektorophobia."

"The what?" She picked up on his sarcasm, her smile meeting her eyes.

An eager kid in a blue coat raced to the glass wall, knocking against her knees. She kept her eyes on him while stepping out of the kid's way, her palm pressing against the glass.

"Fear of chickens. Terrible, horrible fear of chickens. Can't even see eggs. IHOP is my nemesis."

"IHOP," she repeated, "is your nemesis."

Jett saw Bree swimming over before Cassie did, and following his eyes, Cassie turned too. As if realizing she had touched a hot burner, Cassie's hand slipped off the glass.

"Ready to move on?" she said hurriedly.

Jett grinned and planted his boots where they were. "Oh, look, Cassie. That diver's coming our way."

She shook her head. "No, I don't think so."

"Sure." Jett pointed to Bree, now squarely in front of them. "Look, she's waving at us. How nice."

He started waving back heartily, and Cassie began alternating between what was obviously a wave and a clear false-alarm-go-away sign. Instead, to Cassie's horror and Jett's mirth, Bree put her fist to the window and banged against the glass.

Bree had been right. That definitely gathered a crowd.

"Bye-bye, now." Cassie waved to the diver and, obviously at a point of desperation, slipped her arm around his elbow. "I'm starving. Do you want to get something to eat?"

Jolted by the sudden lock of their arms, his eyes broke from the glass down to Cassie. Back in his youth, she'd been the towering royal elf, Galadriel in bell-bottoms, the five-nine queen. Now he had over six inches on her, high enough to smell the coconut in her conditioner. Her eyes were begging, imploring him to move on, move away.

His smile gentled, voice softening. "You're stealing my lines now, Cassie Everson."

And as he urged her with a flick of his eyes to look through the glass, he watched her read the words scribbled across the underwater writing slate in Bree's hands: *Congratulations! You are our 100,000,000,000th visitors! Enjoy complimentary meal for two at The Cobbler's Steakhouse. Reservations: 7 p.m.*

"How many is that, Mom?" A kid tugged and pointed at the excessive zeros carried across the slate.

After one very, *very* long minute of reading and rereading the slate, Cassie looked up to Jett. There was an insuppressible grin and distinct sparkle in her eyes, as though he had at last pressed the right combination and the vault had clicked and opened. What had been the merest flicker of a dying bulb finally struck full power.

And all it took was dragging a thirty-five-thousand-pound fire engine across town, handing over every piece of his criminal and financial activity of the last twenty-nine years, and convincing both her friend and his to join in on the fun.

"One hundred billionth visitors," she said, her arm still looped around his. "That's a very big deal."

"Something worth celebrating as fast as possible, I'd imagine."

He turned her to the hall, enjoying the press of her arm between his own and his side.

"In that case, it's a good thing I know of a quick exit." She danced them backward through the crowd to a small, unimportant back door.

Cassie

Oh, that's right. You hung out with Cole and Stephen on the football team."

Jett spun his pasta around his fork, a wry grin on his face. "No."

"I mean, Greg and Jamie from swim team." Cassie smiled. "Remember how they always walked down the hall in their swim caps?"

Jett lifted his fork, his playful smile growing. "No."

"The Carter brothers from band?" she asked, desperation rising.

"No."

"Terry and the chess club?" she asked meekly.

Jett pointed his fork. "Bingo."

"I knew it." Cassie snapped her fingers triumphantly,

then dropped her napkin over her empty plate. Both the heat from the restaurant's crackling fire and the swimming conversation the last two hours was flushing her cheeks.

She practically started laughing before she could finish the next question. "Hey, do you remember that after-prom party at Drake's where Greg Lynley dozed off and woke up floating on an air mattress in Drake's pool?" Her laughter bubbled over into her words.

Jett grinned. Opened his mouth. Paused. "No."

Her laughter stopped. "I thought the whole school was invited."

"Of course you did. You are *the* Cassie Everson." Jett wiped his mouth, then laid the crumpled napkin on his plate. Perhaps it was the fire beside them, but his face, too, looked flushed as he bantered back and forth with her, his back resting comfortably against the dining-room chair.

"All right, then, Jett," Cassie said, flinging her hands in the air. "I've tried desperately to jog my memory of you the past two hours, and I've given you every chance to lie and make me believe you were cooler than you were. I give up. If you don't want to embellish your high school days to impress me, that's your prerogative."

"Does lying impress you? Because I can lie. I can be the best pathological liar you've ever met." He smiled with ease as he took the bill from the waiter, who was looking down at him suspiciously.

Cassie waved a hand in the air. "Forget it. I looked through the yearbooks anyways. I know about the bowl cut." She leaned forward. "How about you stick to the present, please. And leave nothing out."

"Nothing, eh? Don't tell me you have some grand escape plan worked out with The Cobbler's Steakhouse too."

"You kidding me? Guys never make it to the meal portion of the evening. Still, if you see me drop my fork and start crawling beneath tables for the front door . . ."

He laughed. She laughed back.

Both their eyes twinkled.

The luxury-cabin dining room was filled with votive candles and crisp white tablecloths. Busts of deer and elk and bear surrounded them from their lofty positions beneath the ceiling, and Cassie and Jett sat beside one large, roaring fireplace, knees nearly touching beneath the small table.

"Well, let's see," Jett began, sliding cash into the check holder and pushing it to the edge of the table. "You've already heard about my job. What I like to do. My family—"

"Your sister. Yeah. I remember her."

Jett lifted his brow. "Do you *really* remember her?"

"No, I really do."

He leaned forward in his chair. "Impossible. She was a year behind *me*."

Cassie shook her head. "Believe it or not, when I looked you up in the yearbooks, your last name kept popping into my mind, and it took me a minute, but I realized why." Cassie grinned widely and slapped one hand on the table. "Guess. You won't believe it."

"I don't know. You both . . ." He paused, clearly stumped to come up with any possible way their circles could have intersected. When he kept shaking his head, clearly shuffling through possibilities, she interjected.

"She was my reading buddy at Pittman Elementary!"

Cassie exclaimed. "Isn't that amazing? In Mrs. Richardson's class in fifth grade, we'd go every Friday to read to the first graders. And my reading buddy was Trina. Isn't that incredible?"

Cassie took the last piece of baguette from the basket as she shook her head, amazed at the coincidence. First she'd discovered *he* was the fireman she'd watched out her window that day at the Haven. Then she'd realized his sister was her one and only reading buddy. If she wasn't careful, she was going to believe this was fate.

"She was *such* a cute kid too. I remember how she'd get so excited whenever I came, and how she'd grab my hand and drag me to the tent so we could read in it together." Cassie smiled at the memory, practically smelling the crayons and seeing the rose-tinted books filtered by the rainbow tent around them. "I'd love to see her again. I can't believe it's been more than twenty years. Makes me feel old."

When she looked up from her baguette to him, however, she realized his playful smile had shrunk to a mere shadow, his eyes no longer twinkling.

Before she could begin to ask, or imagine, he spoke. "I haven't seen Trina, or my niece and nephew, in a little over a year now. Unfortunately, she's hit a rough patch . . . or rather, been stuck in a rough patch for a while."

He must've seen the way she looked at him, because he shrugged and added, "But I'm sure she'll come back soon."

Cassie felt, and resisted, the far-too-soon urge to reach over and touch his hand. Instead, she clasped hers together beneath the table. "I'm so sorry. I hope so too. So . . ." She searched for a milder topic. "You're an uncle, then?"

"Yeah. They're twins." His shoulders eased slightly as he, then she, stood. "And I tell you, if they all came as cute as those two, I'd want my house to be overrun with them."

Cassie felt her stomach flutter, but not in the way she wanted.

"Thankfully," he added with a wink, "I know all kids aren't that cute."

The knot in her stomach released. "Yeah," she said, releasing a breath. "Well, it sounds like you have the favoritism part down pat. I'd say you are doing your uncle job perfectly."

His smile drooped slightly, expressing the words he wasn't saying: *I want to. She just has to come back first.*

Instead, he motioned for the door. "Shall we?"

Cassie grinned. "I'm the one ambushed on this date. You call the shots however you want."

The parking lot sat at the entrance to the Great Smoky Mountains National Park, the only light around them coming from the streetlamps overhead and the shimmer of the Little Pigeon River in the distance. Cars filled every available space. Carolina silver bells, basswoods, and Frasers towered above and beyond them.

"Ambushed. Hijacked." Jett stopped beside her car. "Call it whatever you like, the point is I had to find a way to get you out to dinner, and I succeeded."

"By stealing my best friend and using my own moves against me." Cassie opened her door with a grin, the plastic bag with the words *The Cobbler's Steakhouse* hanging off her wrist. She set it on the passenger seat and turned back to him, laying both arms across the top of the door.

"Well, I've got just two questions left." Jett stopped at

the other side of her door and zipped up his jacket. Frost blew from his breath as he spoke.

A gust of cold air ripped through her own coat. For half a second, she considered taking the keys in her hand and turning the car on to heat it up. The tips of her sockless toes were already starting to bite beneath the thin canvas of her shoes.

But then, taking the three seconds to draw her eyes from him was enough to make her fold. Plus, the very idea that Jett could take that to mean she was ready to go was enough to make her slide her keys into her pocket altogether. She had tried to play things cool and casual, but the longer the evening wore on with Jett Bentley, the more terrifying it had become to feel the warmth, the zeal, the plain old enthusiasm welling up within her. This was *it*. Finally, she'd found somebody she wanted to be *somebody* with.

"Two questions. I'm listening," Cassie said.

"So, you've told me all about your family. I've met—and commandeered—your friend. You play tough but have a weakness for girlish romances. You're quasi-vegetarian, all rules off for pepperoni and overcooked bacon. Love the girls at your job but don't want the hassle of your own."

Cassie held her face steady but felt the slap of that false statement. She'd never *directly* said that she didn't want kids. No doubt, he'd surmised it from her profile. Well, not surmised so much as confirmed from the statement in ten-point bold: *DOES NOT WANT KIDS*.

"I laid my ninth-grade confessions on the table for you—" Jett continued.

"Which, as a free dating tip, you probably should've reserved such tidbits as Sharpie-ing our initials in your closet for our second date," Cassie added.

"Are you asking me out?" Jett grinned as Cassie bit her lip. "But, all that's to say, given our lifelong history together—"

Cassie chuckled. "Lifelong, eh?"

"The *decades* ago we first met," he forged on. "I only have two questions left. First, what are you doing Wednesday?"

"Wednesday? Aren't you supposed to let me wallow in anxiety and self-doubt for a couple of days before calling for a follow-up date?"

"Believe me, I'd be asking about tomorrow if I wasn't working. But if you want me to wait a week or two . . ."

"No, don't make me suffer on account of *me*," Cassie said hastily. "I can't think of a thing on my schedule for Wednesday. Count me in. Your second question?"

He crossed his arms with superiority. Paused. "Do you still have game?"

Cassie squinted. "You mean, can I still play ball?"

"That's exactly what I mean."

"Oh, I can play ball. Just tell me when and where." Cassie met his challenge with equal force. Half the afternoons a ball swished through the net at the Haven, Cassie was out there with the girls, sweating drops on the concrete pad.

"GP High. Six p.m."

Her brow raised. "You want to break into our high school?"

He shrugged with the nonchalance of a guy who was about to say something cool and knew it. "The athletic director owes me a favor."

"Ah. I see. What'd you do, save his house from burning to the ground?"

"Yes."

Cassie started, then began to nod. "Oh. Literally. Good work, then. Keep it up."

He rested his hand on the top of her car door and paused, the door separating their bodies but their faces suddenly not so far apart. "Till Wednesday, then."

The exposed skin of his neck was red from the chill, and beneath his form-fitting jacket sat a pair of dark jeans that complemented his green, button-down oxford. Any drift of cologne—if he wore any—was overpowered by the thousands of pines surrounding them, infusing their world with shouts of Christmas.

Nat King Cole's melody, "Almost Like Being in Love" came over the outdoor speakers, drawing them toward one another like the red-velvet ribbon draped around the large Christmas trees in shop windows.

"Till Wednesday," Cassie repeated softly.

He inched toward her, and then, bumping into the driver's side mirror, looked down to the door between them, which was currently working as hard as an elderly chaperone separating them at a middle-school dance.

"I probably could've thought that through better." Cassie gave the chaperone door a friendly pat.

He laughed, the mood breaking like a sunny March day on a frozen lake as he moved to the driver's side of his truck. Taking a half step in, his body lifted above the frame. "See you on the court, Everson. Bring your A game."

"It'll be my pleasure, Your Royal King of the Mountain."

They both climbed in and shut their doors. Started their cars.

Cassie's face hurt from smiling. For ten minutes she drove with that smile—a slaphappy grin. When a car cut her off turning into Food City, she had nothing but a Merry-Christmas-to-all grin to give him. As she slowly passed the lights of an ambulance and two feuding citizens beside busted cars, her wide and vibrant smile met them, and with understandable misunderstanding both citizens threw a few choice words toward her before turning back on each other. But there was nothing to be done about it. The smile wasn't going anywhere.

What if he was the one?

Her eyes were forced into a squint with the sudden and impossible burst of smile within a smile, as if it could get even wider. It was terribly embarrassing to even think these thoughts in the privacy of her car. But . . . wouldn't it be something? Everybody who ever got married had a first brush of meeting. What if she was just aware that this was hers? Instead of holding hands one day looking back at the fond recollection of their first date, telling each other cute little things like, "I never would've believed that night would change my life" or "If I had known that was going to be the start of everything," perhaps she gripped the steering wheel now, fully aware that *this* night was it. The first page of a hundred chapters together.

Wouldn't it be something?

Cassie turned on Profit and glanced over to her office. Girls Haven sat quiet, dark but for the blinking lights of the Christmas tree in the game-room window. The fire-engine stunt had been the hit of the season with the girls, many of whom she'd driven to cash in their gift cards on extra-vanilla, extra–white chocolate, extra–whipped cream, sure-why-not-add-peppermint-sprinkles triple-shot lattes that afternoon.

All of them, that is, but Star, who hadn't turned up.

Or returned her texts.

She flicked her turn signal and moved onto Day Street. The small homes there were lit by the occasional string of lights across paint-stripped porches, inflated snowmen, and retro nativity sets—the yellowed Marys seated quietly above baby Jesuses as poor and unnoticed as the renters watching televisions inside.

She slowed whenever she recognized one of the residences of her girls. A silhouette ghosted by of Destiny's mother walking past one of the windows—involved in her daughter's life, grateful for the Haven's services, always willing to lend a hand and dispense doughnuts. The hardworking single mother who'd pushed herself through night school to be an RN. One of her favorites.

Star's home was at the complex at the end of the street connecting Day to Seventeenth, the "ST" of the stop sign blotted out by black graffiti. Cassie neared it, then saw the blinking lights. She slowed as she watched the two patrol cars parked at the front of Star's building. When she spotted Ershanna, she jerked the steering wheel to pull into an empty parking space.

Bold as aluminum foil beneath the lamp post, Ershanna stood in her silvery puffer jacket, talking privately to an officer at the lower end of the building. With receding hairline tilted down, he nodded, listening to her while simultaneously jotting notes on his pad.

Cassie waited a beat while two other cars passed, then opened her door.

It was probably nothing. There were over ten—her eyes lifted to the windows, counting the lights, calculating the numbers—twelve apartments in the building alone, with half a dozen more buildings surrounding them. And Ershanna was a chatty-child adult, her personality one that drove toward drama instead of shutting the curtains and letting the matter deal with itself. Her talking to the officer meant little.

And yet, Star hadn't shown up.

And yet, she so uncharacteristically hadn't returned Cassie's texts.

Cassie hopped onto the sidewalk and quickened her pace. She sidestepped an overturned can as she turned up three concrete stairs.

"Ershanna?" She spoke softly, not wanting to be rude or interrupt.

Ershanna turned her face to Cassie. The mildly puzzled concentration of the girl's eyes told Cassie she had a hard time placing her.

"I'm Cassie. I know Star from Girls Haven."

"That's right." Ershanna's flat expression dissolved as she nodded expressively and turned, opening up the space for the three of them.

Not a good sign. Cassie didn't want any come-to-the-circle-this-involves-you vibe, didn't wish for any welcoming expression or stance.

Reluctantly, she stepped into the circle. "Is everything all right with Star?"

But just as she asked the question she heard a door open several floors above them and the distinct voice of Rachel, the social worker she'd talked with about Cam's case less than two weeks ago. "Sweetie, your sister is going to hold your hand, see?" she was saying through the child's screaming tantrum.

Something to the effect of "I don't want to go" followed by a garbled "Mypapeesndheidr" poured repeatedly from the little girl's lungs and spread out into the night air.

Then, suddenly, Cassie saw Star. She withdrew immediately and began jogging toward the stairs.

"Ma'am. Ma'am!" the officer called after her, but Cassie only stepped quicker, her Toms slipper-soft quiet as she bounded up one set and began another. Perhaps that, too, was something she had in common with Jett Bentley: evading officers.

Halfway up the stairs, she met them. "Star?"

Star was hip-holding Deidre, whose six-year-old legs hung loosely toward the ground. Her youngest sister, Kennedy, the four-year-old Cassie had only heard about in stories, sat in Rachel's arms, though the child seemed unable to make up her mind between tear-filled shrieks toward the door and her older sister. She arched her back, and Rachel gripped the railing.

Cassie grabbed Rachel's coat and held her steady through another round of "Mypapeesndheidr!"

"She wants Tinker Bell," Star explained, her words stiff and emotionless, detached from the chaos around her. "She wants her puppy."

"A puppy?" Rachel craned her neck around the mass of

the little girl's hair to catch Star's eyes. "A real puppy is in there?"

"No, a stuffed one. It's in my room."

Cassie turned to Rachel. She wanted to ask what was going on. She wanted to interrupt whatever swift transition they were making to demand answers. But the child shrieked again, and all Cassie could manage was, "Can I get it for her?"

Rachel's eyes darkened with unspoken meaning. She looked to the child. "Sweetie, we think little puppy—Tinker Bell—is too sick and needs to stay behind. I don't think—"

"*Mypapeesndheid!*"

Cassie held on to the back of the girl's pale-pink shirt as she reared again. Snot from cold and tears was forming a stream down her lips and past her chin, leaving clear circles on Rachel's thick parka. Cassie wasn't sure what Rachel meant by the dog being too sick, but she could venture the dog needed some sort of heavy cleaning. In hushed tones, she spoke, "What if I took Tinker Bell home and cleaned her up? I'd bring her back to . . ."

To where exactly? And for how long? And why? There were a hundred possible places, and reasons, and lengths of time they were going. The questions were building each moment.

With great effort, Rachel regripped the child on her hip. "You don't want to go in there, Cassie. But can you help me get them to the car?"

It was at that moment Cassie noticed the extreme juxtaposition between the dress of the social worker and the children she was trying, with such difficulty, to get down the stairs. While Rachel's blue parka had a thickness hinting of bulky wool sweaters and down feathers, a gust of wind would roar straight through Kennedy and Star's thin cotton shirts. Only Deidre had a jacket on, though the smiling blue princess printed on the back grinned as if she were as cold as the girl wearing it. And while Deidre wore the jacket, the flip-flops were doing nothing for her toes.

"Of course." Cassie reached her hands out, searching for a way to give them use. "Can I carry Deidre, Star?"

But Deidre, wordless in the whole affair, only dug her head into Star's collarbone and gripped her neck tighter.

"Or I can try and hold Kennedy?" Cassie looked to Rachel, whose typically polished, shoulder-length hair was being tossed by flailing elbows.

"Yes."

"Mypapeesndheidr! *I wan my papee!*"

Cassie pried the child off Rachel and, with difficulty, put her on her hip. One arm protectively around her back, Cassie gripped the railing and managed to start down the stairs.

The child gave a guttural cry, her small head dropping on Cassie's neck with a new and different explosion of tears. Her forehead was burning hot.

Cassie rounded for another set of steps.

The little girl began to tremor, and Cassie knew it was because of far more than the icy breeze. It was as though she could feel the little girl's sense of loss now complete, the realization that she was going to lose her puppy, that her hands weren't big enough to reach up those few steps and wrap her arms around it. That no matter how loud she cried or how desperately she asked, begged, pleaded for help, the adults weren't going to hear her. Whatever was going to happen to her puppy, and whatever had happened in that home in the hours, days, weeks, and years prior, was completely and utterly out of this little girl's control.

"Mypapee!"

Four steps to the bottom.

Three steps to the bottom.

"Mypapee! Mypapee! *Mypapee*!"

Two.

One.

"I'm going to go get it." Cassie turned abruptly and handed the child back over to Rachel, not waiting for a response as she darted up the stairs. Come fleas, bugs, human waste, meth, it didn't matter. She would scrub that dog and drop herself in a bath of Lysol if it came to it, just to hear the little girl stop screaming in that manner.

"Cassie, really—" Rachel called after her, but Cassie didn't stop.

A man in an orange hazmat suit stood in the living room. With the toe of his foot he nudged a pile of dirty clothes. An empty pill bottle surfaced, and he squatted to take a look. When she stepped inside, he looked up.

"Just getting something for Rachel."

He nodded and turned back to his work.

Cassie became painfully aware of the inadequacy of her canvas shoes as she tiptoed swiftly through the living room, careful to avoid the piles. After five large strides beyond the front door came the hall to the bedrooms, and she wrapped her arms around herself as she entered the narrow path.

She heard the refrigerator door to her left open and saw

an officer, a man without a suit this time—one she recognized. The cries of the child outside were a continuous reminder of the need to return as soon as possible. Still, the urge to know pushed her to sidestep into the kitchen.

"Mike, what's going on here?"

Mike Slade had run in the same circles as Cassie for years—everything from the same gym membership and friendly barbeque invites to the same geometry class back in middle school. Though she spoke far more with his wife, she'd had a number of conversations with Mike—restricted generally to the cuteness of his kids and work. In one sense they understood each other more than the others. They knew the grit of the other's job in ways mutual friends and acquaintances did not.

He straightened. "This one of your girls?"

Cassie nodded.

He shook his head. "I hate to see it."

She took a step into the kitchen, observing her surroundings. Every cabinet door hung open, either because Slade had just inspected it or because it had been left that way. Whereas the living room was knee-deep in dirty, broken, and used objects best shoveled out to the dump, here each cabinet was empty. No cans of beans and peas, no boxes of noodles, no Cheerios inside the empty boxes of cereal.

She flicked a bag of chips, and it slid across the counter.

How had this happened to another one of the Haven girls in a month? Another girl pulled from her home without Cassie having a clue how bad it was? Another girl living in such conditions that DCS warranted removal?

Cassie felt her throat wobble, and she clenched her teeth

with a determined steadiness. Not Star. She cared for all the girls, genuinely loved them all. But oh, she loved Star.

She felt the urge to run to her car and drive like a wild woman around town, knocking on the doors of each and every one of the forty-eight girls who dropped in every day. What were they doing tonight? What sort of situations were they living in? She wanted to set each one in a chair tomorrow, to give them the inquisition until she knew with absolute certainty their lives were in good shape. That there was nothing to hide.

But Star? She'd *known* something was going on with Star. She knew her stepfather had come back into the picture, knew her mother was unpredictable, suspected worse facts hidden shallowly beyond that. But Star kept coming to the Haven every afternoon. Kept that smile on her face, kept boxing out the questions whenever Cassie tried to move in.

Especially after Cam's departure and the news of Star's stepdad's return, Cassie had been more diligent. She'd "broken" several of those rules in the fat handbook on her desk: Don't give out full-frontal hugs. Don't keep up private communication after hours with the teens. Avoid becoming friends on social media.

Yeah, right.

Those rules were written by the wise, perhaps, but not by the ones personally holding the door open for the kids every day.

Cassie had spent at least fifteen hours a week with Star for the past six years. Fifteen. That meant she spent *at minimum* seven-hundred-and-eighty hours with Star each year. Tack on the summer camps and special trips, and she was at well over a thousand. At some point, "child in question" became "close as blood," and rules went out the window.

Mike spoke. "Looks like someone tried to get a lab off the ground but failed. Hazmat team took a look around, but they're clearing out now."

"Yeah, I ran into one of them in the living room." Cassie took a step closer, catching sight of the two unopened soda cans in the otherwise empty fridge. "Where's the girls' mother?"

"I'm sure DCS will be coming down tomorrow, asking you the same." Mike opened the second bottom shelf, confirmed its lack of contents, and shut it.

"The girls aren't talking much. One of their neighbors made the call, saying their mom split a while ago. Best I can tell, they've been on their own a few weeks."

"Weeks?" Cassie crossed her arms, trying to think of the exact date she had spoken with Star about her stepdad. Her mom had still been home then, hadn't she? She thought so, but Star had been intentionally vague.

"I spoke with Star about her stepdad about three weeks ago. She led me to believe her mother was still around. At the time Star said her stepfather was planning to leave town." Cassie squeezed her eyes shut, remembering. "Actually, she said he was planning to leave that weekend. Oh, I hope they haven't been on their own that long. I can't believe she didn't tell me."

"Maybe the girl thought her mother would be returning soon." He stood and adjusted his belt. "Maybe the mother still plans to. Not that she'll find her daughters here when she returns."

Cassie shivered. It felt like forty degrees in there. "What's going to happen?"

"Well, I don't know what all she'll be charged with, but child neglect alone—"

"Yes, yes." Cassie nodded, well aware of the court procedures ahead. "The girls, I mean. What will happen to them?"

But she already knew. Even while he started to reply, she heard the cries of the youngest in the stairwell and stepped backward. "Actually, I've gotta get something and bring it back to Rachel. Thank you, Mike. I'll see you around."

"I'll see you. Sorry about the news."

"Thanks." Her reply was feeble as she withdrew into the hall and dodged the piles of refuse there. At the first open door, she stepped over a naked Barbie and into the room. Definitely Star's. Besides a couple of aged movie posters, Cassie recognized several sweaters hanging on hangers in the open closet and strewn across the floor. A Pack 'n Play stood squarely in the center of the room. Star's black backpack hung off a chair where a Spanish 2 textbook sat at the top of a wobbly stack.

Cassie gingerly opened the unzipped backpack and peeked inside. DCS was moving too quickly to even pick up her school laptop? She pursed her lips, shivering again.

She slid the computer out of the bag and just as she did so felt the unmistakable tickle of a bite beneath her jeans, above her ankle.

Time to go.

On top of the twin mattress in the corner lay the stuffed dog, its nose pressed into the wall. Balancing on the spring of a second twin mattress on the floor, she grabbed it.

The silver frame on the window sat on the ledge above it. Pulling the frame in for a closer look, she ignored the second bite on her ankle and stared at the photo. The girls pressed in close around their new Santa fireman friend, giddy grins slapped across each face as they delighted in the surprise visit and euphoria around their united project. It had been a good day. Even Star had her lanky elbows hanging over Cassie's shoulder as they pressed their faces together, smiling at the camera.

Star. Whatever would she do without her buddy?

Cassie took a sharp breath. There was a very real possibility that Star wouldn't be coming back to Haven. Not a certainty, no, but at least a fifty-fifty chance. Who knew where the teen would end up. She never spoke about extended family; no support groups ever came to her side at the Haven's array of get-togethers. The Haven was big on encouraging as much family involvement as possible, and yet it was never Star's mother or uncle or grandmother who showed up to volunteer at a dodgeball tournament or start that (albeit failed) community garden. Without family, she and her sisters would be merging into the system. And if the foster family lived farther out—and odds were they would—would they actually commit to picking Star up from the Haven every day? Of course not.

For that matter, was there really a family out there who would take all three? And one a teen? All they would hear would be the ominous word *fourteen* before the fears and statistics started whispering. They wouldn't know what a mother Star was—how Deidre looked to her as if she could carry the city on her shoulders, how Star had always kept an eye out for her at the Haven, even when she was busy doing her own teenage thing.

Potential fosters had never heard Star cackle at her own jokes, had never seen the way she welcomed new girls into the Haven and helped them feel at home. It was a gift of hers, a way of sensing the needs of others without a whiff of explanation. Few could do that.

The possibility that Star—*Star*—had not only gone through this trauma but would now face the potential of being stripped away from her sisters . . .

The silver frame beneath her thumb crackled in protest and she released the pressure, looking down.

Cassie knew what she must do.

She should feel terrified. But instead she felt her body rushing forward, expelling her through the hall and out the apartment door.

"Rachel!" Cassie called, stumbling down the steps as she felt her phone *ding* inside her coat pocket.

Jett

Jett let go of the pull-up bar in his doorway. It was out of character for him to be impatient, but he simply couldn't wait one more minute.

He rubbed a slick palm across his chest as he picked up his phone.

Had a great time tonight.

Jett hit backspace rapidly until the terrible sentence disappeared. *Had a great time tonight?* Of course he'd had a great time. They'd parroted those exact words back and forth several times before even hitting the parking lot.

Home safe and sound?

Nope. Women prone to old-fashioned chivalry would take that as considerate and protective, but Cassie—the woman who prided herself on walking through dark parking lots behind her not-so-suburban workplace—would be more likely to write him off altogether.

He backpedaled until he stared yet again at a blank screen. He took in a deep breath, waited five seconds far too long for inspiration, then dropped the phone on the bed. Ten more pull-ups on the doorway bar and he reached for the phone again.

> If you lose Wednesday, are you going to skip out on dinner afterward? Best to know if I'm going to need to call a backup date.

He read it again. It wasn't exactly a Robert Frost original, but it was better than nothing.

Pressing Send, he tossed the phone on the bed for another set, aware that with every pull-up his ears strained to hear a muted *ding* against the black comforter.

A *ding* came, but it wasn't from his phone.

Jett heard the TV turn down in the living room. The door opened.

"Jett, you got company!"

Jett arched his head back mid-pull-up but only saw Sunny blocking the doorway. He sped up to finish the set, wiped his hands against his sweats, and started down the small hall. When a set of curly blond heads dodged around Sunny, however, he broke into a jog—running until he slid to a halt on his knees and wrapped the twins in his arms.

Dakota and Drew squealed as they squirmed to be free from his embrace, all the while giggling. Drew broke loose and stole a couple of feet away before Jett snatched him by the back of his coat. Drew wailed in glee, his blue snow boots dragging back into the hug.

"Look at you! What big kids you are! Did you miss me?"

Dakota flung her arms around his neck while Drew made for another getaway. Jett closed his eyes momentarily, Dakota's soft, platinum-blond curls covering his face. He kept one hand on the back of Drew's coat, feeling Drew tug and laugh.

"We need to crash here tonight."

And just like that, a frost far colder than the twenty-four-degree air swept into the living room. Jett opened his eyes. Looked up to his sister.

"Hello, Trina. It's good to see you."

She didn't smile. "Hello."

Gripping Dakota on his hip, he stood and faced her. "If I'd known you were coming, I would've made up a bed for you . . . but absolutely. Come on in."

Sunny shut the door and stood between them, frying in the middle of the awkward silence as Jett and his sister took each other in.

"My phone wasn't working," Trina finally said.

Jett nodded, well aware of how "finicky" her phone could be. "Sure."

His eyes tracked across Trina's face. He wasn't surprised by what he saw, but it hurt just the same. Her dead eyes, her protruding cheekbones fruitlessly veiled by dull skin. The same long, blue coat swamped around her skin and bones just as it had this time last year—perhaps even more. Where had his baby sister gone?

It'd been a year since the incident surrounding her addictions and the twins' lack of safety finally scared him enough to make him go down to DCS to file a report. A year since she'd met the social worker at her door and fled—from the worker and from him.

From the way she looked at him now, he knew she hadn't forgiven him, that if she had any other place to go tonight, she would've gone there instead. Everything in her stance made her thoughts clear as crystal. *You betrayed me. You humiliated me. You aren't on my side.*

But, oh, if he could only get through to her how much he was.

Between them, Sunny began to clap. "Reunion! Yaaay."

And that's when Jett looked down, his jaw opening slightly as he saw the car seat at Trina's feet.

"Trina?" He weighed his voice carefully as he took a step toward them. "Is there a baby in there?"

He bent down slowly, Dakota's arms still wrapped tightly around his neck.

"TJ," Drew declared loudly, standing inches from the television, eyes glued on the football spiraling across the field.

A blanket covered the car seat. Jett lifted the corner.

A baby so small it could fit within the length of his forearm lay unhooked in the car seat, fast asleep.

The slap on his arm was loud, startling. "Don't you dare wake him," Trina hissed, then hoisted the car seat up with two hands. "Where can he go?"

Jett locked his jaw, forcing the frustration down. She'd had a baby. Another baby.

Holding Dakota tighter, he put a smile on his face and motioned with his stinging arm toward the back hall. "He can stay in my room. I don't have a crib, of course, but—"

"He'll sleep in the seat."

He nodded, though even to his own childless ears that sounded suspicious. "I'll take you back."

"I remember where it is."

Yes, but he bet she also remembered where he kept his checks. "Even so. Let me help you." He reached and took the car seat from her grip. The whole thing lifted from her slumped shoulders as if it couldn't have weighed more than fifteen pounds, baby included.

"How old is he?"

"Six weeks."

He nodded, his throat constricting. How odd it was to feel something for a kid upon nothing more than a glance. Less than a glance. Another new relative changed things. All of a sudden he had one more being to care about. One more kid to worry over.

Stop this madness! Get your life back, Trina. Now.

He wanted to talk some sense into her, plead with her, *make* her change. Lock her in a bedroom for two weeks, *force* her back to reality, to life. But she'd heard his pleading a thousand times before, and a thousand times before she had walked right out that door again, saying fanciful things about changing but never following through.

The rule was simple: Always love. Always try. But never, *ever* raise your expectations.

And yet he couldn't stop hoping, couldn't stop persisting in the belief she'd someday be freed.

He set the car seat against the closet door, smoothly slid a couple of checkbooks from the desk drawer into his back pocket, and mentally went through the checklist in his room for any valuables. As he turned, he lifted the blanket for another peek.

"TJ's his name, you say?" His voice was low, matching the quiet of the room.

Trina peeled off her coat and sat on the bed. She looked as worn out as any woman he'd ever seen, as worn out as their mother had been, battling those same demons long ago.

She nodded and put her face to her hands. "Yeah. TJ."

Dakota tugged at his arm, then pushed her finger in his face.

"Is he going to need anything? Formula or something?"

"In the bag." She spoke without opening her eyes, and it was clearer than Dakota's baby-blue eyes that he could push Trina over with one finger and she'd be asleep before she touched the comforter.

Who knew where she'd come from. How far she traveled just to get here.

Again, Jett looked to the baby. Maybe the tiny being in that car seat would be her miracle baby, bringing her back to life.

He was breaking the rule, but hoping just the same.

"Boo-boo," Dakota insisted, pushing her finger in his face again.

He kissed her finger and repositioned her on his hip.

"I'll take it from here. You go on and lay down."

She moved under the covers without another word. Jett turned to the door, paused, and looked back to the car seat. Several seconds of deliberating went by before he tiptoed over and pulled back the blanket. He watched TJ's closed lids flutter as he tucked the blanket beneath his small arms, then stepped back and shut the door behind him.

Trumpets blared to the rhythm of a drum line as Jett and his affectionate sloth of a niece moved through the living room. Drew had moved to the couch beside Sunny and was very seriously mimicking whatever gestures Sunny had taken upon himself to demonstrate. Currently, UT was winning.

"Yeeeeaaaaaaahhhhhhhhh, baby!" Sunny gave an exaggerated growl as he pounded the air three times and looked expectantly to his toddler comrade.

"Yeeeeeeaaahhhhh, baby!" Drew jumped on the couch and repeated the gesture.

"I'm going to run to the store." Jett paused, awkwardly uncertain of his new responsibility. "Drew you, uh, wanna come?"

The football on the screen spiraled to the receiver. An eruption of cheers from thousands of orange fans followed.

"We're good here, man." Sunny gave a thumbs-up and returned his attention to the game, giving a hardy slap on his thighs as he and Drew started hopping like monkeys.

Jett grabbed his keys and shut the door. He was halfway down the stairs when the realization hit him.

Car seats. Three-year-olds still used car seats, right?

Up the stairs he started again, asking Dakota along the

way, "You think you can stay with Sunny and your mom while I run to the store?"

But before he could even get the question out, her nails were digging into his neck. She was scrawny, yes, but she held on as though her fingers were Gorilla Glued to his skin.

He stopped at the door, lingering in the hallway. "Just for a few minutes? I'd be right back. You can watch the football game . . ."

And then she began to wail, the note matching the volume of the siren on his Medic 2–10—yet with the added bonus of being directly against his ear.

"I'll bring you back a treat, Dakota." Desperately he grabbed the doorknob. "You still like those sour gummies?"

She raised her pitch an octave higher.

"I'll take that as a no."

"Jett?"

Jett turned to see Sarah in her doorway, swiftly tightening her robe. Her striped pajama pants and socks peeked out from underneath.

She gave a wry smile. "Need I ask?"

Jett swung his body around for Sarah to see Dakota's tear-streaked face. He practically yelled over the crying. "Sarah, meet my beautiful niece, Dakota."

Sarah took a step toward them. "Why, hello there, Dakota." She touched the girl's back lightly before covering one of Dakota's cold, red hands with one of her own. Sarah looked up into Jett's eyes. "Why are you outside?"

"I'm thinking through my options."

"Want to skip the hypothermia and think through your

options in my place?" She pushed the door open with her free hand. "I make a mean hot cocoa. Straight from the packet and everything."

It was two hours to midnight, the kid was three years old, and the last thing he had a feeling his niece needed was forty grams of sugar. Nevertheless, he was also fairly certain the ear-deafening wail she'd so blessedly provided for every neighbor in the complex had all been performed with a single intake of breath. These were desperate times. "Absolutely."

Inside the apartment, tears immediately stopped, wails ceased, and Dakota peeled herself off Jett—more than that, she hopped down and skipped toward a chair at the breakfast table. He could be replaced easily.

"So, what are you going to do?"

After listening to his explanation and preparing everyone's cocoa, Sarah leaned against the kitchen wall and cradled a mug in her hands.

"I'm not sure how long Trina's staying, but no matter what, the kid needs a bed. Right?" He looked at Sarah with uncertainty. Of all the topics he could throw out a sentence or two about at a dinner party, babies were not one of them.

"No, you shouldn't leave the baby in the car seat overnight. That's like leaving them in cars when you go into the supermarket."

His brow lifted. "And that . . . is definitely bad."

"And on that note, let's just be glad they aren't yours."

"Kidding."

Sarah popped her hip off the wall, setting her mug on

the counter with resolution. "You just stay here. I'll be back in less than an hour."

And sure enough, forty-three minutes later, Sarah sent him home with some sort of portable bed contraption from a mother of three two buildings over and a trash bag full of formula, three different kinds of bottles ("for if the baby gets particular" Sarah stated), a pack of newborn diapers, two packs of wipes, and a handful of newborn-sized clothes.

An hour after that, the twins lay on a sleeping bag on the living room floor. Jett had managed to set up the foul bed contraption and had gingerly begun to transfer his newest nephew to it.

Which prompted the tiny blue eyes to open. And the newborn shrieks to begin.

Two hours after that, with the kitchen covered in bags of baby items, formula dust spilled on counters, an unusually fat diaper lying open faced on the carpet, and three dirty bottles lying in the sink (turned out TJ *was* particular), Jett abandoned the portable bed, and all eight pounds of the little guy settled upon Jett's chest. Jett leaned back against the recliner, wearily rubbing his eyes.

He couldn't fathom how Trina did it.

Truly. Some people said that as a means of expressing a compliment at someone's hard work, but in this case, he meant it in the deepest sense.

It was a real miracle these kids were alive.

Then, impossible to his own ears, he heard the faint *ding* of his cell phone, the text to Cassie and his hope for a reply having been forgotten what seemed a lifetime ago. Carefully, inch by inch, he reached for his back pocket. The clock read 1:43 a.m.

> Backup date? You've clearly forgotten where you live, son. The closest decent backup date would live two hours away. Better start getting used to me.

Cassie

She couldn't let this little, tiny, totally all-encompassing thing like harboring three girls stop her from at least *trying* to have the man of her dreams. Even if it meant she was breaking all sorts of social communication rules by returning a text well after midnight.

Cassie's heart felt like Thumper from the old *Bambi* movie had moved in and taken residence. Then again, texting Jett wasn't entirely to blame for that; she'd felt on the tip of a stroke for hours.

Four hours ago she'd shuffled clumsily through a conversation with Rachel about where the girls would be placed, and eventually the girls moved from Rachel's car to hers. Three hours ago she'd foraged through her own totally unprepared pantry for some sort of hot meal to soothe the four-year-old's incessant crying. But Kennedy cried through the offer of elbow noodles and butter, quinoa and black beans, and scrambled eggs. She cried through the offer of chicken noodle soup. She cried through the offer of five different types of cheese.

Despite Star's attempts to calm her sister, Kennedy was clearly terrified. She had a 101.6-degree fever. She didn't like or understand anything about her current situation—including Cassie. The child wouldn't even look at her, and Cassie felt helpless in her own home. And so she kept cooking.

Two hours ago had been the heavy lifting. Cassie pushed a desk to the corner of the "office" she never utilized. Nearly decapitating herself in the process, she folded up the treadmill in the "gym room" she hadn't touched since her short-lived New Year's resolution of 2016. She dragged cardboard boxes of childhood keepsakes off the guest mattress.

Not that any of her work was very useful. In the end, Deidre and Kennedy deserted the beds Cassie made with soft, rose-colored quilts, covered with her own beloved stuffed animals from her own childhood. Cassie had followed a sneaky trail of water from the laundry room to Star's bed, where she found Deidre and Kennedy snuggled up with their sister. Kennedy clutched the sopping wet dog, Tinker Bell, she had stolen from the wash.

At least it was cleaned.

That was more than could be said for the girls, as with

the night they'd already had, Cassie hadn't had the heart to try.

So after all were in bed, Cassie busied herself cleaning all the nonliving things around the house—as in things that wouldn't scream violently whenever she touched them. It was 1:05 a.m. when she finally caught Jett's text and was brought back to her former world.

Four minutes of deliberating passed before she wrote the short, playfully committed text and pressed Send. Cassie waited on her bed, knees bent to her chin, mildly aware of her own bated breath.

His reply was instant. Whoa, now. Didn't realize I was signing up for dating a night owl.

The corners of Cassie's lips twitched as she began to type. A turnoff? Tucked yourself in early?

When his reply didn't come immediately, she picked up the cup of hot tea. She wasn't worried.

Still, communicating without the ability to catch his facial cues or tone was enough to build up a little doubt. Perhaps she had annoyed him. Perhaps her message had woken him up and he was being serious.

She held the cup closely to her lips, focusing all her energy on watching the little tea grains floating in the tawny water. More specific, she was *not* focusing on his reaction. She was *not* focusing on potentially passive-aggressive responses or the growing feeling of regret.

Could she help it she was too excited to wait until the morning?

Finally, the phone beeped.

Nope. Still wide awake. Just tucking in all the kids.

Cassie exhaled, grinning at his joke.

Naturally. I almost forgot about the secret wife and kiddos.

She put her cup back on the bedside table and rubbed her eyes. The adrenaline of the day was wearing off like a drip pulled from her arm, and before she could get to the point of being too lazy to get up at all, she moved to the bathroom and took out her contacts. Her phone beeped as she spit toothpaste into the running water.

What about you? Night on the town? Or were you busy tucking in all your kids too?

If he only knew.

She rubbed her mouth on the hand towel and replied the only way he wouldn't take her seriously. The truth.

Just hanging out in potential meth labs. Washing the kids' clothes. Moving treadmills.

Your usual, then.

She grinned. Naturally. Off to bed now.

Night-night.

Cassie set her phone on the stand and switched off the light. She heard one of the youngest cough down the hall.

The image of two diverging roads sprawled across the back of her eyelids, and with quickening breath she opened her eyes, staring up at the blank ceiling.

This was going to be fine.

This wasn't going to be an issue at all.

Cassie adjusted the feathery pillow beneath her head.

If given the time, she *would* fall for Jett Bentley. She knew it with a certainty that betrayed her slow and methodical methods.

It wasn't just about settling for what was left of the litter. He was kind. He was fun. He made her laugh in the middle of a serious conversation. He was the kind of guy who leaned on the side of down-to-earth experiences, but at the same time knew how to take a girl out.

And most important, he had a credit score of 747. And a beat-up truck with 319,000 miles. *Clearly* she was well on her way to becoming a trophy wife.

But then, there were the girls.

Rachel had been vague about the children's future. She'd said a meeting with DCS would come in a few weeks after Rachel gathered more information about the situation. The decision to bring the girls in right now had been only as a temporary haven.

Even so, Cassie wasn't stupid. She knew Star's family tree fairly well, and none of it included some benevolent aunt about to step up. So unless there was some long-lost relative willing to take the girls in, they were going to be displaced for a while. Maybe a long while.

What would Cassie do then, faced with that reality?

One day at a time. She'd just have to take it one day at a time.

Two separated, curvy roads shifted back into her mind and she punched the pillow beneath her once more, forcing her eyes to shut, and with it, the worries that would have to wait until tomorrow.

Had she told herself she would take it one day at a time? Silly her. She meant hour.

"No, no, Deidre. Let's leave the doctor's—" She blinked, unable to remember the word. Long sticks. Cardboard. No, not cardboard. Stickish. Of wood. It was only one o'clock and she felt like she needed an espresso IV. "Let's leave the doctor's bowl of sticks alone."

"Tongue depressors," the doctor said with a mild grin. He tried, yet again, to press the stethoscope to Kennedy's back. "Can you hold her still?"

"Believe me, I'm trying." Cassie regripped her arms around Kennedy's waist. Kennedy arched back, another successful four-year-old thwarting two grown-ups.

At least for the moment she wasn't crying.

The doctor pulled back after one more attempt, rolled his chair over to where Deidre was now inching her hand toward the glass jar of cotton balls, and picked up his clipboard. "I'm going to jump next door while we wait on the results. I'll be back in a few minutes, Ms. Everson."

Oh, sure. Super. No problem. These were all words

she would've calmly said in her former single life. *Are you crazy*, however, was the phrase that now came most clearly to mind.

"Okay." Cassie kept her voice calm while hoping he saw the screaming in her eyes. She was currently at that level of desperation—not yet pleading out loud for mercy, but begging without words.

"You're doing great. But I would try to keep that one from licking the floor again."

She nodded as she regripped Kennedy, the slippery worm who had in fact been caught licking the floor ten minutes earlier. The sound of the door shutting was like the nail in a coffin.

For not the fifteenth time today, she wished Star had stayed back from school to help *her*, not the other way around. Star was the one who was transitioning into all of this like the real adult. In fact, at 7:00 a.m. Cassie had walked into a kitchen of stacked plates and used frying pans, where Star had created a breakfast fit for queens: toast, bananas, and whole slices of cheese covering scrambled eggs. Kennedy ate three helpings of Star's concoction, including Cassie's share.

Star was the real grown-up here. And really, who needed algebra?

Kennedy squirmed her way off Cassie's lap again and moved toward the doctor's computer plug.

"Who wants another story?" Cassie plucked the book from the office's top stack. Gingerly she turned the page, trying not to think about how many illnesses lived on it. She began reading the story of a big red dog making well-meaning but silly mistakes. In seconds Kennedy dropped the cord and jumped back onto Cassie's lap as if they were the closest of friends. It took a couple of pages to draw Deidre in, but eventually her bony elbows pressed against Cassie's thigh as she leaned over her to see the pages.

Which led to the questions.

"What's that man doing?" Kennedy asked.

"He's painting his house."

"Why's he painting his house?"

"Maybe the paint was peeling off."

"Why did the paint peel off?"

"Maybe because it was old." Cassie turned the page, reading the text above the furry feline in the tree. "'As they walked along the sidewalk, they heard a strange sound. Why, it sounded like it came from the sky!'"

Deidre pointed. "What's that man doing?"

"He's going up a ladder into the tree."

"Why's he going up a ladder?"

Cassie took a new approach. "Because he's a fireman, and that's what happens when cats get stuck in trees. You call the fire department and they come to save your kitties." Cassie turned to Deidre. "Do you like kittens, Deidre?"

Deidre looked up at her, the same serious expression in her gaze. She turned her head back to the page.

Deidre had not spoken since Cassie had found her hanging on Star's hip at the apartment. Not one word.

Three more books and 120 questions from Kennedy later, the doctor returned and gave her the news.

"You have one tough cookie on your hands, Ms. Everson. Kennedy's test came back positive for strep, plus a double ear infection. Ten days of amoxicillin should do it." He ripped off a sheet and handed it to Cassie. "I'd also like to see them on a diet plan until they are up to full speed."

Cassie scanned the list of food recommendations as he talked about their BMI.

"And . . ." Cassie hesitated, casting a glance to Deidre, trying to figure out how to word the question without her knowing. "About the . . . nonverbal . . . issue. Is there anything you would recommend? Anything I should be doing?"

His eyes dropped to Deidre as she flipped through Cassie's keys. He held on to his clipboard. "I've added the numbers of a few specialists at the bottom of that page for that very reason. It could be a speech impediment, possibly a delay—" He glanced to his sheet. "—though everything else seems to indicate she's right on track. Has she *ever* spoken to you before?"

Cassie shook her head, flooded with guilt at the knowledge that Deidre had been coming to the Haven for four months now and she'd never noticed. She saw her smile on occasion. Knew she was shy. But how could Cassie have not noticed that she wasn't talking? Did she do her job at all?

"Well, I'd call Dr. Mernit first," the doctor continued. "She does great work using play therapy. She'll be an excellent resource. Otherwise, just keep doing what you're doing."

Cassie thanked him, signed the lengthy medical form Rachel had forwarded to her at midnight the night prior, and discussed scheduling for a follow-up appointment in two weeks.

The next three hours, however, slipped by in a blur.

Picking up pills at the pharmacy should've taken ten

minutes. The grocery stop on the way home should've taken twenty. A quick, spontaneous trip down the toy aisle of Target shouldn't have been more than five.

And yet somehow—she couldn't pinpoint how—it was four o'clock and there were still groceries on the counter to unload. As Cassie drew a bag toward herself, she caught Star looking at her from the bar stool, an environmental science book open beside her school computer.

"Are you going to quit your job?"

The question came out of nowhere.

"What?" Cassie pulled out one of five boxes of macaroni. "No. Why would you think that?"

"You skipped today."

"And?"

Star shut her computer. "And you haven't skipped a day since I started coming."

Cassie shrugged, opening the cherrywood cabinet. "Sure I have."

"No. You've made appointments and stuff, but you've never missed a whole day."

"So I'm a genius, then, because I now have enough vacation days to roll me over to July." Cassie took a few steps toward the window to glance in on the living room. Deidre was still at the coffee table coloring with the new glitter markers picked out on the toy aisle; Kennedy watched Mr. Jeeves slip up several steps. She stood at the bottom of the stairs, waiting.

"You going to be gone tomorrow too?"

"Of course. Kennedy's sick." Cassie grabbed the frozen corn. "What else would I do with her?"

"Yeah."

Star looked down, and suddenly, realizing what she'd said, Cassie did too. It was painful to be reminded of how different Star's life had been before, how different the expectations were. To Cassie, this was exactly what happened when you were a sick child; you stayed home with a parent. You drank Sprite and ate loads upon loads of macaroni and cheese in bed. You watched way too much TV. When she was really sick, Cassie's mother had even left a brass cowbell by her bedside, just because Cassie liked so much to see her mother come up the stairs when she rang it. Sure, she could have yelled, but that was the point. When you were sick, you got to be spoiled.

And here Cassie was, seeing firsthand exactly how Star and her sisters were treated. Forget the TV, the cowbells, the cookies. Their mother had put them in playpens. Their mother hadn't even stuck around to make sure they lived.

The cupboard shut loudly, victim to Cassie trying for the umpteenth time not to hate a woman she'd never met or judge a person whose story she didn't know. She forced herself to refocus. "Anyway, I'm planning to take the rest of the week off. That is if that's okay with you, Supervisor Star." Cassie attempted a grin as she leaned on the counter opposite her.

But Star just shoved her computer into the blue-and-white canvas bag temporarily serving as a backpack. It was one of Cassie's bags she'd bought for a family beach trip the summer before, and even before Star slung the leather strap over her shoulder, she could tell it was entirely too adultish to be trendy. Nothing about it screamed cool, fierce teen.

"We can stop by Target and get you a new backpack

after school, too, if you want," Cassie added. "And anyway, Bree was pretty devastated she missed out on the toy-aisle trip today. The way she acted, you would've thought we went to Disneyland without her. But, if we pick her up from work on the way there tomorrow—"

"So, you're not going to leave, then?"

Cassie paused, stood upright. "Not unless you want to pay me a salary plus benefits. What makes you so worried about this? Really?"

"Because everyone at the Haven would kill me if you quit. Because of us." Star's eyes darted to the window. "Because of me."

Stilling, Cassie caught the significance of her words. If there was one thing Star was, it was confident.

Cassie wasn't touchy-feely by nature, but even so, she reached forward and gave Star's forearm a quick squeeze. "You know what, Star? I would gladly quit my job if I had to for you. Any day."

Star returned her gaze at the touch, nodded, then shrugged as she pulled her arm back. "Yeah." She tried to play it off, but she couldn't keep the light grin from playing at her lips as she reached in for another notebook. "Anyway. I just wanted to make sure."

It was one of the wonderful things Cassie and Star had in common: being terrible at public displays of emotion.

"Want to take a homework break and do a round of DB?"

"Seriously? You keep it here, too, Miss C? You're such a nerd."

Still, her lit-up eyes betrayed her words. Cassie took that as a yes and opened the junk drawer—an insufficient term, as even the pencils faced north. It wasn't long before Dutch Blitz cards were flying and tea bags steeping.

On the third game, however, came a distant but familiar sound.

Cassie's shoulders jerked up. "What is that?"

Star wrinkled her forehead, her tone heavily suggesting she was questioning Cassie's intelligence. "A . . . fire truck."

"Thanks, Captain Obvious. I mean—" Cassie set her cards on the counter. "—why is there a fire truck coming down *our* road? Our totally unpopulated, three-mailboxes-on-the-whole-street road?"

"You're getting paranoid." Star followed on Cassie's heels to the living room. "You know, Miss C, just because one guy steals a fire truck and bribes everyone with presents to get in good with you doesn't mean it'll happen again."

Cassie flicked open the blinds, watching the flashes of red lighting up the neighbors' fields. It had already passed one driveway. There was only hers and Betty's left. "Want to bet?"

She turned around and found the two younger girls beside the Christmas tree, grinning proudly. Too proudly.

"We did it! We did it!" Kennedy's shrill voice filled the living room as she clutched Cassie's phone to her chest.

Cassie's stomach sank. "Did what, girls? What did you do?"

"They're going to save Mr. Jeeves, just like the book said!"

"Save . . . Mr. Jeeves?"

Cassie followed Kennedy's pointing finger to the top of the Christmas tree. Through the branches, she could see her cat's jewel-toned eyes. Though impossible, she felt she saw him smile.

Oh, no. No. No. No.

Cassie bent down to Kennedy and Deidre's level. "Girls, I am so—" Nope, *mortified* wasn't the best word choice just now. "—*proud* of you for knowing who to call in an emergency. Just like the dog book showed us." Note to self: screen all children's books from now on. "But you know what?"

Deidre blinked.

"What?" Kennedy said.

"I'm going to have to talk with the nice firemen for a minute, so how about you go with Star to—" Cassie fumbled momentarily, searching for some interesting, quiet activity "—get ready for bed?"

Their eyes stared back at her blankly.

Yeah. She'd have to work on her motherly, summon-inspired-ideas-on-command skills.

"*And* . . . ," Cassie said with emphasis as the sirens grew louder. They blinked their glassy eyes. "Wear your pretty new pajamas!"

Kennedy's brows furrowed. Cassie was getting worse.

"And eat brownies? In bed?" Cassie asked.

Bingo.

"All the brownies!" Kennedy squealed, hopping a few times.

"*Sure*!" Cassie responded with equal enthusiasm.

"And a movie!" Kennedy added.

"Why not?" Cassie said, hopping along with her.

Kennedy's voice shrilled like an excited kitten. "And Mountain Dew!"

A squeal of brakes sounded at her doorstep. Cassie's hopping stopped. Not even forty-eight hours in, and all her grandiose plans for healthy snacks and activities were flying out the window. She nudged the girls toward the steps. "Yeah! I don't have Mountain Dew, but yeah! Whatever I can find in the refrigerator."

Television. Chocolate. Soda. Might as well throw in a cigarette for the road.

She kicked a box of crayons underneath the sofa, crammed a stack of construction paper into the drawer of a side table, shoved the glittery unicorn backpacks into the closet. Catching sight of herself in the mirror above the fireplace, she pushed down the lump at the top of her messy bun. The sounds of vehicle doors opening and closing came just as she tossed the last can of Coke to Star up the stairs.

She paused and took a breath. It felt awkward hiding the girls upstairs like a big secret. Awkward. And made her feel a bit guilty.

But if the man of her twenty-four-hour dreams just so happened to be on the other side of that door, and the girls were all sitting around eating bonbons, two things could happen. Jett could shrug his shoulders, laugh about the little mishap with the cat, and—without showing any recognition of the three strange children in her house at all—go about his merry business.

Or, and what was about 99 percent likely, he could ask.

Oh, and who are these lovely ladies? Oh. How long are they staying? Well, what did their social worker say? And if she can't find any other relatives? Insert the bulging eyes. *You mean you are planning to adopt these kids if given the chance? These three kids? The teenager? All three?*

And then he'd trip over his own ax as he stumbled out the door.

There was another rule for her future bestseller on dating: never freak a guy out with three kids twenty-four hours after your first date.

No, she wouldn't lie to Jett about the girls if he asked. Not on a matter this significant to her heart. She wouldn't lie . . . which was exactly why she had to hide them.

It was the only moral thing to do.

A knock sounded on the door. Game time.

"Jett. Why, hello." Cassie plastered on a cool and confident smile as she swung open the door.

"Cassie?" Jett popped off his helmet and put it to his hip. He grinned. "Gotta say I wasn't expecting you here."

"You either." Boy, was that the understatement of the year.

"Was expecting someone half your size, actually." He volleyed his head, his gaze roving around the living room.

"Oh? Well, you got me."

"It was *you*? Really? Dispatch said it was a kid."

Her voice lifted several notes. "I have a very young voice over the phone."

She gave a high little laugh. He echoed with a low, uncertain one.

"Well?" he said, as though dubious on how to proceed. "How about I come in and see to this cat problem?"

"Oh. Sure." The problem. Cassie turned on her heels.

He followed behind her, stopping at the Christmas tree.

"Where are we looking?" He turned in a circle, searching the ceiling.

Cassie took a breath.

Pointed. "In there."

Jett lowered his gaze to the direction of her finger, a finger nearly parallel to her head. He touched a branch. "Here?"

She closed her eyes. Nodded.

He stepped closer. "In this tree?"

She nodded again.

The room was silent as Jett reached in and pulled out Mr. Jeeves. He set him on the ground. Mr. Jeeves gave him a distrustful blink before whisking his tail and moving into the kitchen.

Cassie's grandfather clock informed them of the hour, and for eight long chimes they both watched the ground intently.

She felt him quietly assessing her sanity.

She fretted with the hem of her blouse. "I have a thing about pine needles."

Excellent. So apparently small lies that did not, in fact, help with the case for her sanity were just fine.

"Ah. See, we didn't cover that at the aquarium." His eyes fell on the pine-scented candle on the coffee table, drifted over the twelve-foot garland hanging over the mantel, and stopped on the miniature Christmas tree cheerfully lit on the floor beside the glider.

"It's a really new thing," Cassie added.

"Uh-huh." Still, he smiled, clapping his gloves. "Well, would've preferred knocking on your door with flowers instead of a firehose, but I'm still glad to drop in. You've got a nice house out here, Cassie. I like your mantel." He put one gloved hand on the dark wood over the fireplace. "And these windows. Good insulation."

Cassie locked her fingers together. "Thank you. I always try to have good insulation."

"Yep. A very important trait in a woman." He paused, seeming to wait on her to say something, ask something, do something.

Though it came at a volume of a mouse's scuffle, Cassie heard a break of laughter floating down the stairs from the girls' room. She gave a loud cough as she grabbed Jett's arm by the coat. "Where are my manners? I'll give you a tour."

Jett obligingly let her speed him through the kitchen, dining room, living room, and bathroom of the first floor.

"I see we have a mutual fondness for macaroni." He stopped at the oversized pot. Coupled with Kennedy's discovered obsession for the sea-shaped cheesy animals and Cassie's complete inexperience in cooking for four, Cassie had gone a little overboard. Seven boxes later, the stockpot was still full from dinner.

"You never know when a midnight craving will strike."

"You mean, all this is for you *after* dinner?"

"Are other guys waiting outside?" Cassie swiftly walked him through the hall and parked him at the front door. "Well, thanks a million."

A corner of his mouth lifted in a sideways grin. He put his helmet on. "A day in the life, ma'am."

She opened the door to let him out. He'd be out of his mind to go on another date after this.

"See you tomorrow, crazy cat lady." He winked and hopped down the front steps.

Her icy breath of relief formed crystals in the air. "Looking forward to more compliments on my insulation."

Jett stopped at the fire engine, calling out as he put his hand on the passenger door. "Just so you know, I'll be covering the three-point line in pine needles."

"Sure." She laughed. "Whatever it takes to give you a leg up."

Back inside, Cassie waved from the living-room window as she watched the engine roll out of the driveway, then collapsed on the couch, her head falling into her hands.

Well, that had gone worse than she anticipated.

She had to tell him. Surely she had to explain everything, emphasizing that nothing about her situation would change anything for the two of them.

Right. Because a heavy conversation on a second date wouldn't make him flee like a spotlighted convict.

She rubbed her temples, eyes closed. It was a catch-22 all the way around. If she was a proactive communicator, she could scare him away; if she hid the situation, she was playing with fire—and looking a little insane over cats and pine trees. Not to mention all this trouble could be for naught. How could she successfully date a man who didn't want kids? She couldn't change the man. She knew that from painful personal experience.

But was it possible she could turn the girls away if the time came to make that decision?

Cassie squeezed her eyes tighter, then opened them. Straight in front of her sat a red streak of crayon across the perfectly white sofa. She hesitated, then ran the tip of her finger along it.

Another muted giggle floated down the stairs, and Cassie rose.

Another day. She would just have to table the worry for another day.

"Making room for me up there?" she called, and legged it up two at a time.

10

Jett

"You hear that, man?"

Even Sunny sensed something was wrong.

A newborn had been in their apartment less than three days, and already they could tell the different types of TJ's cries through the front door. Jett turned the lock and pushed it open.

The light of early dawn was just starting to break in through the living-room window, but otherwise the place was dark. No light came from the lamp on the table beside him at the door's entrance. No light came from the kitchen or bathroom or hall. The TV was off.

Still, Jett felt an impulse that made him push the door open wider, ready to charge to TJ, pick him up, and start scouting out the rooms.

At least he *tried* to open the door wider. But something pushed against it from the other side.

He looked down and around. Dakota and Drew were pressed up against the wall, faces toward the crack beneath the door.

"Guys?" Jett knelt down and touched their shoulders. They were breathing heavily, Dakota's blond curls covering her face. Drew was shirtless, his belly pressed against Dakota's back. The room smelled so foul it suffocated.

How long had they been sleeping there? More specifically, why?

"Man." Sunny covered his nose with his T-shirt, stumbling over couch pillows and toys for the deck window. "Your kids made our place smell like Donna Gene's," he said, throwing the window open.

Jett dropped his overnight bag and moved swiftly to the Pack 'n Play beside the dining room table.

"Oh, buddy. Hang on."

TJ was flat on his back, staring up at Jett with freshwater-blue eyes that contrasted deeply with the red, almost purple, splotches covering his face. His cries were hoarse, cracking at each tail end, and his small fists pulsed up and down with what little fight he had left in him. Half of his sleeper was covered in a dark-yellow stain.

Jett put one hand gingerly on his bottom as he picked him up.

"Trina?" Jett stepped down the hall. "Trina?"

The door to his bedroom stood ajar. He knocked once, then pushed it fully open.

His gray comforter lay crumpled in a heap in the middle

of the bed. The blinds were shut. Each of his dresser drawers was opened, looking the same as when he was late for work and had to quickly rifle through. His watch—hardly worth the fifty dollars he'd paid for it—was gone.

"Trina!" he bellowed. He threw open the door to the bathroom, giving in to one last blind hope she'd be in there. But instead, all he found was an open medicine cabinet, toiletries fallen into the sink.

"Uh, Jett."

Jett heard Sunny's footsteps down the hall, saw him stop behind him in the medicine-cabinet mirror.

"I think you've got a problem." He handed Jett a piece of paper.

Jett read the words hastily scribbled across the Pack 'n Play's manual:

> I'm sorry. I can't handle it anymore.

Jett stared at the words. Squeezed his eyes shut.

Gave himself one deep breath.

And threw the manual against the shower wall with a force that would break glass.

"Annnd let's give Uncle Jett a minute." Sunny took TJ from Jett's shoulder. A definitive *squish* sound came from the area of TJ's diaper now placed firmly on Sunny's forearm. "*Abort. Abort.*" Sunny started to push the baby back toward Jett.

Jett turned his murderous gaze on him.

Sunny pulled back. "I mean, I totally got this. You just have your moment." Sunny repositioned both hands beneath TJ's armpits, holding the baby as far out as possible from his chest. TJ's scrawny legs kicked as Sunny walked him down the hall. "Oh, little man. This is serious."

Jett shut the door to the bathroom, raked a hand through his hair. All of a sudden the world was collapsing, thoughts and emotions whipping by so fast it was hard to specify any one thing. He forced himself to take a breath, tried hard to focus on one aspect at a time.

His sister had come back. That was good.

But then she was gone again. She'd left, and in leaving had left her three kids. *Three* kids. All left . . . to him. For today. The next day. The next. How long?

He took another breath, the bathroom suddenly confining.

Trina. What have you done?

He pulled out his phone and dialed the last number she'd had. The familiar recording, stating the number was not in service, played. He shut it off midsentence.

He turned on the sink.

He slapped icy water over his face.

This was good, though. Better than at least one very real alternative.

Because how many times had his heart stopped beating over the past year whenever Dakota and Drew crossed his mind? A hundred? A thousand? Late at night when he'd looked up at the ceiling, wondering what kind of ceiling they were under at that moment. At least she hadn't left with them, making him worry all over again. At least right now he didn't have to worry if they were fed, warm, remembered. Safe.

Three kids.

Jett looked at himself in the mirror.

His own niece and nephews. Carrying, Sarah had said, the same wavy hair as his own. He was their uncle, and they had nobody else in the world.

He was their uncle.

They had nobody else in the world.

He was their uncle.

Nobody else.

Ten minutes later, he opened the door.

His niece and nephews were safe, and that's what was important right now.

Well that, and the minor fact that he had no idea what he was doing.

"You got this, man? Because I'm here for you. I just also gotta get some sleep."

"Yeah, Sunny, you go on. Sarah will be here any minute." He checked the clock again, ignoring the stress level rising with each passing second Sarah was not there. Without kids, he would've thrown his shoes on and been out the door—sometimes not even worrying about the shoes part. Now, if his neighbor didn't get here in the next three minutes he would definitely be late.

Jett slapped pickles on five turkey slices. He squirted each with ranch. Dinner a la mode.

The last twenty-four hours had been a marathon. After

the surprise visit to Cassie's house, he'd made the regularly unscheduled visit to Donna Gene's and worked a 2:00 a.m. wreck. It had been a long night, a particularly bad night. Yet neither he nor Sunny had anticipated coming home to spend the next eleven hours watching the twins bounce on couches, narrowly miss a stabbing after Drew got hold of a knife, and clean up after the successful breaking of a lamp. And a glass. And a plate from Sarah's cookies with a label on the bottom stating it was fine china.

He had a hundred things on the mental to-do list that took form the moment Trina walked out the door—somewhere before midnight, from what he could gather by the twins' shaky accounts.

His blood pressure started rising whenever he thought too long about it, knowing how terrified the twins would've been watching their mother push away from them, shut the door, and abandon them in the dark. Alone. Eight hours. Ten. However long it had been was long enough to make the twins anxious whenever Jett so much as stood up. Just trying to go to another room was an ordeal, and thanks to today, he could now say he knew what it was like to have two pairs of arms wrapped tight around his legs while in the bathroom. It'd been an eventful day.

Still, *nothing* was going to stop him from seeing Cassie tonight. Not even this.

The knock on the front door came, and Jett called out before she could knock a second time. "Come on in!"

"Well, well, well, what do we have here?" Sarah stepped into the kitchen and placed a tote on the counter.

Jett cast a glance over to the breakfast table, where the

twins were sliding ice cubes on it until they took the three-foot plunge to the kitchen floor.

He shrugged. "All I know is they have a thing for ice cubes. They've been doing that for half an hour."

Sarah dodged TJ, who was lying on a towel in the middle of the floor. She looked down at the puddle of ice water with bobbing, melting ice cubes. "Now I see why the landlord is just *super* thrilled about renters with kids. You got a towel?"

Jett took an orange-and-white T-shirt and tossed it to her. "We ran out of towels two days ago. Down to T-shirts now."

She stretched it out and raised an eyebrow at the college intramural print. "Badminton? Somehow I didn't see you as a badminton kind of guy."

Jett grinned as he threw the sandwiches on a plate and set the stack between ice cubes on the table. "Never underestimate the power of a girl's persuasion. Particularly spicy redheads in Spanish class."

Dakota and Drew snatched at the sandwiches.

Sarah's brow raised. "I see. And how did that relationship turn out?"

"I'm using the T-shirt as a floor wipe right now. That just about sums it up."

Sarah smiled and turned away. "Speaking of your very . . . innovative use of towels, I thought you might want this." She turned the corner of the kitchen and came back with a large box. On the cover, a baby about TJ's age was smiling in some sort of reclining contraption, several colorful objects dangling overhead.

Sarah set it on the ground. "Unless you like the towel-in-the-middle-of-the-floor deal. I just thought TJ here would like it."

Impossible. After a mere eight hours of this parenting thing, he felt a strange stirring as curiosity moved him closer, an unfamiliar enthusiasm toward items devoted to house and home.

A recliner for a baby? A place to set the kid down? The chance for Jett to have his arms all to himself for the span of fifteen minutes? At the moment, it was more beautiful than a Model 70 Super Grade Winchester Magnum.

"Wow, Sarah. TJ will love this. Thank you." He picked up TJ and smiled gratefully, looking into her eyes. "Thank you so much."

That was interesting. He'd never noticed her wearing so much mascara. She blinked, her green eyes softer than he'd ever observed before. He wondered momentarily if there was something different about her eyebrows. Less . . . hairy.

Her smile reached her eyes. "If you want, we can put it together right now. I'm pretty handy with a manual."

Just then TJ spit up, for the fifth time that day, on his shirt. "I would. I really would. But I'm about to be late as is."

He handed TJ over, now very aware of how important it was not to disappoint the woman who had agreed on a whim to watch the kids. "But that would be great when I get back. TJ is going to love it. Aren't you, buddy?"

"And where are you going again?" she began just as he spoke loudly over her to the kids.

"Guys? Remember Sarah? She's going to hang out with you for a little while."

He grabbed the T-shirt towel and began swiping at his shirt.

Out of the corner of his eye, he saw a shift in the twins' postures that made him look up. They wore that same forlorn, don't-leave-us look Sarah also seemed to be wearing. It made him uneasy. "And you can show her all the things you can do with ice cubes. Won't that be fun?"

Dakota dropped her sandwich.

Jett dropped the T-shirt on the counter, sensing the beginning of the battle. "And you can jump on Uncle Jett's bed as much as you want."

Both of the twins hopped down from their chairs and headed toward him.

"And Sunny's! He has a great big giant king bed! Wake him up and go crazy."

The kids kept coming.

Backing up, Jett bumped into the wall, his hand fiddling for the fridge. He opened it quickly. "See this?"

They stopped just before clutching his legs.

"Ice cream! Ice cream for everyone!"

He was yelling so loud that Sarah's eyes widened. When the twins started jumping with him in enthusiasm, however, her lips upturned.

It wasn't too hard to get out the door after that.

With lucky green lights and a sprint from the parking lot, Jett managed the easygoing stroll into the gym a mere four minutes past six. He stripped off his jacket. Cassie waited at the three-point line—void of pine needles—of the old gym, a ball in her hands, her chestnut hair pulled back into a playful ponytail. She was just as beautiful as the day she'd stood on the same court fifteen years ago.

"Why, you look stunning, Miss Everson."

Cassie laughed, looking down at her athletic pants and T-shirt. "Man, your bar must be really low. And anyway, where's all the trash talk you've been throwing down the past few days? Don't tell me you're going soft now when it counts."

She bounced the ball toward him and he caught it with both hands.

"Oh, no. I'm not backing down. I just think it's time we let actions speak for themselves." He dribbled the ball to the three-point line, positioned himself, and threw it. The ball swished with such perfection through the net he could hear the angels singing.

Or rather, that's what would've happened if he'd been in charge of the moment. In reality the ball soared through the air, missed the backboard completely, and slammed into one of the hanging blue mats on the back wall.

Her laugh wasn't one of those sweet, jingly types that came off like a polite wind chime. No, as he jogged after the ball, she cackled at megaphone volume.

"I just need a warm-up," he called back, searching for the ball now hidden among the bleachers. "You'll be sorry soon enough."

"You keep telling yourself that," she said between laughs.

Already, the night was perfect.

Old metal halide lighting dangled from the forty-foot ceilings. Yellow walkways and blue bleachers covered the gymnasium where echoes of old memories lingered: the feel of the ball on his fingertips, the cheers in the stands, the shouting of his old coach.

The smell of spit-up on his chest.

Jett pulled down on his jersey, grimacing at the six-inch spot against the gray. Oh, perfect. Nothing said romance like spit-up tie-dye.

"You going to pass me that ball or what?" Cassie called.

"Yeah, I've, uh—" He turned his chest away from her and tossed the ball, making a beeline for his athletic bag. "Go for it."

Cassie turned and made a shot, the ball *swishing* through the net. "Actions speaking yet? Or are we still warming up?"

"Once you get three in a row, we'll be done warming up." He unzipped the bag quickly. Several toys spilled out. *Drew.*

He heard the net swish again as he stuffed a boat—still dripping in bath water—and about forty-seven cars back into his bag. Yanking out his water bottle, he squirted a couple drops on his shirt. Began rubbing hastily on his chest.

The spot sucked the water up and—from his angle—took on the shape of a submarine headed directly for his armpit.

"What are you doing over there? You're not taking a water break already, are you?"

"No, no," he called back. "Just seemed to—" He rubbed fiercely. "—have something—" The submarine was morphing into a warship. "—on my shirt."

He stared at the water bottle for a long moment. Looked to his jacket. Imagined what it would do to him if he tried to play basketball for two hours in a coat. Considered stripping off his shirt for half a beat and shuddered at the image of himself brazenly passing her the ball like he was The Rock and knew it.

Instead, he doused half the bottle on himself. Water spread and covered the top half of his chest, turning the gravel-shaded shirt into one the color of Cassie's cat.

Well, that solved the warship problem.

Finally, he turned around.

She saw him and stopped dribbling.

When he reached her, he could tell she was on the cusp of rolling over in laughter, yet again.

He tilted his chin upward. "I see sympathy isn't one of your strengths."

"Oh, I'm not saying anything. Did I say anything?" She threw him the ball. "Now, let's play."

Jett grinned, started dribbling, and hedged around her for the basket. She chased after, trying several times to knock the ball out of his hands before he reached the net. He made the shot.

The ball *swooshed*. He caught it with a grin. "*Now* warm-up's over."

For the next hour they dribbled and shot, dodged and blocked, and elbowed their way to the basket. Discreet fouls turned to overt ones as they started to snatch at the other's shirt, take hold of each other's shoulders. At one point Jett lifted Cassie—and the ball—completely off the floor, enjoying the feel of her wrapped inside his arms.

Three games later, and stomachs rumbling, it was time to call it quits.

"Not bad, Everson. You gave me a run for my money." Jett wiped the perspiration from his eyes, his shirt so sweat soaked at this point all memory of the spit-up incident was gone.

Cassie, on the other hand—with that mysterious ability available only to women—managed to show no signs of exhaustion besides a damp hairline and a disheveled ponytail. She slid an arm into a long-sleeved maroon zip-up. "Not enough of a run, Bentley, if you still got me on that last one 21 to 8. Whatever happened to a little flirtatious losing? I'm the girl here. You're supposed to drop a few shots so I don't get too far behind."

"Are you telling me that would've worked on you?" He held one hand out to the three-point line. "'Cause we can go right now."

She zipped up her jacket and waved him off. "No, it's too late now. I'm just going to have to throw a pity party for myself later. Where are we eating dinner?"

"Loser picks, if I remember correctly."

"Have you been to Abram's? Not the refined feel we'd get at Cobbler's Steakhouse. More of a kid place. But seeing as you look like you went under a waterfall, I'd say we're better dressed for fried okra and biscuits anyways. Don't you agree?"

Jett nodded, all the while well aware of the way she had referenced the restaurant. It was a kid place. Given her tone, that wasn't a compliment to the restaurant.

Kids weren't in the cards for her, as she had made clear. What had been nice to hear a few days ago was now a point of concern. Should he tell her what was going on?

Absolutely not.

The girl was a flight risk. She even had her own escape door.

And besides, Trina could be back tomorrow. Heaven knew he'd keep calling her until she was.

So, the hazards of his current situation were most definitely *not* on the tip of his tongue as he watched Cassie let her hair down from her ponytail and reshape it again. She smoothed tendrils back as she started throwing out suggested dishes from the restaurant, her perfectly clear, carefree eyes dancing through the conversation. A night with Cassie Everson was even better than he could have imagined. Sensible, capably independent, yet with a streak of delicateness, he wanted to swoop her off her feet then and there without the poor excuse of going for the ball. The way she paused as she teased him, gauging with a sensitivity if he was still laughing too. The way she tried hard to show she didn't care, and yet even in the old lighting he could see a bit of golden bronze highlighting her already naturally tan cheeks. She smelled of clean cotton fresh from the dryer, of marine mist drifting across a dawning beach.

Which couldn't be said for him. He'd had better days.

And yet here she was, looking just as happy as he was to be here.

He took a step toward her. "You know, you are standing on the exact spot I stood at the end of regional championships my junior year."

She stopped, looked down at her sneakers touching the three-point arch. "Is that so?"

"Yes. Thanks to the square foot of maple wood you're standing on, there's a trophy in the main hall." He stepped a little closer. "Does the air feel cleaner where you are? Can you smell pure triumph?"

Her eyes sparkled a bit. "Well, I don't know, Mr. He Who Brags While Flirting. But you could step inside this winner's circle and see for yourself."

Jett closed the distance between them.

Bent down.

Just as he watched her take a breath, his pocket began to ring.

As did Cassie's.

The clash of both jingles worked its magic in removing all magic, and reluctantly, after several seconds of pretending not to hear them, they moved back.

"Just one second," Jett said and quickly slipped his phone into view.

Sarah.

His jaw clenched, and he forced himself to step away.

"I am so sorry. I have to take this," he said, but she hadn't heard him. Her ear was pressed to her own phone, her legs already moving toward the far end of the bleachers.

Jett moved in the opposite direction. "Sarah. Hey."

There was immediate screaming in the background.

"Jett? I'm so sorry to be calling in the middle of—" She paused, seeming to wait for his revelation. "—your thing, but I think we have a problem with Dakota."

"What sort of problem?"

"I don't know how, but I think she got a piece of pickle stuck up her nose. She keeps saying it's burning. I looked at it with a flashlight and thought I saw something, but I'm not positive."

Jett stuffed his hand into his jacket. "You think you can get it out?"

"I tried. Sunny's here too. He gave it a shot. But now he's pulled out a vacuum and says he wants to suck it out—"

"*Don't* let him do that."

"I know. I'm not an idiot, even if he is." She paused as Drew's voice came into the background. "No, Drew. We don't call people idiots."

The screaming multiplied, now including the well-known newborn wail from TJ in addition to the frantic, high-pitched shrieks from Dakota.

Jett exhaled, hearing his own exasperation in his breath. The woman refused payment. There was only so far he could infringe upon her goodwill.

"All right, Sarah. I'm on my way."

He hung up the phone and turned back to Cassie. She was on the opposite end of the room, shoving her phone in her pocket, walking toward him.

How on earth could he avoid explaining himself? A man didn't just step back from a near first kiss and dash out the door. *So sorry, I've got to kiss and run. I know we were going to eat dinner, but . . .*

But . . . what?

But his niece had a pickle stuck up her nose.

If she ended up asking him about it, he'd just have to tell her.

Fine.

They stepped back toward each other.

"I'm so sorry. I have to head out."

He couldn't tell who'd said it first, but somehow they had managed to speak the words at once.

They both smiled, both seeming to be bitterly aware of the broken mood.

"Okay, then." Cassie rubbed her hands together. "Thanks for the game, Jett. I'll see you around."

Jett started nodding. "I'll call you."

As they walked to their cars, it was difficult to tell who was walking faster.

11

Cassie

I don't know. She shut herself in and locked the door almost—" Cassie's mother checked her watch, her hand trembling slightly. "—forty-five minutes ago now. I'm so sorry to break up your big date, sweetie. I just didn't know what to do."

Her mother crossed her arms tightly over the chest of her Christmas sweater. Her toe nervously tapped the floor as if to wear out the floorboards.

"It's fine, Mom." Cassie jiggled the knob. "These things happen." And of course they happened now, not in the other twenty-three hours of the day when she wasn't with Jett. Of course they happened just on the tip of a very romantic kiss. What felt at the time like it could've been the kiss of a lifetime, she might add.

But, no, thank *goodness* Deidre and Kennedy hadn't waited until she was home to lock themselves in a room full of staplers and scissors and thumbtacks—all of which she realized in hindsight weren't the best things to leave around. Other parents got a year of figuring these rules out before a baby got their feet beneath them and walked into major messes. Even when they were walking, they were only a foot tall and there was time to figure out what to do with dangerous things on higher ground.

But for her? She'd become a parent overnight and all of a sudden was having to think about both parental controls on the computer *and* hiding bleach. It was incredible how many oversights were possible. Locks? On doors? She couldn't understand how any house in America had locks on its doors when there were so many millions of children running around just waiting to lock their parents outside.

"Girls?" Cassie bent down to the brass knob, peering inside the lock. The hole was small and round. Basically, if she was going to try to be a lock picker, her observational skills started at ground zero. "Girls? Can you unlock the door?"

Silence fell on the other end, and her mother started worrying with her hands. Cassie looked to Star. She was still wearing the purple, destroyed-at-the-knees jeans Cassie had dropped her off in this morning, her face still carrying the zest of hanging out with friends. "Please tell me you just got here, Star. Please tell me Keely just dropped you off and you haven't tried getting them out yet."

Cassie's mother put a hand on Star's shoulder. "She tried talking to them—"

"I told them I was going to whoop them to Tuesday morning if they didn't come out—"

"I'm sorry, sweetie," Cassie's mother interjected, clearly uncomfortable with teenage words and ways. "The girls weren't eating dinner, and I was nudging them along, but then . . ." She waved a hand toward the door. "They bolted and sealed themselves inside. I thought I was just giving them a little encouragement, but I believe they felt pushed too hard."

"It's okay, Mom. They hardly eat for me either." Cassie straightened, looking up and down the sides for a hinge. That was a thing, wasn't it? Slide it out with a screwdriver somehow? The point was moot, however, as the hinge must've been on the other side. "Girls? Deidre? *Please* open the door."

Cassie pressed her ear to one of the panels. Sure enough, the drawers of the desk on the opposite wall made a sound as though being slid open and closed. Cassie mentally went through all the items they could possibly be touching, all the horrendous things they could possibly be doing. Taking out the scissors. Cutting each other's hair. Spilling five hundred thumbtacks around them so that every precious step became a real-life game of Don't Step on the Tack (what on earth was the point of buying those colorful needle puncturers anyway?). Having a sword fight with sharpened pencils. Making paper airplanes out of all her tax returns. Seeing how much lead they could fit up their noses.

Cassie jiggled the doorknob once more. She slid her fingers over the sturdy, beautiful, five-paneled door. "Stand back."

"Oh, honey, you can't be serious." Cassie's mother held on to Star and pressed them both to the wall. "What about a window?"

"The window's on the second floor, Mom. And even if I did get a ladder, you think they'd let me in out there? I'd have to break a window." Cassie moved until her back touched the door to her bedroom.

"Let me call your father," her mom pleaded, gripping Star, who was now holding her phone up, videoing the whole affair.

"Girls, last call!" Cassie cried out across the hall. "Either you open up or I'm breaking in!"

Five. Four. Three. Two. One.

The door stared back in silence.

Summoning all six months of karate training as a child, Cassie ran like a wild boar and threw herself at the door. Just before slamming into it she kicked squarely at the center of the door with all she had.

The door rattled. Slightly. As if laughing at her pathetic attempt.

It was the second time tonight she'd been easily defeated.

She bounced back, stumbled, and crumpled on the floor.

"Sweetie!" Immediately her mother was beside her, while Star's phone hovered over her head.

Star didn't even try to mask her mile-wide smile. "Miss C? You okay?"

Cassie held onto an aching shoulder, groaning as she rolled over to her right side. "I've never felt my age before. You guys are making me feel my *age*."

The door made a clicking noise, and two faces appeared cautiously in the two-inch crack.

"Deidre! Kennedy!" Cassie sprang up, pushing her hand through the open space before they could even think of closing it again. The door gave way, revealing faces covered in every Sharpie color in stock. Cassie snatched at the scissors so casually dangling from Kennedy's hand.

"Well, well," her mother said. "I misjudged you, dear. Looks like you got it open after all."

After an hour of bubble baths, of scrubbing faces and arms, her mother gave each girl a hug and headed for her own home. Nobody else in the world would have noticed just how eager she was to get into her nice, peaceful car after such an arduous evening. But after apologizing to Cassie for the fiftieth time and then highlighting each of the wonderful character traits she had witnessed in the girls, she quickly slipped into her driver's seat and backed out without even looking twice each way. Cassie watched. She understood. There had been more excitement in these three hours than her mother normally had in a month.

With Star's shower running down the hall, Cassie sat with Deidre on Star's bed. Kennedy lay beside them on her tummy, turning the pages of the big red dog book, their new favorite series. The room smelled thickly of lavender from the girls' baths, but there was also a mildly sour smell Cassie couldn't put her finger on. Minus all the deadly office supplies, the room had been put back in order. The desk sat crammed against the window, and two mismatching antique bedside tables from Cassie's great grandmother had been placed on either side of the queen-sized mattress. The closet was newly crammed with twenty shades of pink. Tags still hung on most items.

Cassie peeked an eye over at Kennedy's page—hoping for no more grand ideas like calling the fire department—while she cautiously began to rub a piece of Deidre's coiling black hair. Like most things these days, Cassie was clueless as to what she was doing.

Her phone sat beside her, open to a blog article on African American hairstyles for little girls. She fumbled with reopening the coconut oil lid with her now oiled hands and looked at the array of bows and large colorful beads that lay across the quilt in front of her. "Did you pick out your favorite bows yet?" She hoped desperately Deidre didn't choose one of the mysterious beads—another blog post tutorial entirely.

Deidre had been playing with the hem of her Disney-themed pajamas, remarkably patient for being a girl of only six. Silently, she handed over a red bow and a green one.

"Oh, I like that. It's very festive." Cassie's eyes shifted to the Rudolf sweater and matching green corduroys on the hanger for Deidre to wear to school tomorrow.

Deidre picked up a polka-dotted white-and-black bow and handed it to her. Then an orange one.

"All of these?" Cassie asked.

Deidre turned her back to Cassie, hands once more in the pile of bows.

"Well, now that's a nice arrangement you have there. I wouldn't have thought to put the orange and green and red and polka-dotted—" Cassie watched Deidre add a purple one to her growing bouquet. "—and purple. Pretty soon you'll have all the colors of the rainbow."

Kennedy shut the book and rolled over to the bedside table. She opened it and wedged the book inside.

Cassie's mouth fell open.

The sour smell was coming from the drawer—the distinct smell of rotting food.

In a blink of an eye, Cassie was jolted back to the reminder of where these kids had come from. In a room thick with lavender, a house of bubble baths and cozy comforters, food for today and someone to tuck them in at night, there were still the small, intruding reminders that everything was not fine. Reminders that shattered her romantic ideals and forced her to keep a spry eye out for pocket-sized clues.

It amazed her that these girls could laugh so loudly, embrace life so merrily twenty-three hours of the day and yet also know fear and hardship in ways she could only imagine.

Struggling for nonchalance, Cassie set the coconut oil down and picked up the detangling spray and comb. "What's going on in that book, Kennedy? How did that doggie end up in the swimming pool?"

Cassie listened and combed as Kennedy gave her four-year-old summary of each page, throwing in additional bits and pieces totally unrelated to the story. She listened until Deidre's head was entirely combed and braided in five separate sections—a foolhardy move for which no amount of blog posts could give her adequate talent. When Star came in from her shower, she laughed at Cassie and pointed at

Deidre's head for five minutes. Then she took pictures and sent them to Bailey, Keely, and Cam—who Cassie had heard was now somewhere in Florida. Cam, of course, wrote something cheeky back.

Cassie never once looked at the drawer while sitting on the edge of the bed, watching Star teach by demonstration as she rebraided Deidre's hair with fingers so nimble she didn't have to look.

Cassie waited an hour after the girls had been tucked in bed and then found her way back to the room. She cracked open the door, the light of her phone guiding her to the bedside table. Quiet as a mouse, she opened the drawer and set to work. She scraped bowls' worth of macaroni from the interior wood, three slimy hot dogs, two pieces of quiche, empty yogurt cups, half of one old chicken breast. Dipping her rag in cleaning solution, she scrubbed the interior and dried it with towels. Then, legs going numb from her awkward squat, she restocked the drawer with a box of Triscuits, cheese crackers, animal crackers, and a zipped-up bag of dried fruit. Tomorrow she'd see about finding some pepperoni sticks, which Deidre loved.

As Cassie crawled into bed, she tried to imagine what it would be like to live like them, tried to prepare herself to anticipate issues like this that could come down the road. They were little girls, yes, but they were also little warriors, always looking up to their mighty big sister who, in certain lights, proved still so small herself. Having no answers, only guesses, about the future. Right now, all the three of them knew was that they were here today. But what about tomorrow? They could be stripped from her, from their schools, teachers—everything—tomorrow. And they, she, all of them, were powerless to do anything about it.

Tomorrow.

For their sakes as much as hers, Cassie was going to get some answers tomorrow.

Jett

"Hurry up, man. Little Dude is peeing on my chair!"

"I can see that, Sunny, thank you," Jett said tersely, flapping out what felt like the fifteenth diaper of the morning. The diaper wasn't unfolding, however, and with his other hand wrapped around TJ's feet, Jett was powerless to cover the baby's bottom. TJ wailed, grinding on Jett's ears—ears that hadn't touched a pillow for more than four hours at a time in days. This included the night prior when he'd had the joy of dropping five hundred dollars at the ER so some resident doctor could pop a piece of pickle out of Dakota's nostril. It took a sum total of twenty seconds, with three hours of paperwork and waiting.

This was why family men got fat. It wasn't that they were

lazy—as was made clear by the fact Sunny was lounging, feet up, on the recliner while Jett scrambled on the carpet. The small humans just sucked out all the dad's energy. Like vampires. It was their lifeblood.

"*Dude!*" Sunny pointed as TJ wailed and let loose another fountain of urine, this time making a perfect arch onto Sunny's shoes.

"If it bothers you so much, get up and help!" Jett shook the unyielding diaper.

Dakota came around the corner, one hand clutching a half-eaten peanut butter sandwich. Barefoot in pajamas, her long, blond hair was wound up on top of her head with a rubber band. She impatiently held out a finger, pushed it to Jett's face.

"Not now, Dakota."

"Little man's making that face!" Sunny lifted his legs up suddenly, as if TJ could reach him. "He's making the gonna-blow face!"

Sure enough, TJ's expression had turned beet red and pouty. In seconds the carpet that was already starting to be covered in splotches of juice stains and diaper fails would get another murky addition.

Not this time. With a determined shake, the diaper finally cracked open. Jett dropped TJ's ankles and pushed it beneath him.

Dakota pushed her finger back in Jett's face, blocking his view. Despite Jett dodging her digit while trying to get TJ covered, she persisted.

Finally, he gave in and kissed it. "There." For whatever invisible boo-boo it was. "Better?"

Dakota brought her finger close to her eyes, examining it seriously while Jett strapped on the rest of TJ's diaper. Once done, Jett wiped his brow, feeling the intensity of the moment lessen.

"Nope. Still poopy," Dakota announced and pushed her finger back in Jett's face.

"*What?*" Jett's arm shot to the wipes and he then rapidly began wiping at his lips. Sunny started to cackle. Obviously disappointed in Jett's parenting skills, Dakota disappeared in the direction of the kitchen.

Why in the world did people *opt* to have kids? Seriously.

Of course, that wasn't a question he was going to be allowed to ask at his meeting with Rachel Henderson, DCS child specialist, this morning. Nor would it be beneficial to express the uncouth tone and choice words currently shouting in his head.

He picked TJ up and stood—just in time to hear a crash in the kitchen. Thankfully, just as he felt his sanity slipping, a mild knock came from the door and Sarah peeked her head in. The smile on her face pulled him back from the ledge. She held up a basket. "Blueberry muffin for the road?"

Jett gave his lips another wipe. "You are a lifesaver, Sarah. Thank you."

She shrugged. "Well, it's a big day for you." The basket swung in front of her. "And Sunny and I will make absolutely sure that no more pickles go up anybody's nose. Right, Sunny?"

Sunny scrubbed pee off his shoes. "Yeah."

Though it was absolutely uncalled for, Jett could still see

the guilt lingering in her eyes. "It wasn't a big deal, Sarah. Really. It took less than a minute for them to get it out." He smiled good-naturedly, all the while trying not to think too hard on the memory summed up in three words: tears, chaos, money.

Jett craned his neck as he pulled on his coat. "Hey, guys! Sarah brought you muffins."

"Saaaraaaah!" The twins rounded the corner full speed. Both faces were covered in what he guessed was mayonnaise. Maybe whipped cream. The point was they weren't crying.

Sarah took in the twins' hugs and passed them each a muffin. Her eyes passed to the baby recliner still in its box in the corner. "Maybe when you get back we can put that together."

He followed her eyes to the recliner. "Yeah. Definitely."

"Good." She gave a pleased smile. A smile that looked a whole lot like the kind Cassie gave just before their almost kiss.

Jett scratched the back of his neck, feeling very uncomfortable. If he was a wise man, he'd stop asking for Sarah's help. But what were his options lately? Sarah had volunteered herself, every time, with no expectations. No *spoken* expectations, at least.

Still, with every kind word or deed, he felt the debt getting heavier and had a growing feeling he knew in what currency she dealt.

"You know, Sarah," Jett began, "you have done so much for us. I know you've said no already, but really, let me pay you."

Sunny perked up from the couch, several potato chips falling to the floor. "Her? What about *me*? I woke up to Drew in my bed this morning. You know how I knew he was in my bed? He peed in it. You know what it's like to wake up to the growing sensation you're in an ocean?"

Jett stepped toward Sarah, taking out his wallet.

Sarah's basket, along with her body, backed up. "No, Jett. I couldn't."

"I insist."

"No. *I* insist."

Sunny waved his hands all over. "You heard her. She insists. I, on the other hand, am not insisting. I *need* the money. Drew ate one of my shoes yesterday. *Ate it*. Like a li'l puppy dog."

Jett forced himself to overlook Sunny's concerning statement, giving one last push for Sarah. He pulled out a couple of twenties. "Just enough to cover some food, then. You guys can order pizza."

But Sarah put a hand over his, pushing the bills away. "No. This is what neighbors do. We are there for each other when they need help. I'm sure you'd do the same for me."

"It depends on if your plight included kids." Jett paused, feeling himself giving up. There would be no winning this battle. He pushed the wallet back into his pocket. "You set the bar pretty high for neighborly conduct, Sarah."

"Yes, she does." Out of nowhere, Sunny snatched the twenties from Jett's hand. "You're a very honorable neighbor, Sarah. We are in awe. But you and I will also need some pizza."

"Well . . . oh." Jett paused, then looked down at TJ in

his arms. He had held him so much the past few days he was starting to forget when the kid was there. "Probably should take him before I go."

"Probably." Sarah grinned as she took TJ, waving his little arm as Jett closed the door behind him.

He would not feel guilty. He'd done his duty. He'd tried several times to pay her for her help.

Still, Jett couldn't help wondering, as he drove downtown, what a bum deal it was for her. She was a nice woman, a beautiful woman. Friendly. Easygoing. Tidy—although what woman really wanted that as a top-five characteristic?

Perhaps that was what was wrong. He could write down plenty of good traits, but the missing piece was still missing. What would he call it? That gelling. Conversation unstifled, words and unspoken wishes mixing with laughter that came only too easily, breaking layers with each smile, digging deeper each time their eyes met. In two—and a tenth—dates (counting a failed one), he had already rooted himself too deep to move planters now.

There was absolutely nothing wrong with Sarah. Just that Cassie was everything right.

A light dusting of snow covered the sidewalks of downtown Gatlinburg. Shop windows decorated by the marketing savvy caught the eyes of pedestrians with their glittering merchandise beneath festive trees and waving snowmen. The town of Gatlinburg conspired together to create an even jollier atmosphere for potential shoppers, offering the siren call of conveniently placed speakers playing holiday songs. Jett gripped his lifeline of late—Guatemalan coffee, black—and moved along. The backside of his hand was already starting to stiffen in the cold.

He couldn't remember a December in Tennessee this chilly. Georgia winters had been far more temperate, and if he recalled correctly, this time last year he'd been cruising along in a coworker's speedboat on an unconventionally warm weekend day. Jett zipped up his jacket; just thinking about gliding through the lake at thirty miles an hour on a day like today made him shudder.

He let go of the zipper. His fingers felt oddly wet all of a sudden, which, as he was learning in his new state of life, was never a good sign.

He grimaced and with deep hesitation put his fingers to his nose for a quick whiff.

Not again.

One glance down confirmed TJ's gift upon the brilliant green of his down jacket.

These kids were merciless.

Through the thick crowd he spotted the DCS building a handful of buildings ahead. He started to pull off one sleeve of his jacket.

"Jett?"

Cassie?

His smile brightened as he watched her part from the sea of oncoming pedestrians. Her legs looked particularly long and lean in jeans that clung to her calves. Sleek gray boots with tiny heels covered her feet, and she looked warm in a white pea coat and thick collars wrapped in one of those uneven, stylish ways around her neck. Her hair curled around her shoulders, framing her heart-shaped face, highlighting a relaxed smile and pink lips. It was clear as day she'd put more time into her appearance today than for any of their two-and-a-tenth dates.

"Well, look at you. I hope you aren't off to some lunch date with another man." Jett paused, his arms halfway out of his jacket, as she stopped before him. "He'd fall for you in a second."

"Look who's talking here. I don't recall you wearing a fancy polo on our date. *And* I believe you called my T-shirt-and-ponytail ensemble stunning. What about all this talk about going for the outdoor-girl type?"

"Oh, believe me, with you I can be both." But the charm of his words diminished significantly, he realized, with the fact he was currently trying to pry his fingers out of his feces-covered coat with coffee in hand. He successfully yanked one arm out, and her attention was drawn to the jacket.

"Um, Jett. What are you doing?"

He pulled his arm from the other side. "I'm warm."

"It's sixteen degrees outside."

"Surely not," he said, cautiously laying the clean part of his jacket over his arm. "I'd say it was well over thirty. Practically balmy."

Cassie pointed to the First Tennessee Bank sign directly above them. It proudly stated the weather, all sixteen degrees of it.

His "fancy polo" proved to be about as useful as a paper towel as his chest left the safety of the warm down and faced the bitter wind alone. He tried with everything in him not to shudder.

"Hey, crazy." Cassie's brows drew together as she leaned in, eyes on the jacket. "I think you got something on your coat." A breeze lifted her hair and left a few sweet flurries.

"I don't think so."

"Right there, see? Looks like maybe a bit of mustard . . ." Suddenly she began rummaging in her purse.

"Oh, yes. Maybe so—"

But just as he started to relax, waiting for the pack of paper towels to appear—women were always *so* resourceful—she whipped out an old, crumpled, impossibly thin, single-ply tissue and held it in the air. She began to straighten it out, and even then, it began to tear.

"It's not much, but maybe it'll at least keep it from dripping until you find a towel—"

"No, that's okay."

"Really, it'll just take a sec." And then her hand moved toward him, her perfectly soft, delicate fingers—protected by just a whisper of cotton—drawing in toward their filthy target.

He wasn't about to explain. Twenty feet from the DCS building he wasn't about to get this close and open that can of worms.

In a moment of either sheer brilliance or absolute panic, he took a step back, twisted his ankle, and flipped his entire steaming cup of hot coffee on his coat. "Whoa," he said loudly just as Cassie reached out and grabbed him by the arm.

"Jett!" She stared. "What just happened?"

"I slipped. Watch out for the—" He looked down to the pale slab of dusted sidewalk. "—black ice."

"Black ice?" Her gaze moved to the ground beneath him. "There's no black ice."

"That's exactly why black ice is so dangerous. It's invisible." He scraped his boot against the perfectly safe, non-slippery surface. "See? We'd better move over there. I practically did it again."

His entire body started to tingle from the cold as she let him guide her toward the window of a store, amusement highlighting her face. "Oh, sure. This is terrifying. I can only imagine what you'd be like in a real snowstorm."

"Look who's talking, Girl Who Calls 911 Over Cats in Pine Needles."

"We're a real pair, aren't we?" Cassie grinned, several snow flakelets resting lightly on her rose-brushed cheeks. "So," she forged on, "besides dousing yourself in coffee and trying to get hypothermia, what *are* you doing out and about?"

"Me? Oh—" A holiday bag wacked him on the shoulder as a shopper passed. "Christmas shopping. I was just about to go in here." He jutted his thumb behind him.

Her eyes drifted dubiously over his shoulder to the awning. "In there."

Vaguely, out of the corner of his eye, he saw a silky robe covered in paper hearts. No doubt one of the general stores selling everything from root-beer-scented candles to beef jerky; tourist traps like that were a dime a dozen around town.

"Yeah. Still looking for something for my aunt and uncle. These places are corny, I know, but they're great for one-stop shopping. I can always find something eclectic for my uncle."

Her eyes became mirthful. "Is that so? You've done it before?"

"Plenty of times. You can only buy so many ties before you have to get creative."

Her smile widened. "Right. 'Creative.'" Her phone beeped, and her expression changed. "Well, I'd love to stay and watch *exactly* what you pick out, but I have to meet a friend. Are you going to the parade Saturday?"

"I'll be in it."

"Really?"

"Sure. What's a parade without a fire truck? We're runner-up to Santa Claus as far as enthusiastic kids are concerned." He hesitated, the choice of words reminding him of the impending meeting, a meeting he was getting later for by the second. "Anyway, it was great bumping into you—"

"And watching you spill coffee on yourself," she added.

"But, uh, see you Saturday, after the parade?" Then he remembered the little hitch—or rather, three little hitches—getting in his way. It would be painful to ask Sarah again, especially the way things were heading. "Maybe?"

Oddly enough, the same cloudy expression fell over her face. "I'll be working that night. Doing a volunteer thing with the Leadership Club for some shut-ins. But maybe. Either way, I'll be sure to wave from the crowd."

"I'll be on the lookout."

Both Jett and Cassie backed away slowly, regretfully, she seemingly as committed to her appointment as he was, yet seemingly wishing just as much as he to stay. He backed up to the storefront door, turned the knob, gave her one last wave. Her grin was as bright as a lightbulb as she watched him turn. Her steps seemed to slow, in fact, until he had no choice but to actually go in after all.

The smell of spandex met him, and even before taking in the floor-to-ceiling rows of cheap, lacy intimate wear on plastic hangers, he knew his mistake. A neon-pink sign hung above the register, and a woman with thin, permed hair teased into a ponytail began striding toward him. "What'll be your pleasure, sir? Looking for something—"

Jett scrambled back out the door and practically tripped, this time for real, on the sidewalk. Even several buildings down, from the front of the DCS building, he heard Cassie cackling.

He straightened his shirt. "That's not Buck's General Store, in case you're wondering," he called.

"Oh, really? I didn't know," she called back, grinning elfishly before stepping inside.

She had just gone into the very building he needed to go into.

Not to mention the top half of his body was numb.

There were a few other stores in the immediate area to solve that problem, but hiding out in nonlingerie stores wouldn't help in the matter of getting to his meeting. He'd have to chance it.

Cautiously he looked inside the windows of the government building before stepping inside. Cassie was nowhere to be seen.

He made his way to the front desk.

The receptionist, a man wearing what appeared to be a permanent work frown, looked up. "May I help you?"

"Yes, I'm here to see—" But just then he heard Cassie's voice floating through the hall. "—the restroom."

The man's eyes didn't so much as blink. "You're here to see the restroom," he repeated.

Jett nodded. "And then I have an appointment."

"To the left, down the hall. Make a right after the water fountain. Hit the cat poster, and you've gone too far."

"Left, then right after water fountain but before poster. Got it."

"Cat poster," the man corrected and set down his pencil. "There are other posters, but turn before the cat poster. Not the vaccine poster or the domestic-abuse poster or the poster with the statistics about tax fraud. The cat poster. The cat is a Siamese with a ball."

Cassie's voice grew louder, and Jett saw her silky hair peeking above the window in the hall door to his right. He put up a hand. "Cat poster. Got it. Thank you," he said and scurried to his left and around the corner.

"I'm just beginning to call around, Cassie," the woman was saying. "I wish I could give you and the girls something definitive, but one of their relatives hasn't even called me back yet—"

Cassie sounded deflated. "No, I understand. I just feel, for their sakes, how imperative it is to know what to expect in the near future. Or far future."

Jett caught a glimpse of the woman touching Cassie's arm. "Believe me, I wish for that kind of answer in this job every day too. But right now, there's so much potential for the unknown that I don't feel comfortable leading you guys one way or another. Let's keep our appointment for after the holidays, and, at the very least, I'll see you at the first PATH class on the thirty-first. Until then, know that unless I give you a call, nothing has changed. And if something does, trust me, I'll be calling you as soon as I can."

"As *soon* as you can," Cassie repeated. "Really, Rachel. Please."

The woman nodded.

Cassie's voice was empty, all the bounce in her step from those former moments with him gone. "You have a Merry Christmas."

Cassie Everson. It was impressive how much she cared for the girls at her job, endearing to see her standing up for them firsthand. Those kids were lucky to have someone like her in their corner.

Jett waited until Cassie was safely out of sight before venturing into the waiting area. Rachel leaned over the desk, checking the clipboard.

"Have you gotten a Jett Bentley in yet?" she was asking just as he stepped up.

"So sorry I'm late." He put out his hand. "I'm Jett. Thanks for being willing to meet with me."

Rachel shook his hand. "It's fine. I've been behind all morning anyway. Come right this way."

The moment Jett sat in the chair opposite her desk, he set his crumpled jacket on the floor. He saw a Purell bottle and quickly gave himself a couple squirts. "I'm here to discuss my sister's children. They have recently come into my care."

Rachel nodded. What was earth-shaking, life-altering news to him didn't faze her—someone who dealt with misplaced children for a living. Nevertheless, her lack of reaction was disappointing. Calm, much too calm, for what it meant in his life.

"You should already have a file on them. I, uh . . ." Jett rubbed the knees of his pants uncomfortably. "I had to file a report sometime about a year ago."

"I see." She reached for her cup of coffee. "How many children?"

"Three. The twins are just over three years old, and the youngest, a boy, is somewhere around seven weeks."

"Quite the newborn." Rachel sipped her coffee. "And under what condition did they come to you?"

He paused. "As in . . . ?"

"As in are they healthy? Are they dealing with medical issues, abuse?"

He dodged the question. "To the best of my knowledge she never hit them."

"Yes, but I think we both know physical abuse isn't the only type out there."

Rachel asked him several more questions and listed off a dozen potential behavior responses of a child affected by different forms of trauma. A few of the issues hit the target for Dakota or Drew, or even TJ, and he shifted his legs uncomfortably.

How much could he share here? How much did she need to know about Trina for this conversation? He found himself afraid to be too specific. Instead, he avoided details for her sake, choosing to round up his answers by saying, "My sister was in no shape to take care of the kids at this time. Several days ago she took them to my home and left them. Now I'm struggling to know what to do."

"Well, you have a few options here, Jett." Rachel set her coffee cup down. "You can continue as an informal kinship caregiver, taking care of the children until she returns to take the children back. Or . . ." She went through several other options, including gaining temporary legal custody, finding other relatives, or assuming temporary guardianship in the case his sister was prosecuted on charges of neglect and possession. He shook his head after each one, including the last, which was turning the children over to the State.

Rachel clasped her hands together and leaned forward in her chair. "Well, that's all I've got here, and you don't seem pleased with any of them. So tell me, what do *you* think is the best option for yourself and these kids?"

"I want—" He pressed his thumbs together, watching through the open door as another case worker walked by. What did he want? He'd realized five minutes into their conversation that his situation might not be the norm, that people didn't usually come to DCS telling them about a child in their care. DCS usually called relatives trying to drop off nieces and nephews, not the other way around.

From what he could tell, the easiest path for him was to be an informal caregiver—to welcome life as a single uncle of three little kids, to feed them and clothe them and send them off to school and help them with homework and coach their Little League games until the day Trina popped back in their lives and tossed them into the back of her duct-taped car.

He couldn't imagine living with that uncertainty.

But there was one thing Jett knew. "I want them to

have everything my sister and I didn't have, and should've. We've lived firsthand through a childhood example of how it shouldn't have been. It haunts me to imagine Dakota or Drew, now TJ, going through that too. But . . ." It pained him to be so honest, so selfish. "I just don't want that to mean giving up my life. I was prepared to be the fun uncle who dropped by. I wasn't prepared for this."

Rachel's look turned, a steady dose of empathy breaking through the face that had heretofore shown nothing but routine and protocol. "You said you have an aunt in South Carolina."

Jett nodded, this conversation making him feel that all-too-familiar sense of suffocation.

"Talk to her. There's nothing selfish in placing your niece and nephews in the care of a loving relative, especially if you feel you are unfit for the financial and emotional strain of taking on three children. Perhaps she can be the kind of caregiver these children need. And, worst-case scenario, if she can't take them in, I don't think I'll have too much trouble finding a foster placement. Plenty of foster parents out there would jump at the chance to give children this young the bright start they deserve. Just this morning I met with a single woman who dropped everything in her life to take on three emergency placements—one a fourteen-year-old."

"Does she want three more?" he said, smiling lightly at the joke, then shaking his head.

Foster care for his own kin. The very words were painful. No doubt compounded by the days of disrupted sleep, he felt overly emotional, raw. He was coming face-to-face at last with the realities of his situation, and after an hour with a professional the answer was as clear as muddy water. Could he talk with his aunt and uncle, the mildly close relatives he saw every holiday, whom he made a point to visit about every six months? His aunt had her own realty business, her own grown children, even a couple of grandchildren. They already had a full-time life set up just as they wanted.

But then, so had he, hadn't he? Or rather, he was at the *brink* of having the life he'd always wanted—settling into a great job in his old town, starting a relationship with Cassie. Whereas his aunt and uncle had already lived a long and full life and were now enjoying the fruits of their labor, he was just on the cusp of his. To have it soiled, quite literally, by his niece and nephews—cute as they might be—wasn't fair.

Then again, none of this was fair. Not to the kids. Not to him. Not to Trina.

Not to anyone.

Foster care wasn't an option. Letting Dakota and Drew and TJ walk into the arms of someone outside his bloodline wasn't an option. If it came to that, he would just do what he needed to do.

His aunt, however, was another story. He'd call her today, and maybe, just maybe, reclaim his life.

He stood. "Thank you for taking the time to meet with me, Rachel."

"Thank you for seeking me out." Standing, she followed him out. "I'll e-mail you some of the information about our programs. And if or when your sister returns, please have her contact the office. It would be far better for her to come to us than for us to have to find her. In the meantime, if I come across something of benefit to you, I'll be in touch."

13

Cassie

Move over, laddies, you're blocking this old lady's view."

Several youths in dark-gray and green plaid jackets stood huddled in front of the row of elderly women and men. It was five to seven and it looked like everyone in town had come trooping through traffic and frigid temperatures for the show. Which wasn't surprising, as the Christmas parade was one of the local highlights of the year.

One of the boys cocked a brow at Donna Gene then slowly started to move. They weren't moving fast enough, evidently, because she—seated in a lawn chair—picked up her umbrella from the ground and began prodding them.

"Okay, Ms. Donna Gene. That's good, I think they're moving along." Cassie grasped the tip of the umbrella and lowered the weapon.

With their combined powers, Girls Haven Leadership Club had managed to secure an excellent block for the event, and with twelve lawn chairs and wheelchairs in place for their elderly patrons, the girls had grabbed their plastic bags and dispersed among them. Most of the Leadership Club service projects were thought up by the girls themselves, demonstrating creative planning, budgeting, leadership, and logistics, but this one—gathering a list of shut-ins from Cassie's church and chauffeuring them to the most beloved community event of the year—was hers.

Cassie felt the tug on her collar and looked down to the honorary teen-club member in her arms. Kennedy, who had picked out her own winter wear, was a Pepto-Bismol commercial in her thick pink coat, pink snow pants, pink boots, pink mittens, and pink hat. One arm wrapped around her empty pink basket. "Where's the candy?"

"It's coming soon. See?" Cassie pointed to the two high school girls bouncing in their short-skirted dance uniforms, each holding up one side of the Gatlinburg Christmas parade sign. "They'll be throwing candy any minute."

"Here, sugar. Take one of these to hold you over." Donna Gene put her hand out, holding up a peppermint.

Cassie hesitated, having experienced the condition of Donna Gene's home when they helped the woman and her elderly friend out to the van this evening. Still, Kennedy's face blossomed at the sight of it, and there was no going back now.

"That's very kind. Can you say thank you, Kennedy?"

Kennedy, with great difficulty from her bulging coat and mittens, took the candy between both mittens. "Thank you."

She opened her mouth wide as Cassie tore open the wrapper and popped the mint in for her.

Trumpets and drums sounded together, and Donna Gene smiled and turned her face to the oncoming band. "It's no problem. I must've had that swimming in the bottom of my purse for years. Oh, look." Her plump hand dug into what appeared to be a black snakeskin purse straight from the 1950s. "I found another."

Cassie alternated Kennedy, who was already sucking away at her mint, to the other hip. "Oh no, no. This is just enough. Thank you."

Everybody watched in anticipation as flutists marched past and groups of ten-year-old ballerinas danced heartily across the road. Clowns in white-and-red faces passed candy out to eagerly awaiting hands and bags. Antique cars and waving homecoming queens. Floats, whether of the duct-tape-and-stringed-lights-on-a-truck-bed variety or robust themes of the Grinch sponsored by a large electric company, played jingles loudly through speakers.

With a pound of peppermints, Tootsie Rolls, bubblegum, and church flyers with attached candy canes in their baskets, Kennedy and Deidre hung on to a street lamp and leaned out with their baskets as far as they could as kids from the YMCA passed. A girl not much older than Deidre poured a handful of Hershey's Kisses in both baskets.

Then, finally, her new favorite vehicle came into view, and for once it wasn't sounding the sirens. "Rocking Around the Christmas Tree" played loudly through the crowd, the electric guitar echoing cheerfully back from brick buildings. String-lit garland draped across ladders the width of the fire engines, and firemen dressed in bunker gear waved heartily to the crowds.

Cassie's heart momentarily paused as Jett—with arm hanging out of the front passenger seat—spotted her. Lifting his Santa hat off his head, he waved it and winked at her. She felt her cheeks heat as she waved back.

Both Donna Gene and her elderly neighbor turned in their chairs.

"Why, do you know that man, Patsy?"

"If I'm not mistaken, I'd say he was sweet on you." Mrs. Kolak crossed her frail arms across the blanket on her lap, and it was hard to tell just then if that was a compliment or criticism.

Cassie tugged on the red scarf wound around her throat. "My name's Cassie. And yes, Ms. Donna Gene, I've just started seeing him, actually."

The wrinkles on her forehead shoved up as she lifted her brows and looked at Cassie as if it was the first time she was really seeing her. "Why, that's a fine piece of man right there, I daresay."

"Anybody would be lucky to have 'im," added Mrs. Kolak tartly, facing straight as an arrow ahead while a group of accordion players passed.

"Don't mind Edie," Donna Gene said, patting her neighbor's lap. "She's just mad the boys don't trip over themselves to light her cigarette anymore."

"They used to too," Mrs. Kolak muttered.

Donna Gene pushed her bags off an empty lawn chair. "Anyway, indulge us. Tell us all about you two."

Both women seemed to have forgotten completely about

the parade. Instead, they watched her as though she were now the man riding the oversized unicycle.

With traces of warmth still on her cheeks, Cassie glanced at the retreating fire engine well down the block. In her line of work, this type of nosiness was standard. In fact, she kind of preferred it.

Day and night she had been focused on the kids' needs, trying desperately to tiptoe around potentially disruptive conversation topics, trying to make them feel happy and at ease. It was exhausting work, physically and mentally. Frankly, besides sitting down with Jett himself, there was nothing she'd rather do at that moment than talk *about* him—even if it was with two odd ladies. Not to mention, being a friend to a shut-in was the point of the Leadership Club's outing tonight. If she had to talk about him, she had to talk about him.

Cassie glanced around to her charges: the fourteen teens seated beside their companions, Deidre and Kennedy circling the lamppost. She sat down.

Donna Gene, looking pleased, patted her knee.

"Well," Cassie began awkwardly, crossing her boots at the ankles, "his name is Jett. He's twenty-nine—a little younger than me, I admit—and works with the fire department."

"Tell us something we don't know," Edie chirped. She sprayed hand sanitizer in front of her face.

"Of course he's a fireman, she means. He was sitting in the truck." Donna Gene laughed and gave Edie a hearty, slightly startling slap on her frail shoulder. "Anyways. What else?"

"Why do you think you deserve him?" Edie added.

Cassie laughed. "Well, given I deserted him on the first date and almost deserted him on the second, I'd say I don't deserve him, really."

"Oh?" Evidently this was more what Edie wanted to hear. With perked ears she leaned forward while Cassie, with their prodding, went into full details of their meeting, of his relentless pursuing, and where they finally were today.

"And what about those two?" Donna Gene pointed her umbrella at the girls jumping at the finale of the parade, Santa aboard his luminescent sleigh, perched atop a float carried by Billy's Tow Services. "They yours?"

Cassie hesitated. It was the first time anyone had asked. "They're . . . with me. Yes."

"And how's he taken to them?"

"There's three of them, actually," Cassie said. "And he doesn't know."

"Tell him after the wedding." Edie was nodding, the sequins of the belt buckle around her wool hat jostling. "I did the same thing, and I was married forty-two years."

"The same thing? What do you mean the same thing—"

"Take it from Edie." Donna Gene waggled her finger. "As Dr. Bob says, we must learn from the experienced, or we'll never find our way. She was happily married—"

"Married. I never said it was happily." Edie sprayed the air again.

"And her marriage lasted half a century—"

"Forty-two years. Not a day longer."

"And you do want to marry him, Patsy, don't you?" Donna Gene unwrapped a Tootsie Roll. "Now I haven't talked official with Edie yet, but on her behalf and mine, I'd like to offer our little patch of earth for the ceremony. It's not much, what we have up there, but there's a nice good space in the woods that would make for a marvelous backdrop with the snow."

If Donna Gene wasn't gripping Cassie's hand, she would've stumbled out of her chair. "Whoa, now. I think we're getting a little ahead of ourselves here."

"You thinkin' spring?" Donna Gene replied. "Well, you'll have to hide the children that much longer, but if that's what you want to do, I suppose you could keep them in the basement—"

"That's what I always did." Edie primly popped a mint in her mouth.

"And just eyeballing it here, I'd say you're a size 6? Or 8?"

They were talking dresses now? And harboring children in basements? Cassie stood abruptly, the conversation sixty miles beyond the point of control. "Oh look, there went Santa. Parade's over. Girls! Deidre! Kennedy!" Cassie beckoned them over, and with baskets overflowing, they readily jumped to her side. She then called to the teen leaders, "Haven teens, let's assist all our new friends to the bus."

Cassie tried her best to delegate any tasks related to the two women to the teens, and between gathering thirty people and packing them into the borrowed church bus, she had just about succeeded in avoiding Donna Gene and Edie the rest of the evening. They dropped every man and woman off one at a time, Donna Gene and Edie seated in the row farthest back. Star and Bailey sat in the row ahead of them like angelic guards at the entrance of Eden.

But as Cassie turned the steering wheel onto Rattlesnake Hollow, she heard the squirt of sanitizer behind her and felt the distinct smell of disinfectant tickle her nose. She looked into the wide, overhead mirror and jumped at the sudden figures seated behind her. So much for them being elderly.

Edie readjusted her vintage hat.

"Now, where were we?" With hovering pen, Donna Gene lay the crumpled back of a receipt across the top of the bus seat as though it were a doctor's legal pad. "You'll need flowers, of course. You can't have a good wedding without flowers."

Cassie checked the mirror for the back seats. Were her teens alive?

"And we'll need a cake." Donna Gene pointed her pen in her partner's direction. "Edie, I trust you can take care of that. She's a wonderful cook. Watches *Cake or Steak* regular, don't you?"

Edie lifted her chin. "Fondant or funfetti?"

"Ladies, thank you so much for wanting to coordinate my—" (unscheduled and absurdly forecasted) "—wedding. But I've only been seeing Jett two and a half weeks. Barely two and a half weeks. And that's counting a date that lasted all of five minutes."

Edie sniffed. "I had Frank at the altar in twelve hours."

"And yours is . . . quite the example. But I'm going to need more time. Who knows what he'll think after I tell the man who hates kids that I just added three? He'll probably run for the hills."

Donna Gene watched Cassie closely, then patted her shoulder. "Don't you worry your pretty little head about it anymore. You just leave it up to us. We'll see that everything gets sorted out."

Leave it up to them?

"No, really, that's not necessary," Cassie started to say, but when she looked in the mirror, the seat behind her was empty, only the scent of alcohol disinfectant lingering in the air. Inching her chin down, Cassie saw both women securely back in the farthest row, looking as though they'd never moved a muscle.

Jett

He was going to church 40 percent for all the appropriate reasons, 60 percent for the free babysitting. And no, at this point of sleep deprivation and sanity loss, he didn't feel bad about it.

Sunny tucked his slightly rumpled button-up into his jeans. "You sure you don't want to come with Sarah and me?"

"Yes."

Kneeling in his grey slacks, Jett crammed Drew's wiggling toes into socks and then pushed his feet into lime-green sandals. Everything in his life felt like it had to be done quickly. Quickly he pushed feet into socks or else Drew would wiggle himself out of his grip and be running down the hall yelling like a wild monkey. Quickly Jett had to throw cereal into a bowl or else the twins fell into hysterics of hunger. Quickly he had to mix formula. Quickly he had to pick up Dakota when she fell down. Quickly he had to grab Drew before he squeezed through the porch bars and fell two stories.

It was incredible how he could watch his roommate talking, walking, dressing at a snail's pace with a snail's attitude all while he himself was running with a blood pressure of 170 over 90. Work was a break. These days, knocking down a door in a burning building of 1,100-degree heat was a day at the beach.

Grabbing Drew by the underarms and lifting him to stand, Jett held a firm grip and reviewed the trio beside the door. Dakota had a lopsided ponytail, a pink sweater, and a lollipop she'd been licking passively the past twenty-four hours. Drew had a Cheerio on his cheek, a Thomas the Train T-shirt on, and socks peeking through sandals. TJ was in his car seat, a large stain on the same fuzzy sleeper he'd worn to bed. Time to roll.

"You sure?" Sunny said.

Yes. Simply, the answer was yes. If he was stuck between a rock and a hard place and had to take up Sarah's offers for babysitting, he at least could try to avoid her on Sundays, when he was off. Also, there was another, equally significant, reason for going his own way. "Cross Point doesn't have a double service. I'm going somewhere they have two services."

"Why's that?"

"So for two and a half hours I can breathe."

"Let me get this straight." Sunny slid on his only pair of nice shoes—one in fact disfigured by Drew's chew marks.

"The service is going to end, people are going to leave, and you are just going to keep sitting in some pew, going through the whole thing again."

"That's right." Jett adjusted his tie, then picked Dakota up. "And I'm going to relish every moment of it."

Sunny laughed and opened the door. "Whatever floats your boat, man."

Sarah's own door opened.

"Ready, boys?" Sarah turned the key in her deadbolt and faced them. Jett had never seen Sarah wearing earrings so large before, and the thick eyeliner above her lids made the almond shape of her green eyes seem almost catlike. Catlike . . . in a pretty way. She tied a decorative belt around her pea coat.

Jett picked up the car seat and grabbed Drew's roaming hand. "Not for us today. We're going to try another church down the street."

Sarah glanced to Sunny, the gears clearly turning behind those catlike eyes of hers. "Oh? We could . . . go along with you if you wanted. I'm sure you could use the help."

He felt the tug from Drew toward the stairs, and gladly obliged. "No, you guys go on. I had to get out of the house with them eventually. Might as well be today."

Sarah seemed hesitant, uncertain as she watched him take the car seat from Sunny. "If you're sure . . . Will you still meet us for lunch?"

It was painful hearing how hard she was trying to sound nonchalant. He didn't want to hurt her feelings, which only pushed him more to know what he had to do: refuse the babysitting offers as much as possible, show an obvious nonchalance toward her, emphasize as much as possible that their relationship was utterly, wholly platonic. In essence, dig himself out of this grave of kindness. "We'll probably lay low after service—or rather, services. You guys have fun."

She fiddled with her keys. "Oh. Alright. Well, we're just a call away if you end up needing us. Right, Sunny?"

"Oh, sure. Definitely. I'll definitely not have my phone turned off the second you walk downstairs."

"Thanks, Sunny. You're a true friend." Jett let himself be pulled down the stairs by Drew, which didn't feel too far off from getting yanked by a Doberman. "I'll be sure to keep the kids away from your DVD collection while you're gone."

Cross Point, the old grocery building turned church he'd attended the past few months, was nothing like First Community. The church itself looked like an ancient European monastery with a mall parking lot, all plotted on no less than seventy-five acres. Just to get into the parking lot there were three volunteers in orange jackets directing him. Still, he got lost twice.

"Stick on that roof!" Drew proclaimed, pointing out the window. "There's a stick on that roof, Uncle Jett!"

Jett squinted. "That's what we call a steeple, buddy."

Three car seats to unbuckle, one pair of shoes kicked off to replace, and several hands to hold, and Jett finally made it into the stream of churchgoers in the main lobby.

He searched around for a sign. Women in skirts carefully climbed the stairs to a second level. A group of men gathered in the center of the ornately red carpet, chatting. Three couples were standing next to various doors leading to what he could assume was the church sanctuary. They passed out sermon notes while someone inside struck the piano keys.

Finally, a break in the crowd led to a sign, where the word *Nursery* was followed by an arrow.

He pulled the kids left. Hey, this wasn't so bad.

Dakota was in one arm. TJ was drooling, fast asleep in his car seat in the other arm. Drew, for once, was calmly walking beside him down the deep and long hallway. The large, wallpaper-type pictures of people from around the world caused Drew to slow to a stop several times as he became fascinated by the face of an elderly Indian man or a Filipino child. For a minute Jett waited, letting Drew look at the photograph of two women washing their clothes along the Nile.

He took a breath, eyes skimming over the card beside the photo describing the church's work in that area. Despite the commencement tune on the piano down the hall, despite the rush of latecomers kicking up their heels and oxfords as they rushed by them into the sanctuary, the kids were quiet, and everything felt calm. Maybe he wasn't so bad at this parenting thing after all. The kids were here, weren't they? They were happy; they were clothed.

In this moment he felt a sort of sweetness as he held his niece close and watched Drew's wide eyes take in something new. The kid was always learning. Every day they were learning. And for the thousandth time he felt a pang, trying to imagine where Trina was, how she was faring, knowing she was missing this.

He set TJ's car seat down and leaned back against the wall, letting Drew take his moment to observe. Maybe, just maybe, this wasn't going to be impossible. If he just got himself together, got a sitter when he was working, made a schedule, read some parenting books. He might have to find a bigger place, but the dream of settling into his own home had already started churning a few months ago. Gatlinburg had plenty of good houses out in the country, where you could open your blinds to something else besides a parking lot. Where you could drop a dumbbell on your floor without getting a complaint from downstairs tenants. He'd always liked the idea of having cows. Plenty a meal at work had come from the beef raised on the farm of one of the guys. He could call up his old buddy from high school he'd run into the other day, a realtor—

"Are you looking for the nursery?" A middle-aged woman paused in her passing, her arm tucked around a stack of hymnals.

He straightened up. "Yes, actually. This is our first time here."

"Wonderful. I can walk you there." The woman smiled to Dakota and TJ as she spoke, her accent deep and rich. "Oh, how *precious*. And how old are they?"

He picked up the car seat, took a step beside her down the hall. "This little guy is TJ. He's—" He paused. How many weeks was he exactly? He'd never been told TJ's exact birthdate. "Two months. Give or take a few weeks."

The woman's brows rose.

Jett pressed on. "The twins just turned three."

"Oh? She's a twin?"

"Yes. Her brother here—" He looked down to his side. Turned his head. "Her brother . . . Excuse me a moment."

Clinging tightly to Dakota on one hip and hauling TJ's car seat in the other arm, Jett started jogging down the long, wide hall like a quarterback on the field—only this time his pale-green tie was slapping him in the face and the ball was an eight-pound baby.

He'd only let his mind and eyes wander for a *minute*, and yet somehow there was no sign of his nephew at all. There were side halls that went off from the main hall every few seconds, but as his face swiveled from one side to the next, he found no sign of the wandering two-foot toddler. The piano ceased playing from inside the closed doors of the sanctuary, and vaguely Jett heard the group rise and begin a group call and response.

The hall spilled back into the main lobby, and Jett swiftly turned in a circle in the center of it.

Then he saw him.

"Drew!" he hissed, sprinting across the lobby floor.

Blood-red communion wine covered the front of his Thomas the Train T-shirt as he leaned against a small metal cart on tiptoe. Hundreds of tiny plastic cups filled the cart, which shook dangerously as the toddler picked one up and held it, the ounce of communion wine shimmering a candy-apple red.

Jett dropped the car seat midstride. Abruptly he set Dakota down as well. She tumbled to her bottom and began to wail beneath the glittering chandelier.

Drew tipped the cup back just as Jett cleared six feet in one jump. He grabbed his nephew's pudgy hand. Drew stumbled back a step, the cart shaking vigorously.

An elder turned, suddenly aware the communion cart he was charged to protect was under siege.

Gripping the empty communion cup, Drew looked up to Jett with a red stain already forming on his lips. He smiled. Several empty cups lay on the carpet around his feet.

The car seat began to rock as TJ, alone beneath the three-tiered brass chandelier, gave a high-pitched scream that easily eclipsed his sister's howls.

The elder's mouth couldn't have gaped any wider.

Jett picked up Drew. Chest heaving, he pointed to the cart. "Wine or grape juice?"

The flabbergasted man looked as pasty as raw dough.

"Is that wine or grape juice?" Jett repeated.

"It's—it's—it's juice. Just juice," the elder replied, then gripped the cart protectively as though the pair was about to make another run for it.

Jett let out a breath. "Thank you."

The elder's mouth took ages to form words. "You're . . . welcome."

Five minutes later, and one emergency bathroom trip (in which Drew rolled underneath the stalls, Dakota "missed" the potty, and TJ grabbed Jett's tie midhandwashing, giving it a nice, deep soak), he hauled the trio back through the wide hall.

Miraculously, the woman was still waiting, although she'd craned her neck uncertainly, as though unsure of his promised return. She said nothing as Jett held a teary-eyed

TJ in one arm, the empty car seat banging against his hip. Clingy Dakota wrapped her knees deep into his stomach and back from the other side, and if Jett held Drew's hand any tighter he would've been called out by social services.

"So, where were we? Ah, yes. This is Drew."

"Hi. I'm five." Drew held up four red-stained fingers and smiled with red-streaked teeth.

The woman smiled at him. "Oh, my, isn't that—"

"He's three." Jett cut the southern charm. "Where is that nursery again?"

Three turns, one water-fountain break, and a staircase later, he was finally, *finally* scribbling their names with numb fingers onto a check-in sheet. A young girl and waiting couple watched him silently as he wrote the contact information while gripping TJ in one arm. He finished, and pushed the clipboard the girl's way, trying to manage a well-adjusted smile while every piece of evidence suggested the contrary: He was thirty minutes late to the service. Freshly splattered grape juice decorated his white button-up and crooked green tie. He felt the sticky residue of Dakota's sucker on his neck.

The door to the room opposite opened. A single line of toddlers obediently marched out.

Drew, in the meantime, was rolling in the middle of the hall.

"Oh, Mrs. Davis," the girl called out. "We have two more who'd like to join you all today."

Mrs. Davis took one look at the twins and kept walking.

"Mrs. Davis," the girl called out again. She snapped her fingers. Leaned over the counter. "Mrs. Davis!"

"Hm?" Mrs. Davis paused, as though giving in to the fact she was actually going to have to take them. "Oh, were you talking to me, dear?"

With a bit more prodding, for the twins *and* Mrs. Davis, Dakota and Drew finally joined the marching line and headed down the hall.

Now, just one more kid to unload, and he'd be free.

"And if the baby falls asleep?" The mother beside him clasped tightly onto an infant twice TJ's size while the father held a supportive arm around her shoulder. She was bouncing as she spoke to the girl at the desk. "Do you lay them on their stomachs or on their backs?"

"On their backs, ma'am. We follow safe-sleeping guidelines."

"And during diaper changes? You wouldn't put some synthetic cream on my baby without consent?"

"No, ma'am. But to make sure, we can write that as a request on your family profile."

"Oh, yes. Please do." The mother squinted toward the caretakers behind the girl—three ladies in their mid-seventies wearing white aprons and rocking infants. "They have all had their background checks?"

Check-In Girl nodded patiently, as if such paranoid behavior was routine. "Yes, ma'am."

"How about your cleaning supplies? Do you know if you use bleach? Or vinegar?"

"I—" The girl looked uncertain this time. "I think so. I can ask if you'd like."

"You think so, what? Yes, to bleach?" The woman bounced more rapidly on her toes and shot a glance to her husband.

"Honey, if they're going to use bleach on the toys, and then Thomas goes around licking them—"

"Darling, he can't even crawl yet. I doubt he'll be licking the toys."

Jett leaned against the counter while the check-in girl stood on a chair, moving bottles around above the diaper-changing station. At this point, he would've taken an hour of lying in the middle of the hallway so long as he could just do it without kids. He could sleep on this countertop if they just let him.

Six more questions, a handoff of a diaper bag larger than some suitcases, and one painfully long good-bye to their child with fourteen kisses—he counted—and it was finally his turn.

"Here he is. I think he's pooped." Jett held TJ out, sans diaper bag, sans directions, sans kisses and painfully long hugs.

She took him in her arms, calling out as he started around the corner. "Sir? About TJ's date of birth."

He squeezed his eyes shut, cursing his feet for obeying and turning around. "Yes?"

"You left it blank."

"October." He threw out a number. "Let's say October 25th."

"Sorry, sir. But childcare is only available for children eight weeks and up."

"The first, then. Does that work?" He adjusted his crooked, dripping tie.

Her lips parted, then shut, then opened again. She patted TJ's back. "Yes, sir. Okay, I'll write that down."

"Thank you."

The preacher was well into the sermon by the time Jett slumped into a pew three rows from the back. He exhaled. Then a prayer started, and for one glorious minute there was silence in a room of well over one thousand people.

A loud chime echoed from his pants pocket, loud as the drop of a headlamp echoing through a soundless cave. Perfect. Just perfect.

Several eyes opened. Fumbling to pull out his phone, he caught Sarah's text as he silenced it.

Just checking in. You doing ok?

Clinging to the single thread of dignity he had left, Jett jammed the phone into his pocket without answering.

For the next forty solid minutes, he did nothing but breathe.

It was heaven.

"Let us stand." The preacher lifted his arms, the cart of communion cups beside him. "Whenever you are ready, come."

Jett merged into the long line. A pause caused him to stop, and he looked ahead, two rows up, to see several women breaking into the crowd of people. His eyes started to move on. But then, like a lulling baby jerking awake, his gaze snapped to the two women he knew only too well.

Donna Gene, standing out like a purple Easter egg in a basket of black eggs, adjusted her broad-rimmed violet hat just before pushing a walker into the line. Edie wobbled close behind, spraying her hand sanitizer in the air just before merging.

"Excuse me." Jett gestured for another woman to go ahead of him and ducked away. With a church that size there were two other lines on this floor, and another two on the floor above. He'd just have to move to another—

A hand gripped him by the shirt and tugged him back.

Cassie, grinning elfishly at the sight of him, pointed to his shirt.

"What happened?" she whispered. "You look like you broke into the wine early."

"It's grape juice, actually," he whispered back. "And as a matter of fact, I did."

Her smile dropped slightly. "You did what now?" she hissed.

Oh, right. As if he was going to explain everything here. In a silent sanctuary, with award-winning acoustics.

Quickly, Jett flashed a warm, somewhat apologetic smile as if to say, "Oh, I'd love to chat, were it the right time," and turned his face forward, head bowing reverently. Nobody ever interrupted a person with a bowed head; it was one of those universal rules. And sure enough, they silently went forward, took communion, and found their seats.

A few final words and ten minutes later, Jett found himself back in the foyer among a sea of people—most important, the woman in the comfortable-looking gray-and-white striped dress who peered up at him.

"What are you doing here?" Cassie stuck her arms into her dress pockets, a tease in her grin. "Are you stalking me now? I've never been stalked before. I probably shouldn't sound so excited."

"This was my first time." Jett crossed his arms, trying to cover as much of the stain as possible. At least the tie had stopped dripping at this point.

"Sure. Sure. If you're stalking me, I guess you're not supposed to give it away. Well, what'd'ya think? Think you'll stick around?"

"I think I might." The memory of Drew standing on tiptoes for the communion cups came back to him. "It took some work getting here, but it was worth it." His smile tilted. "And no, not just because of the present company. Although it certainly is a plus."

And for several minutes he felt as though they were alone in the middle of the large foyer, standing beneath the chandelier amid a whirl of men greeting each other with friendly slaps on the backs, families toting children toward the nursery, and attendees leaving to make room for those coming. It was calm, it was normal. For the first time that morning, he felt like a decently pulled-together human being.

A carpeted, quiet-looking area in a room to the far left caught his eye behind her. A coffee station stood in its corner, a red plastic tablecloth covering what looked like a simple metal table. Two large white containers of generic sugar and nondairy creamer stood next to a stack of coffee cups. He wasn't sure from this angle, but it seemed reasonable to assume there were at least a couple of chairs in the otherwise empty room. And right now, with the second service still ten minutes away, he had one hour to spare.

Sure, three weeks ago cheap coffee in the corner of a

church would have been the worst date ever, but right now the room shone like the mountain of gold the dragon Smaug protected in his fiery den. It sang to him, lured him. An hour in some folding metal chairs with Cassie today would be worth a hundred dollar bill. Maybe two.

He nodded in the coffee station's direction. "You know, I could do with a cup of coffee. You care for any?"

She turned toward it, and he realized his error. Just because he was stranded here for the next hour didn't mean she was. What would he say if she suggested they take this date somewhere more official—like a real coffeeshop or a restaurant?

But to his surprise, her smile widened. "Sure. Maybe I'll get to see you add a coffee stain to your shirt as well. You know, for being a decent baller, you're *the* clumsiest person I know."

His fingers tingled as he touched her shoulder, and together they moved through the crowd. Through the soft knit material of her dress, her figure was lean, her shapely calves silhouetted beneath her black leggings. She was the perfect mix for him—feminine but strong, soft yet capable, kind while carrying an air of quiet intelligence. She knew herself. She was the type of person who was confident of her tastes and acted upon them, knew what was expected of her and followed through.

He used to think he was that way. But right now, he was only too aware of how far he fell from that line. What was expected of him? What was *his* right way?

One phone call and the kids could be shipped off to his aunt's. One phone call and he could put on a shirt without it smelling—or looking—like it'd been dunked in a compost bin. He could sleep again. For hours at a time.

Take Cassie out. Get prime seats at UT games. Have day hikes in the mountains.

Is that what he wanted?

Is that what was best for the kids?

He hesitated in his thoughts, unable to stop the question that he'd asked himself most: was it possible to make both answers align?

He didn't know. He felt stagnant, his ankles dug in quicksand, only capable to live in this moment.

Edie and Donna Gene, clad in their vibrant dresses and hats, chugged with their walkers into the bursting foyer, parting the people like the Red Sea. He ducked his head, just low enough to be level with the crowd around him. He was fond of them in teaspoonfuls. But letting his personal love doctors see him with a grown, beautiful female around? He'd already had enough drama for one day.

He turned his head slowly by equal degrees, keeping the ladies in his line of sight as he moved around Cassie like a circling shark. "I'm clumsy, eh? Well, I don't recall being clumsy when you called us to save your cat from the burning skyscraper and lethal pine needles."

Cassie swatted his arm playfully. "M-hm. So, do you care to explain what you are doing?"

"I'm hiding."

"From whom?"

He pointed to the duo, who were currently sliding all the mints out of a decorative silver tray into their purses. "From the two women who keep our station in business."

She leaned back, getting a view of the two before straightening up again. A smile crept up her face until it shone like a lightbulb. "They call the fire department often?"

"They're on the once-a-week plan."

"Well then, let's not linger." She bent several inches and began creeping for the coffee station.

He grinned, enjoying how utterly unconcerned she was about how she looked, and followed.

When they made it to the table, one glance back confirmed they'd reached safety; the women were now out the doors and moving slowly onto an idling bus.

Cassie wiped her hair from her eyes. "I'm afraid I'm to blame, actually, for your two fawning friends coming here today. The Girls Leadership Club took them to the parade. Afterward, I got them hooked up with a couple people from the church."

"Well, they need a place like this to come to." He picked up two of the upside-down cups from the sleeve on the table and passed one to her. "But for your sake as much as mine, I'm probably going to keep ducking out in public for a while. Hope you don't find that too strange."

"Ducking? Not at all." She poured herself a cup and then poured a full amount into his. "I hide from my teens all the time."

Her teens. The way she always spoke about her work at the Girls Haven, about the kids, denoted a relationship far beyond an hour or two of life spent together each week. Those kids took up a significant portion of her heart. Kids. Adolescents, younger than eighteen, well above the age of Dakota and Drew and TJ, but still in the same category nonetheless: kids. She loved them. Perhaps, when she found out the whole situation with him, she could make enough room in her heart for three more.

People everywhere, all the time, could change their minds when given enough motivation.

Was he, though, after only a handful of dates, enough motivation?

It was only then that he realized she had been as silent and thoughtful as he was, staring into her coffee as she stirred. He wondered what sorts of thoughts were running through her mind.

"Hey, Cassie—"

He heard a faint buzzing from somewhere inside her coat.

"Yeah?" she said as she pulled it out to check it. Her face changed.

She set her coffee cup down. Not a good sign.

"So sorry, Jett. I have to take this."

Jett waved it off, shielding his disappointment. "Sure. Go ahead."

"This might take a while. I'll, uh, call you soon? Maybe see you sometime this week?"

"Yeah, I'd love that," he started, but she had already pressed the phone to her ear and slipped into the emptying foyer.

In her wake, a cream-colored, still-swirling coffee sat on the table, untouched.

So much for revealing his hopes and dreams.

15

Cassie

Rachel. Hi." Cassie tried not to sound breathless as she pushed open the doors of the church and stepped into the December air.

"Hey, Cassie. I hope you don't mind me calling on a Sunday."

"No, of course not. I said anytime, remember?" Cassie leaned a hip against the waist-high concrete ledge. "What's up?" She tried not to sound too concerned. Rachel could be calling about any number of children at Girls Haven besides the three currently residing beneath her roof. This could be a call about Cam's situation. This could be a call verifying information on another one of the girls.

Or it could be about Deidre and Kennedy and Star.

It was Sunday. Of course it was about Deidre, Kennedy, and Star.

Cassie found herself pacing the length of the sidewalk, the nutcrackers on her Toms staring up at her. Their enormous teeth gritting with each step.

"We found the girls' mother."

Cassie nodded, hearing Rachel's words over the phone.

"It wasn't pretty," Rachel continued.

Cassie felt her head pulsing. She would have to tell the girls. Or at least tell Star and let her decide whether they should tell her sisters.

Cassie knew from experience that fostering was hard. She'd known several foster parents along the way. "Prepare for the rollercoaster" were their general words of wisdom. Reunification of the biological family was always the goal, unless the case was too extreme. But how extreme did the abuse need to be? How long was neglecting your children too long? How many days, or weeks, did they need to face malnourishment and an environment broken by addiction and the dangers of abandonment before the government took away someone's certificate of motherhood?

If Rachel was calling to say the girls' mom was back, that she was sorry, that they were going to start the process of reunification, could Cassie's heart bear it? Could she bear standing idly by week by week, month by month, dropping the girls off for visitations, packing their bags for overnights? Could her heart withstand the trembling as she counted the minutes, trying not to imagine all the possible, painful scenarios, until they returned?

She couldn't handle it.

Maybe she'd thought she could two weeks ago, but now she knew: she wasn't strong enough if something like that happened to her.

What a fool she was.

Cassie found her voice. "Where is she?"

"They're holding her right now in Memphis. Seems she'll be facing charges of possession and distribution. That plus a mounting case of child neglect and abandonment." Rachel paused, and the seconds mounted. "Cassie, she signed over her rights."

Cassie stopped midstep. It was her turn now for silence.

"Do you hear me?" Rachel continued. "Those girls are legally up for adoption as of twenty minutes ago."

Cassie's throat began to close, her vocal cords straining as she found her next words. "What about relatives?"

"I've looked into all the Allen children's potential relations. I spoke with two leads, and both were either unable or unwilling to take over custody. Believe it or not, you're actually the closest relation they've got . . . Cassie, those kids are yours if you'll have them."

She found she was still nodding, though the parked cars straight ahead were starting to blur. *"Have them"?* Have *them*? How could she feel anything *besides* wanting to have them?

Over the past two weeks it had become pretty clear the girls were going to need extra help in a variety of areas. Deidre still hadn't spoken a word. Kennedy erupted into loud, sometimes violent tantrums that required moving fragile items and potential weapons out of the way. Just the few snippets Star had shared about life in that apartment warranted regular visits with a professional counselor. Lots of people around the world would say Cassie was completely, totally in over her head.

And she was.

But it wouldn't stop her.

Rachel spoke into the silence. "Are you still there?"

Cassie pulled the phone to her hip for a moment and coughed, trying to pull herself together. Even so, her voice sounded raspy in her own ears. "I'm here. I—" If she attempted the words "I want to adopt them," she most assuredly wouldn't be able to hold it together any longer. "Just tell me what I need to do next."

They talked over details, court dates, the lengthy process and paperwork to be done in the coming weeks and months, and when Cassie ended the phone call, a breeze nearly lifted her off her feet.

It was official, or as official as official could get before becoming signed-and-signatured official. She was going to become a mother.

She checked the time and started jogging for the front doors.

More specifically, she was about to become a mother who had forgotten her children in childcare.

Cassie had reached the emotional state that, if someone touched her as she raced down the hall, she would've burst into tears. She ran up to the check-in girl—who was currently cleaning a rather large amount of spit-up off her blouse—and was directed to the gymnasium.

"Here to pick up?" a man said, leading her into the busy room of second-service children.

Cassie nodded silently. Pick up. Ready to pick up *her* kids.

Set up between two basketball goals on either end, a manger scene stood on a portable stage. While one group of eight-year-old angels practiced on it, huddled groups waited offstage beside teachers, appearing to be split up by age.

Deidre stood among a group of six-year-olds, clearly more interested in watching the director flick her conductor's baton than listening to whatever direction her teacher was currently giving. The director made the dramatic motion of cradling a baby in her arms, and the child angels—sans Deidre—followed suit.

Kennedy was huddled with the rest of the four-year-olds, tugging on her braids.

Star stood off to one side with the rest of the teens, listening to a man who looked more like a football coach than youth pastor as he pointed rapidly, seemingly spouting off placements.

The man turned to her. "Which one of them is yours?"

Cassie felt the air catching in her lungs, her throat constricting in the same unyielding way as before.

Well, there it goes.

She was not a crier—a fact in which she prided herself. Now, however, one simple question tipped her over like a wobbly stack of dominoes.

A croak—not too far from a real frog's—spilled out from her. She pressed a hand over her mouth as he jerked his head back to her. *Pull it together, Cassie. Pull it together.*

She pointed with her other hand. "The six-year-old girl in the striped pink."

Another sniff. "And the four-year-old with the two yellow pom-poms in her braids."

He rocked back on his heels, crossing his arms uncomfortably, doubtless rethinking this whole "volunteer in the children's program" thing.

"And—And Star. One of the bravest—" Tears filled her eyes. "—most beautiful, relentless girls I know."

Her face pinched, her skin both hot and cold. With a chin making heroic attempts to stay strong in the war against becoming a human water faucet, she knew she looked like a pig who'd eaten a frog. Another muffled sob escaped her. She was *not* a pretty crier.

She turned around abruptly and retreated down the hall toward the restroom. It was quiet, empty. Perfect for her to pull herself together.

She yanked out a tissue and blew her nose. Then thought about all the times she would get the privilege to blow Kennedy's nose.

And the waterworks started.

The problem was the news that she could have three adopted children—one whom she'd already known and loved for years—kept hitting her like a ton of bricks. The consequences of what that meant slipped into her mind one at a time, as if demanding individualized attention.

Anticipated dreams—the opposite of memories—drifted into her mind like videos in iridescent bubbles. Her and Star sitting on the couch, talking about Star's day while the youngest two lay tucked into their beds. Star closing up the Haven with her and dropping her backpack into the back seat of her car. Easter morning, when the girls would scavenge the yard in pastel dresses with baskets full of Easter eggs. Going over to her sister's, drinking tea and turning barbequed chicken as cousins jumped on the trampoline. Sitting around on a regular afternoon with them, doing nothing at all.

All beautiful bubbly little videos.

Life as she knew it as a black-and-white world now shifted to color. Nothing in her own life, not one thing, was unaffected by the fact she was choosing, wholeheartedly, to raise these kids. Not one thing.

But two points had to be discussed.

The kids had to choose her too—in particular Star. Any child fourteen or older had to consent to the adoption. Did she—did they—even want her?

Second, she had to tell Jett. This was no longer a potential reality; it was her future, and if he was as interested as he acted in her, it was only fair to tell him the truth.

The smell of gardenias from that night those years ago suddenly overwhelmed her, the feel of her fingers against the brown tweed of Matt's suit while he looked her in the face, telling her flatly he no longer wanted her.

Cassie felt her confidence wane as her hands gripped the vanity.

Five years she had committed to that man. Through two blissful, adventurous years of college, through the painful months she sat by the phone, waiting for every one of his late-night calls while he "found himself" in Colorado. Through graduate school when they ate buttered noodles off paper plates like they were kings and queens. Through it all, she'd stuck by his side.

But then Matt hadn't wanted her, as he'd informed her days after a surgery revealed her life would be changed forever. Was the timing pure coincidence? Maybe. Had their relationship already sagged from issues they kept pushing on the back burner? Certainly.

But she'd seen his face when she told him she couldn't have children herself anymore. She'd felt the coldness grow in the following weeks.

Now, here she was, with the forecast of a home not empty but filled to the brim. But at its core was a replica of the conflict that had first broken her heart. No matter how nice Jett was now, the fact remained: he'd stated very clearly he wasn't interested in the sort of family life she was about to lead. Could he change his mind? Could she persuade him? Sure. Maybe. Possibly. But, again, their relationship had barely begun.

If she thought about what she'd *really* known about Matt in that first month of their relationship, it'd come to this: zero. Jett was charming and sweet and funny and responsible and all these great things, and part of her *felt* that he would respond to the truth of the situation with an enthusiastic open mind. Part of her *dreamed* that he would fall in love with the girls, just as much as she had. Part of her *hoped* they would get their family cross-stitched together on a pillow, holding hands. But there was still a problem: she was going off of a perception of him built upon mere weeks.

If she adopted the girls, she would have to come to terms with the reality that she might be single forever. However scarce the possibility of her falling in love and getting married was before, well, now it definitely rested solely on the shoulders of a miracle maker.

She stripped off a paper towel and wiped the mascara beneath her eyes, then tipped her chin up, staring at herself in the mirror. Put her hand against her flat waistline—unaffected, for the first time in years, by the thought of the scars hidden underneath.

She had tacked on another fifteen minutes to her long-overdue pickup by the time she again pulled open the door to the gymnasium and stepped inside. The man she'd spoken with before saw her and practically jumped over a stack of chairs to get away. He nudged a woman, and the woman, after some prodding, made her way toward Cassie.

Kids were playing a game of Mr. Fox on one side of the gym while several teens shot hoops on the other. Beside the stage, a couple of platinum-blond toddlers chased Kennedy in circles around Star and Deidre. One of the children, a toddler boy running madly with one sock on, threw his arms around Kennedy. She giggled with his hands locked behind her neck, turned, and the chase started again in reverse.

That is, until Star pulled on the sleeve of Deidre's sweater and gave a furtive glance to three teen girls standing six feet off. They chatted wildly among themselves, shifting from one hip to the other in colorful leggings and matching pairs of furry boots. Cassie hadn't thought twice when Star put on her worn-out turquoise Chucks this morning. At the Haven, Chucks were the norm, rain or shine. But of course, Star wouldn't care. She was one of those who led the pack, not followed along blindly in it.

Listen to her, she was pulling all the proud mom moves already.

The three girls laughed loudly, and Star turned her face

away. When Kennedy ran by again, she snagged her by the dress and set Kennedy on her lap on the ground.

"Want to play a game?" Cassie read Star's lips as she watched her pull a wrapper from her jeans. Star rolled it into a ball, then hid it in one of her fists. She knocked both fists together, and Kennedy's eyes lit up, trying to guess where it was hiding. The two furry-headed blond children stopped, quick to follow in the new game.

Enough of this. She could stand in the corner watching them all day, smiling as she watched her three soon-to-be *daughters* be their normal, delightful selves. But then that would scare the poor man off volunteering in the children's ministry forever, and she was too anxious to get them into her arms anyway.

Cassie called out to the three of them, her smile as high as her waving arm. "Hey, guys! Time to go!"

Star's gaze lifted to Cassie. The wadded ball dropped to the floor as she stood and lifted Kennedy onto her hip. Her hand reached out for Deidre while Kennedy waved goodbye to the toddlers.

The trio began walking toward Cassie.

Then, without slowing, they walked right on past her, Star turning at the last moment to knock Cassie's shoulder, hard, along the way.

16

Jett

Radiator fluid leaked all over the pavement, and all Jett could think was how Drew would've loved to be a fireman on this call. He would've pressed his hand against the neon-green fluid, probably would've licked it when Jett wasn't looking. Then he would've chased all the white-feathered chickens clucking hysterically around the sideways truck leaning against a tree. He would've splashed his feet in the freezing-cold brook where a headlight lay submerged, glowing like hidden gold.

This Norton Creek crash site would've been a downright playground.

Overturned and opened cages littered the mountainous road as he walked past the exposed undercarriage of the vehicle. Even that looked like a gigantic Hot Wheels (Drew really was hacking into his brain these days) with bumper stickers slapped all over the backside of the jacked-up, three-quarter-ton diesel.

Jett's eyes skimmed each sticker:

KEEP HONKING, I'M RELOADING
DUE TO PRICE INCREASE IN AMMO, DON'T EXPECT A WARNING SHOT
EAT MORE POSSUM

Well, with the thirty-six-inch mud tires, he didn't expect the bumper sticker to say EAT ORGANIC or MY DAUGHTER IS AN HONOR STUDENT AT PI BETA PHI ELEMENTARY SCHOOL.

This guy was a real piece of work.

The narrow road was completely blocked off now, turning the wreck into a logistical nightmare as officers scrambled to organize detours. If he had to guess, it'd be an hour yet before the tow truck arrived.

Jett gripped the jaws-of-life to the crushed door. The frame bent further as he began to pry it open.

With a loud *clip* the door yielded to him, and together with Kevin, they pulled it off. Jett reached in, extended a hand. With a truck like this, he was surprised the guy inside hadn't swung open the door like a rocket and dragged his own body out with his two behemoth biceps.

But instead of accepting help getting out and onto the unsteady bank, a bony hand swatted his arm.

"What the [*bleep*] did you do to my truck!" the man

roared. Only it wasn't a man. It was the squeaky voice of a teen without a filter.

With arms skinny enough Jett questioned he could even hold a rifle, the boy pulled himself to a standing position. He yanked up the camo pants threatening to fall to his ankles. Pointed to his door.

"What the [*bleepity-bleep-bleep*] business do you think you have [*bleepity*] . . ." The teen raged on while chickens flapped around them in a white-feathered dust cloud.

Unbelievable. Twenty guys were out here wasting the day on a kid who couldn't steer his own truck, and this was how he thanked them.

Teenagers. He didn't know how Cassie did it.

They wasted another two hours at the site and finally made their way back to the station, hours late on a meal and starving. Not ten minutes later the alarm rang again.

As the dispatcher's voice laid out the details over the speakers, Captain Ferraro dropped his fork. "That's it. Bentley, when you get back, I want you to make sure those ladies haven't planted cameras in here." He pointed up to the corners of the ceiling. "Somehow they always *know* just when you're on the clock."

"Maybe they're tracking your phone," Johnson grunted, his face in a second bowl of Mac's fire-alarm chili. "I do it on my girls. One of 'em's twenty-two now, and she's still not privy to it." He lifted his gaze with a mischievous smile, a chili bean hanging on to his beard. "But I can tell you one thing. The boyfriend hates me."

A few chuckles went around the table before the men returned to their dinners. Captain Ferraro called out as Jett,

Sunny, and two others started down the stairs. "You give us so much business, Bentley, I don't know whether to fire you or promote you."

"I'll take that as a compliment, sir," Jett replied, pausing on the stairs.

The captain fired back, "Don't."

Jett pressed his lips together, followed with a muted nod.

The seat was still warm when Jett slipped into the driver's seat. Sunny swung the passenger door of Medic 2–10 shut and switched on the lights. Then, out of nowhere, he raised a bowl of chili to his chin.

"You know," Jett said, pulling into the street. "Ferraro will have you on dinner duty for weeks if he catches you eating on the job."

"I have to, man. Between calls from your elderly sweethearts and your minions eating all our food, I'm whittling away to nothing. You know how much little man Drew ate yesterday for lunch?" Sunny didn't wait for a reply. "Three hamburgers. Three. Dakota nibbles on half a chicken nugget while Drew demolishes his cheeseburger like a T-rex on steroids. Then he goes after one of mine, and I have a benevolent moment, thinking, 'Hey, I'm a good godfather—'"

"You're not his godfather."

"I'll steal his fries and let the little guy have a few bites of my one-and-a-half pounder. It's covered in jalapeño sauce, after all. Best he can do is take a bite and start crying."

Jett turned on the blinkers. "And that's not what a good godfather does."

"Sure it is. Anyway, you know what the little terror does?"

"Godfathers probably don't call their godsons terrors."

"He swallows half of it. In *two* bites. At one point he rubs jalapeño sauce in his eye and starts to cry, and I'm thinking, 'Oh, good, I'll get it back now.' But you know what happens then?" He looks at Jett. "Do you?"

Jett sighed. "No, Sunny. Please. Tell me. What happens next?"

"He keeps on crying, tears running down his face, and stuffs the rest of it in his mouth. It was like tears were the fuel that kept him going. I can't put it into words, man, but it was creepy. Inspiring, but also creepy. Like a rabid squirrel."

"So now your godson is a rabid squirrel."

"You admit it!" Sunny pointed and exclaimed, his spoon knocking chili to the floor.

"I admit nothing," Jett replied, turning the wheel.

Airbrakes squealed as Kevin parked the engine at the turn for Skyline Drive. Jett turned, the trip ending with the well-known chassis-trembling, move-at-a-snail's-pace drive up the rocky gravel.

As Jett turned off the ignition, sauce dribbled down Sunny's chin and shirt and dashboard.

Jett opened the door with an I-told-you-so grin.

Snow crunched underfoot as they followed the small, female footprints—and one long streak of cane—to the porch. Jett tried knocking the snow off his boots on the thin welcome mat reading *Animals Welcome People Tolerated*, but with no luck, he kicked lightly against the burgundy frame of the front door. As snow reluctantly gave in and dropped to the ground, he heard Donna Gene call to him. "Well, c'mon in, boys. We haven't got all day."

Sunny and Jett exchanged looks before Jett grabbed the screen handle.

There, hanging from the ceiling in the middle of the room, was a suit. Edie took one long, squinty look at Jett, then took a pin out of her mouth and slid it into the waist of the jacket.

Donna Gene hobbled a step to the table, leaning on the chair for support. "What'd'ya think, Jetty boy? We've been working on it all day."

He lingered at the unwelcome mat. Sunny gave him a firm elbow in the back, and Jett stumbled forward.

"It's . . . very nice." In addition to not wanting to be there, he also didn't want to ask. Whatever reply came out of their mouths he wasn't going to like. But there it was, the question a mosquito in front of his face, a sting on his neck, then forehead, then arm. He had no choice but to give in and swat it. "What's it . . . for?"

"For you, of course. Don't think we don't know about Ms. Everson."

"Or your little rendezvous on Sunday." Edie lifted her cane and hit the burgundy jacket. Dust exploded as though the cane had wacked a cupful of dust. "That's right. We saw you all cozied up in the church parlor."

Jett stepped lightly around the coffee table—littered for once in things besides empty cans and chip bags. An open sewing kit, scissors lying on a pile of bridal magazines. A roll of lace, partly unwound until a foot or so dipped onto the matted carpet.

He lifted his head, sensing the silence. He turned his head to the television, where it stared blankly back.

The TV was off. Repeat, the TV was *off*.

"Well, ladies, I appreciate any . . . designs . . . you might have in all of this. But if you don't mind, I'd just as soon focus on the emergency you called us in for." He hesitated, finding it wrong to hope yet hoping all the same. "There *is* an emergency?"

"Just missed it." Edie wrapped a tape measure around his waist. "Donna Gene had one of her dizzy spells."

"Is that so?"

Donna began fanning herself with a magazine, her chest rising beneath the pink bathrobe. "I'd say it was a miracle. Edie pulled me back up with brute strength. What's his waist, Edie?"

"Thirty-four inches." Edie moved the tape measure across his shoulders, which Jett, as politely as he could, started swatting off.

"Well, in that case, we ought to be going. Lots of work today. Isn't that right, Sunny?" Jett took a step back, then bumped against Sunny.

"Oh, I think we have enough time to sit a spell," Sunny replied with a wicked grin.

"What about the suit, Jetty boy?" Donna asked.

"What about it?"

"It's the perfect shade for you, isn't it?" Donna leaned the pant leg toward his side. "Matches your skin tone and everything, I'd say."

"Worn at my late husband's funeral," Edie clucked. "Suitable for all occasions."

Sunny slapped Jett on the back, stopping him from even trying to move away. "Now did you hear that? The lady is offering you custom tailoring on a bona fide vintage suit. That's not something to take lightly. How about you get up on that coffee table for some proper measurements?"

Sunny crossed his arms across his chest, blocking the door with a smile as wide as Texas. He was getting back at him for the twins washing Sunny's toothbrush in the toilet without telling him—well, not telling until they were watching Sunny brush his teeth.

Jett was going to have to talk his way out of this, but the only thing he could think of was the truth. "The thing is, ladies, I don't think there's going to be a wedding anytime soon."

"Oh, we know. We've already talked it over with Patsy."

"Who's Patsy?"

Donna frowned. "Why, your sweetheart, honey. You need to sit down? Have something to drink?"

"No. Thank you." Jett shook his head. This was getting out of control.

"Anyway, it should take us a few weeks to get everything sewn up just right."

"No. I mean, ever. There may never be a wedding. So you don't need to worry about making a fuss."

Donna started fanning a magazine. "Surely not. There's not one fault she can find in you."

"On the contrary—" Jett slammed his boot on Sunny's toe and hip-checked him out of the way for the door. "—there are exactly three faults she can find with me. I'm just going to have to figure out how to tell her."

"About the children?"

His hand paused on the handle, a gust of wind pressing against his tension on the door. He turned his head. "You know about the children?"

Donna Gene paused, then tapped a finger twice to her temple. "Jetty boy, you'd be surprised all the secrets the old lemon holds. That's why you oughta sit on down and let old Edie and D take a hatchet to your problems."

"Maybe some other time, ladies. Okay, then. Bye-bye." He all but ran back to the truck, purposeful not to turn back as he heard Edie call after him. Sunny followed, snickering all the way.

In the safety of Medic 2–10, Sunny spoke. "Well, you're fully justified now. I think you can go check for cameras."

Sure, Sunny could laugh it off, Jett thought, but the question remained: how did they know? The twins and TJ had left the house once, maybe twice, in the last two weeks. Jett nodded. "Church. They must've seen me walking around with them at church."

It had to be. He would just keep telling himself that until he believed it.

A minute, then two, rolled by in silence.

"What you said back there about three problems. You still thinking about keeping them?" Sunny asked.

Jett looked out the window. If anyone knew the harsh reality of his life right now, the day-in, day-out consequences of that question, it was Sunny. "I don't know. But after I meet with Aunt Neena, I'll have my answer. One way or another."

"Drew, pick the macaroni up off the floor."

Drew, sitting at the antique-white, farmhouse-style table, shoveled another scoopful of macaroni into his mouth.

Jett leaned forward from his chair opposite. "Drew. Pick up the macaroni."

Several seconds went by. Jett gave a polite smile to his aunt, who smiled politely back.

Her husband coughed at the head of the table and set his fork down. "This tenderloin is delicious, honey."

Aunt Neena, holding TJ awkwardly while his head kept falling forward, tried to pick up her fork for a bite of salad. It slipped off. "I'm so glad you like it."

Jett leaned so far forward his white upholstered chair tipped up and his face came within inches of one of several tall candlesticks lighting their dinner of tenderloin, glazed asparagus, and Caesar salad—which had been, it should be noted, the original planned meal for the kids. That was before the twins gave their long, loud, and unending opinions on the matter. And before one of the gold-rimmed china plates shattered on the white shag rug.

Now they were eating macaroni in Tupperware.

Jett whispered tersely, pointing to the thrown items. "*Drew. Pick. Up. Your. Macaroni.*"

Drew looked up at him while shoveling another handful—literally, as in *hand* without the spoon—of macaroni into his mouth. "Can't. I'm a dinosaur. Dinosaurs don't have hands."

Jett's uncle stifled a smile.

Jett himself stifled a look that would've slid that smile

right off his uncle's face. He set the fork down and stood. "Young man . . ."

Working with Drew at an agonizing pace to place thirty-three pieces of macaroni back into the Tupperware, Jett resettled in his chair just in time for coffee.

Aunt Neena, still attempting to hold TJ, settled a quaking cup and saucer before Jett.

"Honey, let me have him for a minute. I've hardly gotten a chance to see him." Jett's uncle reached up for TJ, but his wife turned away.

"You'll get your chance, too, Ron. This is my time with my great nephew." She put a protective hand around TJ, whose wide, blue eyes stared at Jett as she settled back into her high-backed, button-tufted chair. Unsteadily, she picked up her cup. "These children have the sweetest smiles."

That was false. When Dakota and TJ smiled, it was sweet. When Drew smiled, you got the feeling it was because he'd discovered your weakness.

"So, Jett, tell us about this new situation of yours."

"Sure, I, uh—" Jett pinched his forefinger and thumb together as he picked up the exceedingly small, ornately curved handle of a porcelain Turkish coffee cup with roughly a third the capacity of TJ's bottle. "Trina showed up at my apartment last week when—" He raised his voice, interrupting himself. "*Guys*, get off the couch. *Stop.* Do *not* throw the pillows."

Drew and Dakota paused, both arms loaded with one of the half dozen throw pillows arranged on the white canvas couch. When had his aunt and uncle become so civilized? In his childhood, visits to their home meant watching baseball games while eating corn dogs on a green plaid couch. Everything back then was striped wallpaper and wood paneling.

Now the place was covered in white: white walls, white couches, white dining room tables with white candlesticks lighting white china over a white rug. As a conscientious temporary parent in the dead of winter, all he wanted to do was round up all the interior designers and shoot them with paintball guns. With brown paint, for all the mud the kids inevitably carried in the house. With red, for all the juice spills and blood. And with every other color of the rainbow so no stone was left unturned.

Jett took a sip of his coffee—thereby draining it—and prepared to start again. Before he could do so, he was interrupted by the squeaking of springs. He stood quickly. "*Drew*, what did I just tell you? Get off of the couch. No, stop jumping—Drew—"

An aching fifty-two minutes later he clicked the last of the children into their car seats, feeling like he'd just barely survived a tornado. He turned for a hug, then handed his aunt the doorknob Drew had managed to pull off. "Thank you for letting us come."

Aunt Neena, a stain on the shoulder of her white blouse and necklace turned backward, hugged him in return. "I loved every minute of it." She squeezed him tighter, then gave him a peck on his cheek. "Truly. And don't you worry about the coffee spill on the couch. I'll have the stain out before you hit the interstate."

His smile tightened, remembering well the second Dakota, in an unwatched moment, had picked up a cup of coffee, brought it over to the couch, and, naturally, immediately dropped it.

"Just focus on bringing those babies back down for Christmas, okay?" she continued. "I'm going to have so many presents under that tree they won't know what to do with themselves."

He nodded and smiled through the rest of the partings, but he felt he wasn't actually breathing until he hit the highway. Dakota was crying over the *Better Homes and Gardens* magazine Aunt Neena had given her that had fallen to the floor mat, out of reach. His seat was being kicked at sporadic moments by his nephew, who was also singing the ABC song loudly. Despite it all, *this* was the first time all night Jett felt himself relaxing. He rolled his head to one side, neck and shoulders tense enough to beg for an Advil. Never had a visit been so stressful.

This was how it was going to be forever. He knew it.

For the next seventy years, every time he went out in public he would be hauling these three little goldilocks-headed minions around, catching glass objects and scooping them up before they plunged off stairs. Eventually he'd become so terrified of going out he'd become a hermit, and together the four of them would inhale the same stale air while he watched them destroy the furniture and crayon on the walls. Forever.

And from the way things had gone tonight, his options, really, had plummeted to none. None. The one measly hope he'd had in his aunt and uncle had been held out, tenuous as a snowflake. Yet tonight that dream had been sufficiently thrown to the ground, crushed underfoot, picked up, lighted on fire, and taken flight, and the ashes were now scattered somewhere over the Pacific. In other words, he couldn't ask them to take on the kids.

The way they'd enjoyed being casual onlookers while he struggled to get the kids under control. The way they'd carried TJ as though he was a football. It wasn't that they didn't want the kids. It was just that the idea was so impossible that it hadn't even entered their radar.

They had presented empathetic expressions and listening ears as he shared the situation. Aunt Neena squeezed his hand as she watched him struggle to explain the difficulty of the past two weeks. But there had been a line there, unseen but no less impenetrable, that said that was as far as it would go. Throw in a boatload of Christmas presents on the holidays. Invite them to birthday parties. Come visit sometime for a Little League baseball game. But as far as taking over parental responsibility, he was on his own.

He hadn't even bothered to voice the actual possibility to them.

Drew kicked the back of Jett's seat again. Dakota's wailing finally reached a breaking point, and Jett blindly reached into the backseat for the magazine. He passed it to Dakota, who stopped crying instantly.

"Drew, look out the window." Jett's voice tipped up. "Do you see that? What is that big thing right next to us?"

The kicking stopped. "A truck."

"A *sixteen-wheeler* truck. What else do you see?"

Jett cruised down the interstate, playing the amateur league of I Spy.

Breathing. Driving.

He'd be worrying right now about his future, if he only had the time.

Cassie

A storage bin for the car. Now isn't that handy?" Poised in the snowflake sweater she'd knit herself three years prior, Cassie's mother beamed from her perch beside the pot-bellied Christmas tree. The branches were so thick with tinsel and lights her hair blinked red and green.

Despite Christmas parades, the mass creation of snowman jars, the assembling and distribution of shoebox Christmas projects, and the festive window displays that had covered the streets of Gatlinburg since the day after Thanksgiving, there was nothing quite like her mother's annual elephant gift exchange party to really settle Cassie into the Christmas spirit, and let her know Christmas was truly around the corner.

Seven days to be exact. And for the first time in her adult life, she'd have a full house to share it with.

Her mother held the bin up and received a round of simultaneous *ooohs* and *ahhhs* in response from many of the adults—a comfortable mix of friends, family, and neighbors. The few in the room in their teenage or younger years merely clung tighter to the wrapped presents in their hands. But most of the women had a gleam in their eye, clearly considering swiping Mom's present when their turn came up.

Cassie, it was painful to admit, was old enough to see the merits of the storage bin. But for the sake of her aging spirit, she gripped the bright-yellow wrapping paper around the shoebox-sized package in her lap, hoping there was a fidget spinner inside.

"Who's number three?" Cassie's mother raised her gentle voice as she took the bowl from Cassie's father and lifted it, the one of the pair to bravely toss aside her reticent ways for the yearly party. She looked around the room, but none of the twenty-five or so faces waved a slip of paper with the scribbled number in the air.

After a long moment, Cassie realized the missing link and turned to Deidre. "What number do you have?"

Sure enough, Deidre handed her the slip of paper.

"Here, Mom." Cassie put her hands on Deidre's shoulders and spoke quietly. "It's your turn to pick your present, Deidre. Go ahead."

"Actually . . . that's odd," her mother replied, picking up a rectangular box with smooth, metallic-red wrapping paper. "I believe this one has your name on it, Deidre."

She smiled as she handed it to Deidre, then gave a subtle wink to those around her.

It took a little convincing from Cassie, some playful tugs of the large ribbon placed squarely in the center of the box, a little nipping at the tape, but eventually Deidre turned her focus to the mystery of the gift inside. Cassie's mother had generously rigged the game for Deidre, Kennedy, and Star beforehand, so it was no surprise to see Deidre's face increasingly glow as she recognized the light-up tracing pad underneath.

"Well, look at that." Cassie stroked one hand down the girl's freshly braided ponytail. "Isn't that what you pointed out at the store yesterday?"

Deidre nodded, already snapping out the blue-colored pencil.

Cassie heard Star, huddled on a stool in the corner, exhale loudly.

Cassie's jaw clenched. For forty-eight hours she hadn't been able to get anything out of Star. Not a "Good morning," not an "Oh, thank you for getting up at 5:00 a.m. and making me eggs Benedict. That was so thoughtful." For once in their relationship, Star had out-stubborned her. What had originated as hurt after the church service had turned swiftly and concretely into brooding, and with each passing hour, the top of the pot quaked more and more with the threat of explosion. Cassie had realized the grave errors she'd made and apologized. She'd talked to the silent door of Star's room more than once, saying she was sorry.

Nothing came of it but silence.

Now, however, Cassie felt the threatening winds. She

just didn't have a clue how to respond. But for all the things she didn't know, there was one thing she did: not here. *Please, oh, please, don't blow up here.*

Her mother already thought Cassie was taking too much upon herself. She didn't have to say so; it was written clearly in every casserole she brought over to help with dinner, in every piece of laundry she offered to help fold. Cassie came from a long line of traditional home-and-hearth women. To her mother, a full-time job as a single woman was an "alternative lifestyle." Now a single working woman with three kids? It was positively mind-blowing. In the last two and a half weeks Cassie had gained enough casseroles to last a year.

For the next half hour or so, Star stared sullenly out the window, watching the blackness outside while the rest opened presents one after another. Until it came time for number eighteen.

Cassie felt her back stiffen as her mother repeated herself for the third time. "Eighteen, anyone? I think somebody must have it. I wrote down one for everyone." Her mother gazed down at the half-full bowl as if expecting it to sprout another slip of paper.

Finally, Star turned her gaze from the window.

"Is that you, Star?" Cassie's mother gently pressed. "Do you have eighteen?"

Star gave a lazy look at her number. "Yeah."

"Oh! Well, isn't that convenient. There seems to be one here with your name on it too."

Star limply took the present from her mother's hands—a sturdy, wide cardboard box containing what Cassie had been excited about: a pair of sky-blue, Moxi suede ice skates.

Premium stainless-steel blades combined with a vintage floral print, so old-fashioned it was the latest trend.

To say Star would be thrilled was an understatement.

But just as she tugged off one loop of the yellow bow, she stopped. Exhaled, as if the work of unwrapping it was too much. Then dropped it. The box bounced to the ground, knocking against the back of the couch. She resumed looking out the window.

Cassie felt the heat on her neck as her voice rose. "Star, go ahead and open the present, please."

Star didn't move.

Comfortable silence suddenly became very uncomfortable, as the eyes of her neighbors and family began looking intently into the beige carpet or quickly engaged in conversation. "What do you think about that slicer," she heard one of the women ask another. "I bet you'll get lots of use out of it. Is it just for apples, you think?"

The hum of small talk began to fill the living room. Men with even less to say on topics of UT scarves and makeup kits left the room completely, opting for the eggnog station instead.

Deidre stopped doodling the pony on her pad. Her large, round eyes watched Star and Cassie warily.

Cassie stood. She dodged the sea of crumpled wrapping paper littering the floor.

"Excuse me."

Mr. Patterson, the only oblivious one in the room, looked up from his new pocketknife and let her squeeze through to the backside of the couch.

Cassie turned her back to the rest of the guests. She spoke

so quietly even Mr. Patterson and his wife, sitting inches away, would have to arch their backs to hear. "I know that you're angry right now." She wanted to add, *And for the first five hours, through my first two apologies, you had every right to be,* but held her tongue.

"But, come on," Cassie continued. "My mother wrapped that present especially for you. Why don't you just open it, thank her, and let everyone here have a nice time?"

"Or what? I'll ruin the party because I don't open a *totally* adorable pair of boots that's, like, a must-have of the season?" Her over-the-top, preppy voice dropped as she crossed her arms tightly around her, speaking loudly—too loudly—out the window. "I don't want anything from you. Or your *mother*."

The room froze.

The heat that had been sitting in Cassie's neck rose to her cheeks as she saw her mom stock still in the center of the room, a statue holding a tray of her famous crab dip.

"Let's go," Cassie said under her breath.

Star shook her head. "No."

Anxiety was starting to turn into the inability to think clearly. What could she do? At the Haven, the girls worked off their misbehaviors by cleaning the cobwebs off the windows, scrubbing down toilets, mopping scuffed-up floors. If the punishment required more severity, there was suspension. More than that, and the girls were expelled.

But here, what could she say? *You'll obey me, missy, or else you're going to be grounded for two weeks? Scrubbing the bathroom floor of the house you've only lived in a matter of weeks? Suspended? Expelled?*

There was a fire in Star's eyes that just dared her to try, to say those unspeakable words.

Cassie knew she had failed Star on Sunday; the realization had hit her the same moment Star's shoulder had, with equal force. It wasn't about being the new girl in the crowd or the trivial fashion differences between Chucks and boots, sweaters and scarves. Star, of all people, had never been a fearful one or one to bow to the standards of another. She was a natural-born leader. Tough. So tough, Cassie never questioned her. Even when she managed to keep herself and her sisters alive for weeks alone. When every day she showed up at the Haven, shoveling food into her mouth, stockpiling pretzels in her backpack, claiming for days she'd forgotten money to eat lunch and asking Cassie to let her into the storage closet. Even through each of those brave-faced lies that Cassie now knew were part of Star's only concrete plan to preserve their family.

Cassie had messed up. She didn't anticipate how Star would really feel about going to Cassie's church; she didn't know because she had never asked. And without even realizing it, she had let the kids go through the motions of the first service, never imagining how they must've felt as one by one parents plucked up their children until they were the only ones left. The Sunday school teachers checking the clock for the fifteenth time and leaning their heads out into the hall, stretching their necks to see above the departing parents with kids in tow. Saying things in a sing-song voice like, "*Nooo. I don't see her yet. But I'm sure she'll be here any moment.*"

And the girls couldn't even sleep in their own beds.

How had Cassie not thought twice about insisting they get to stay together in their classes? Heaven knew Deidre and Kennedy had clung to Star and then each other, trying.

But they'd trusted her. In the end, they let Cassie convince them it was only an hour, only sixty minutes and then she'd be *right back* to pick them up. The time would fly by with the fun.

So they'd waited, alone, the obvious strangers, sticking out like black swans in a white flock one thousand strong. Hitherto, Cassie had not realized just how homogeneous First Community was; it wasn't something you had to think about when you were the one fitting in. She'd let Jett's handsome offer of cheap coffee, and then Rachel's call, and then her own pathetic crying blind her from remembering she was about to hit the kids' hot spot: abandonment.

And for over an hour, they had sat there, in a new place, wondering where she had gone.

How could Cassie try to discipline the girl whose wound she had just thrown salt on? Star, the one who'd never needed to clean so much as a light switch as reprimand at the Haven?

This was hard.

This was nothing like handling a group of kids from 2:00 to 6:00 p.m.

Why did she so blindly think she could ace parenting so easily?

"I'm going to the car," Cassie said. "I want you to come."

Star inhaled suddenly and kicked her feet off the stool as she hopped down. "I'm going to Ershanna's."

Cassie shook her head. "You're not going to Ershanna's."

"Yeah. I am."

"*No*. You're not."

"*Yeah. I am.*"

"Who wants some crab dip?" Cassie's mother said loudly, and as if in unanimous vote, the group stood, only too eager to rush for it.

Even Mr. Baker, with a shellfish allergy, jumped up to the front of the line.

Her mother turned around. "I think I have more in the kitchen if you want to join me . . ."

The group followed her blindly. If she had said she had a pyramid of toilet paper rolls in the kitchen, they would've stormed for it.

Only Bree stayed behind at her post on the carpet, her braid reaching the floor while she opened the refrigerator of the dollhouse with Kennedy. Kennedy set a plastic doll on the bed, though her eyes were glued to Star and Cassie.

Time for a new tactic.

"Fine. You want to walk eight miles, you go for it." Cassie moved over to her purse, picked up her keys. "Let's go, girls."

Both Bree's and Star's eyes widened momentarily, neither expecting Cassie to call her bluff. Star practically spit as she accepted the challenge. "*Fine.*" And with that she blew out of the room, out of the house, without so much as a glance back. Cassie picked up Star's coat while taking hold of Kennedy's hand.

Ten minutes later, Cassie's headlights spotlighted Star as Cassie gripped the steering wheel, the speedometer reading so low it hovered at zero. Star held on to her ribs tightly as she pushed against the wind, houses of nearly identical designs flanking them on either side. There was no moon tonight; even it had no interest in peeking in on this melodrama.

"You got some sort of grand plan for all this?" Bree murmured from the passenger seat. "Because, just on a hunch, I'd say this is one of those no-no's in the parental rule book."

"I want to go back to the party!" For the seventeenth time Kennedy jiggled the car seat locks, her bottom lip jutting out a mile long as she looked out the window.

The car crept by a waving, blow-up snowman in a front yard. And then a bobbing reindeer. And then a dozen brightly colored lawn ornaments.

Thirty-five houses down, and Star still hadn't acknowledged their existence.

Finally, Star shot her head their way. "Go away!"

"I'm not going away, Star." Cassie leaned her head out the window, heat blasting through the vents. "If you want to walk to Ershanna's, fine. But she's just going to turn you back over to me. Why don't you just get in the car, and we can go home?"

Star shouted something short and vulgar, her words piercing, her tone halfway hysterical, then jumped up on the sidewalk, farther from them.

Cassie threw the car into Park and unclipped her belt. "Take over, Bree."

"You know what you're doing?" Bree asked.

"No clue." Cassie slung her coat around her as she jumped out of the driver's seat.

And without pausing, she pushed her hands in her

pockets and jogged up onto the sidewalk. Star stared straight ahead, jaw so clenched it threatened to break a tooth. She didn't stop.

"Look," Cassie began, "I'm sorry you had to wait around so long at church the other day."

Star turned her head away, walking faster.

Cassie matched her pace. "I'm sorry, Star. I *am*. You know I am."

Star pulled her hair in front of the left side of her face, concealing her eyes.

"But I didn't *forget* you," Cassie continued. "I may have let the time get away from me, but I didn't *forget* you. And I would never, *ever*, *ever* just leave you. You're my Star." Cassie pulled Star's jacket out from the crook of her arm. "Literally and figuratively."

She held it out for Star. Waited.

"And if you don't like that church, I get it. We'll find another one. One we all want to be a part of."

Star snatched the coat out of her hands without slowing down.

At the stop sign she strode even faster across the road, and Cassie sped up.

They walked together silently, Star's breaths coming heavily as the neighborhood houses came to an end. Cars whizzed by as Star stopped, finally, at the stoplight for the main road. Bree slowed the car to a stop beside them, smoke gently curling from the exhaust.

"Look." Cassie's breath materialized as she spoke. "The truth is I don't know what I'm doing. One minute I'm on the best date of my life, the next I'm figuring out how to do laundry for four. You gotta give me a break here. I've never had to be a parent before. Heck, *you're* doing a better job at parenting than I am half the time." She looked at the passing cars. "But, for my part, having you guys in my life has also made it the best weeks of my life—"

"You don't mean it—"

Cassie turned to face her. "Yeah . . . I do. Of course I do."

For the first time Star, too, turned and met her eyes.

The pit in Cassie's stomach started quaking. For as much as she knew about Star, there were still parts she had kept hidden all these years, things about her home life she had kept under wraps. Frankly, Cassie didn't know how Star would respond. To anything. Half of Cassie expected Star to knock her over then and there, shouting she wasn't her mother.

"But . . . there was a reason I was late on Sunday. A reason I've needed to tell you. Something you need to know."

Cassie felt the words being pulled from her. She hadn't been able to bring herself to tell Star about her mother on Sunday, when Star had flown into her room and shut the door for hours on end. Cassie hadn't found the words the morning after, either, when she'd heard Bailey's car pull up in the driveway and seen Star leave for school—she could only hope—an hour early.

She didn't know when the time would be right for this kind of news. Never, it seemed, was the time right for this kind of news.

"It's . . . about your mom."

Cassie could see Star's eyes tighten, a momentary look of surprise before settling back into distance.

"What about her?" she asked quietly.

"They . . ." And suddenly Cassie realized she *really* had no idea how to handle this. Any of this. "They found her in Memphis. I, uh, I think your mom is going to face some charges. She might have to spend some time in prison. I don't know how long."

Star started nodding to the cement, her eyes hard as she bit her bottom lip. The light turned green, but she didn't move.

Cassie dropped one hand out of her pocket, on the off chance she'd have to grab Star before she ran into traffic.

"And what about us?"

Cassie released an icy breath.

"You guys will stay with me. If you want. For . . ." Her words fell heavily. "For as long as you want."

Star lifted her chin, brows furrowing. "What are you saying, Miss C?"

"I'm saying—" Cassie lifted her shoulders and dropped them again. "I'm saying I'd like you to stay with me."

"No," Star said, her voice rising sharply. "What are you *saying*?"

And suddenly Cassie was backed into a corner. Suddenly, she knew she should've talked with Rachel more about this. Should've waited until the PATH foster classes so someone could've gone over this conversation in detail, telling her exactly what to say. She didn't know what she was doing. She hardly knew the meaning of the term "termination of parental rights"—nothing more than what the Wikipedia article had to say.

Someone else should've told Star. Star's guidance counselor. Rachel with DCS. Really, *anyone* would've been better.

But they weren't here, were they? And that's what her job was now, wasn't it? To be the person who did the hard things, sometimes. To be the person they could rely on. No matter what.

Cassie spoke slowly, carefully. "I'm saying that your mother signed over her parental rights." Her voice felt more clogged by the moment.

But no, she couldn't stop now.

"And . . . if you want me to," Cassie continued, "I can adopt you."

Star watched the sidewalk some more. Cars moved around Bree, who waited beside them, wipers on, lights flashing. Cassie glanced back to the girls in the back seat. Deidre pressed her face against the window, taking it all in.

The girls shouldn't have been watching this. Yet another bad parental move, Cassie was realizing.

"You wanna take my sisters?" Star said abruptly.

Cassie stared. "Of course not. I want to take your sisters *and you*."

The light turned yellow, then red. Cars began to line up again.

She didn't have the heart to tell Star it was up to her, that she had to give consent before the judge. Maybe Star would hear that and back out, changing her destination from Ershanna's to the DCS building, so she could be there first thing in the morning to give her statement and get out of Cassie's home. She could do that, too, probably. She was old enough. The courts surely would respect her wishes—

Cassie felt her breath knocked out as she was suddenly hit in the chest. Just when she felt certain Star was in the throes of pummeling her, however, she felt Star's arms wrap around her ribs, her face pressed so hard and so deep into Cassie's chest she felt Star was getting zipper burn. She wasn't trying to smother her. She was trying to hug her.

Relief flooded over Cassie.

Everything was going to be okay.

"*Why doesn't she want us*?"

The almost inaudible, whispered words halted Cassie's thoughts and turned her blood ice cold.

Suddenly she felt the wet tears on her neck, the slight tremors of Star's body through their coats.

"Oh, Star." Cassie wrapped her arms around Star's shoulders and squeezed tight.

For seconds that turned to minutes, they stood in silence.

Eventually, Bree turned the car off.

Finally, after the fourth series of cars went by, Cassie pulled away enough to look down at her, her throat throbbing. "I don't know, Star. No matter what, though, I'd like you to stay. With me."

She swallowed, these emotional moments—especially with the stream of cars watching—foreign and uncomfortable.

Star pulled back and rubbed her nose against her jacket. She didn't move. Didn't seem to breathe.

After a long, thoughtful pause, she nodded.

Slowly they both stepped toward the car and slipped into their seats.

They sat in silence the rest of the way home, even Deidre and Kennedy in tune to the heavy moment. Hours later, after

Cassie had cleared the cookie crumbs from the kitchen table and helped the girls get baths before bed, she quietly shut the door to Star's room and tiptoed down the hall. Part of her felt like her feet were in charge of her dragging body, and catching the sight of her bed through her open door, she was tempted to collapse on it clothes and all. But her mind ached in the way it did after six hours of television in bed on a sick day, overstimulated and too wound up to let her sleep. She turned instead at the top of the stairs and started down.

Hot tea would do her good. Help her process what all had happened that day.

And there, at the end chair of the dining room table, sat her best friend, two cups of steaming tea on the table.

"Bree?" Cassie said, skipping down the last three steps. "I didn't realize you were still here."

Bree turned the handle of the mug in her hand, nodding with a weary smile. "I waited."

Once seated, Bree pushed the mug her way. The way she slid it over silenced Cassie; the lack of animation on Bree's face hushing Cassie's thoughts. Never had she seen Bree look so somber—at least, not since Cassie's accident.

"Cass, I need to tell you something."

Cassie reached out and pulled the mug toward herself. The heat radiated through fingers she hadn't realized were so cold. "What's up?"

"You remember the day we met?"

"Of course. At the park." She'd never forget spying the tall, lanky eight-year-old girl on the swings out her third-story apartment window. How she'd begged her mom to let her fly down those stairs, jump over the creek, and meet her in the adjacent park. The newcomer from Jersey. Her instant friend—rather, her instant bosom-buddy, who-needs-anybody-else, forget-those-mean-third-grade-girls forever friend. How could anyone forget such a pivotal life moment?

"And do you know what that park was next to?"

"There was a Food City nearby. A gas station. A—" Cassie paused, suspicion rising. "A Rebos."

Bree nodded, turning the cup in her hands.

The Rebos facility was simple, just a two-story colonial updated to house a support group for addiction recovery. Rebos. Spelled backward: S-O-B-E-R.

"You know, I was the youngest honorary member of that house," Bree continued. "I wore down those halls with my running. I even once asked if I could be a real member when I grew up, just without the alcohol."

Cassie sat back in her chair, stunned. "I had no idea."

"That place was home back then." Bree shrugged, her smile bittersweet. "Those people were family. In those early years, after getting back together, Mom and I were there almost every day."

Cassie let go of her mug, felt herself stop breathing. She leaned forward. "Bree . . . What do you mean 'after getting back together'?"

"After Mom got me back." Bree took a breath. "From foster care."

The world moved like a great rocking chair, and Cassie felt herself pulled back into her seat, the world suddenly dizzy. "*You* were in foster care? *You*?"

Bree started nodding. "For three hundred and twenty-six

days. Mom got me back June 6, two weeks before my eighth birthday."

Cassie's lips parted, but no words formed. Her? Bree? *Bree*? And *Mrs. Leake*? This wasn't possible. It had to be a joke . . . a terrible joke. But there Bree sat opposite her, her emerald eyes a rich and rare hue of sorrow and honesty and unlocked story.

Cassie fumbled for words. "I—I can't believe this. I don't know what to say. Why didn't you ever tell me?"

"It wasn't my secret to tell." Bree shrugged, but then a whisper of a smile lifted on her lips. "What excuse did I give you for why we moved all the way down here from New Jersey?"

Cassie smiled. "To get cows."

"Yeah. Well, I hate to break it to you, but there are cows in Jersey too." A huffy laugh escaped her, and for a moment they both smiled in recollection before their smiles slowly slipped away.

"What really happened is that Mom wanted to get away after it all, take us somewhere nobody would judge her, and I wouldn't have to remember. Where we'd never have to drive on Scott Street on the way to the grocery store or the elementary school or the movies and see the yellow townhome where I lived for months away from her. Where I wouldn't have to look at the second-story window where I used to sit for hours, watching the road, hoping to see her car pass by. *Making* myself believe I saw her car pass by. Making myself believe she was slowing down and was squinting through the car window to see if she could see me and was waving. That any moment her blinker was about to turn on, and she'd pull in and ring the doorbell and say it was all over and I needed to jump in the car right then. And that she was sorry for everything. And everything was going to be different. And I was going home." She shook her head. "You have no idea how many blue Hondas are on the road until you spend your life looking for one."

Cassie lifted the cup of tea, her throat suddenly aching and dry. "I'm so sorry, Bree. I can't imagine. I can't believe it . . . A year?"

Bree nodded.

Cassie and Bree sat in silence for a minute, Cassie trying to wedge this entirely new set of information into the neatly organized facts of her life. Mrs. Leake had always been a second mother to her. There for every graduation. There for every holiday. Cassie had spent so much time at the Leakes' home she was in half of their framed photographs on the walls. More than once she'd been included in the family photo sent out for the Leake Family Christmas card.

Bree? In the foster system because of something Mrs. Leake had done—or failed to do? Because of addiction? The woman had more self-control than a Shaker, and they'd all but died out in their successful stand on celibacy.

Bree turned the handle of her mug round and round, the skidding of the ceramic bottom across the dining table the only noise between them.

Finally, Cassie heard herself sputter despite herself, "*What happened*?"

She paused. "A lot of things that shouldn't have, Cass. A lot of things no kid should experience." Bree opened her mouth to speak more, then let it hang there a moment before seeming to change her mind. "But that's the thing I do want you to hear from this. The point is those girls upstairs have a *mom* already. And no matter what had happened to me back then, and how wrong it all was, I still *wanted* my mom. I wanted her to get fixed up and get me back. I wanted her to fight for me. And thankfully, in my case, that's exactly what she did.

"Now, I don't know Star's mom. I couldn't begin to guess all the reasons she signed off her rights last week—maybe she felt pressured, maybe she thought it was the loving thing to do. Maybe she really didn't care. I don't know. But I'm telling you now, I don't think she would've hung on to those girls this long if she didn't care about them at all. And I don't know Star's and Kennedy's and Deidre's whole situation, but I can guarantee you one thing: no kid wants to hear their mom is letting go."

Bree's eyes flickered down to her mug as though afraid to say the next words to Cassie's face. "And Cass, I hate to say it, but you need a little redirection."

Cassie swallowed the lump in her throat. Bree had never chastised her. Never. Not once in their twenty-five-year history.

Bree blinked and reached for Cassie's hand. "I *know* you want a family. I *know* it. And girl, you deserve it more than every single person on this planet. But you also gotta realize that what is victory to you is tragedy to them. You *have* to start seeing what is happening through their eyes, even if they aren't showing it on the outside."

Cassie's words rushed out, "But I'm sure these are different circumstances than you faced, Bree. Their mom *left* them without food for weeks—"

Bree shook her head, spreading her hands on the table as though spreading a deck of cards. "You know these facts. These few facts. But what you don't know is every *other* memory these kids have with their mom, every *good* moment. Every possible reason for *why* their mom did what she did. That's the thing. We don't know her why."

Cassie crossed her arms, suddenly cold despite the radiator beside them. She felt silly, sheepish as she defended herself quietly. "I just thought they would want to be out of all that—"

"What I saw tonight is that they want to be with *her*, just *without* 'all that.' This—" Bree waved a hand around the room. "—all of this, is not the plan. This is the backup plan, born out of tragedy. You can cover the place in scented candles and chocolate-chip cookies and bubble baths all you want, but at the end of the day, those girls are hurting."

Cassie felt the hammer fall on her heart, crushing, flattening.

For several minutes they sat there, silent. Finally, slowly, Bree stood and reached for her coat. Cassie stood with her.

"They will be happy with you, Cass. Darn happy. And I'm over the moon to see it all play out. But I want you to remember that grief and happiness aren't always mutually exclusive, okay?"

"I know," Cassie whispered.

"I know you do, but do you know it *enough*?"

Bree's gaze bore into Cassie's for one long moment before Cassie nodded, seeing Bree—her carefree, tropical fish Bree—in ways she'd never seen her before.

Honestly, she'd never looked so beautiful.

Jett

Hearing the knob jiggle on the bathroom door had the same effect on Jett's heartrate as a burglar taking a golf club to his window. From his very private moment in the bathroom, he groaned as the door opened and little Dakota, dragging a gallon of milk, came inside.

Milk sloshed on his toes, on the linoleum, on the black bath mat, as she set it before him.

"Dakota, go put that back right now."

Dakota, however, pushed the sippy cup between his knees. "I want some milk."

Jett picked up the cup and set it on the bathroom vanity, his pulse beating rapidly as he raised his arm and pointed. "Out, Dakota."

Where was Sunny when you needed him? From his seated

view, each and every cushion was thrown off the couch—the new normal. In the center of the rug, Drew was piling them together, building a train or a house or a boat or whatever his imagination had concocted that hour. Unused diapers, known to the twins of late as "snowballs," were thrown in every corner of the room. TJ sat in the handy bouncer he and Sarah had finally put together a few nights earlier. He kicked his feet as he stared at the dangling star above his head.

"Dakota, go on. I'll get you milk when I'm done."

"Make a snowball, make a snowball, throw it now, throw it now . . ." Drew sang to himself as he turned to a couch cushion and began to lift it on one side. "Maaaaake a snowball—"

Milk sloshed yet again over his foot as Dakota turned and began to drag it out the door like a twenty-pound weight.

"Drew!" Jett called out.

Weeks of solo parenting was training his brain to become that of a master chess player. Hundreds of times he had played the game and lost, seeing the lamp knocked over, the kid tumble off the couch, the toilet paper strewn throughout the house. Slowly he was becoming the grandmaster in the chess game of parenthood. Perhaps that would be his new name one day: The Grandmaster.

And today he foresaw the deadly domino effect that would take place as Drew lifted one couch cushion. It slowly ticked upward by degrees, and when it went beyond the ninety-degree mark, Jett could practically see it falling to the other side, knocking onto the coffee table, tipping over the Coke can, pivoting twenty degrees, and landing flat on

TJ. Cue the suffocation. Cue Jett running to lift it from TJ's face. Cue the fifteen minutes of teary scream fest.

Jett *loathed* the scream fest. At all costs, the scream fest was to be avoided.

In the chess game of parenthood, quiet was king.

"Drew!" Jett shouted again, but Drew, with all the focus of an engineer in his career-making moment, was now singing as he got beneath the cushion, using his head to lift the heavy, three-foot cushion.

Jett stood awkwardly. "Drew. Put that down, now!"

The cushion now easily reached the 80-degree mark.

Gritting his teeth, Jett gave in and waddled swiftly to the rescue. He ran into the living room, lunging for it as the cushion began to fall.

Drew looked at the halted cushion and then to Jett, his expression somewhere between seeing him as the man who had impeded him in his ultra-important project and the reality of what he really was: the huge, naked uncle on his knees who had fussed at him for something.

"You have to be careful, Drew. If this fell, who would you have hit?"

Drew watched the cushion silently.

"*Who*?" Jett pressed.

Drew's voice was meek, confessing. "Timothy."

"No, I'm—" he started to say, but then halted. Timothy was Jett's name, but he'd only been known by the first part of his given name, Timothy Jett, in the earliest days of his childhood.

Jett's head swiveled down to TJ, who blinked back at him with his innocent, oblivious eyes. TJ. *TJ*.

"Is this Timothy? Is this what your mother called him?" Jett pointed to TJ, and Drew nodded.

"Timothy *Jett*?" he pressed, but Drew just pointed back to him and replied.

"TJ. Timothy."

Well, what'd'ya know.

"How do you like that, Timothy?" he said, standing, a bit of pride in his face as he smiled down at TJ, and TJ wriggled his pink, sockless toes in return. "Looks like you're named after your dear old uncle."

Maybe there was hope yet.

Whatever sweetness was held in that momentary bubble popped instantly, however, as for the second time in five minutes, a knob jiggled. This time the front door.

"Yeah, of course they'll want some. Come on in." Sunny's voice came loud and clear through the door.

Jett swiftly grabbed the large cushion out of Drew's hands and made for the bathroom. Before he could take even one long step, however, the door swung open.

Sunny put his hand on Sarah's back and led her and her trayful of cake balls inside. Approximately three steps in, she jerked to a stop. Chocolate balls went tumbling.

It was college initiation all over again.

"We had a little issue." Jett started to bend and reach for the sweatpants huddled around his ankles. The cushion slipped an inch, and he snapped it back up with both hands.

"I see." Sarah's cheeks began to turn the shade of her peppermint sprinkles.

Sunny wasn't saying anything at all. In fact, he was hardly visible, hunched over behind her, both hands on his knees.

Then, deepening Jett's frown, Sunny took a breath. And the laughter—howling, police-calling laughter—began.

Sarah whirled around. "I'll just come back later."

"*Look at you*!" Sunny arched his back, and down he went again, howling with both hands back on his knees.

"Yeah, brother, look at me. You were supposed to be watching the kids."

"I got the mail!" Tears started forming in the corner of Sunny's eyes, no sorrow in his voice whatsoever. He tried to point at the stack of junk mail on the side table, but his arm was so off with his laughing he pointed to the couch.

At Jett's ankles came a sudden ringing from his pants pocket.

"You need me to get that, man?" Sunny appeared to be swiping tears from his face as Sarah swiftly placed the tray in his hands and walked out the door. Sunny called after, laughing. "No, Sarah, don't leave."

Sarah's door shut with a resounding *thud*.

Sunny turned on Jett. "Man, if it wasn't so fun watching you suffer, I'd have to kick you out. You guys are terrible for a man's love life."

Were he not in his current predicament, he would laugh at the mere image of Sunny trying to get Sarah, of all people, to fall for him.

"Yeah, Sunny. *We're* the reason for your love hiccups." Jett swiftly pulled up his pants, settled the waistline firmly on his hips. The phone still vibrated in his pocket. He checked the screen. Cassie's name ran across the top. The tempo of his heart quickened even more than before. He hadn't talked to Cassie in days, not since Sunday.

He pointed at Sunny as he strode toward the hall. "Drew! Dakota!" Both kids turned in his direction. "Go jump on Godfather Sunny."

"*Wheeeeeeeeeeeeee.*"

In his periphery, he saw Drew make a leaping dive on Sunny before he turned into his own bedroom and answered the call. "Heeeey." The word drew on until the door was firmly shut. "How's it going?"

"Good. I think. What's a girl gotta do to get a phone call around here?"

His hand slipped off the back of the door as he smiled at her playful and yet sincere tone. He knew exactly why he hadn't called: those three reasons currently screaming approximately fifteen feet away. "Sorry. I worked two days and took a day trip out of town. Things have been pretty hectic." He squeezed his eyes shut, knowing the price he'd have to pay for his next words. It seemed that for every minute he avoided taking Sarah's favors, she ended up doling out two.

"I'm off tomorrow night, though." *I might be able to arrange a sitter,* he added silently.

"Another midweek ballgame? This could become a tradition."

He liked the sound of that, more than he could say. But before he could actually *say* anything at all, he had to press his hand over the phone while another round of wrestling screams kicked in.

Jett opened the door and leaned his head out. Sunny, lying on the ground, grunted as Dakota and Drew bounced repeatedly on his stomach.

"Quiet down," Jett hissed.

Sunny arched his head at Jett, his eyes a clear *oh-no-you-didn't*.

As Jett began to shut the door, he heard Sunny shout, "Who wants to go pound on Uncle Jett's door?"

The stampede began.

"You know," Jett stumbled to say quickly, "I'm going to have to go, Cassie. That sounds great. See you at six."

"Alright. Well, I'll—"

"See you soon. Yep. Terrific. Bye." Jett barely managed to hang up before the screaming, giggling, pounding began.

He could do this. He *would* make a relationship with Cassie work.

Two and a half hours later, Jett pushed the sleeping bag around both Dakota and Drew's chins as they lay on the living room floor, chocolate from peppermint cake balls smeared like poorly applied lipstick around Dakota's lips.

"Kiss," she said, and he hesitated before begrudgingly leaning down for another wet one. She lay her head back on her pillow.

"Mmm," he said and wiped his mouth with his hand, tasting the mint. "Ready for prayers?"

Dakota grabbed onto his hand, now accustomed to what had been so foreign weeks ago. Drew nodded sleepily with the other. His curls covered his forehead, the ends touching the tips of his long, blonde lashes. He needed a haircut, had needed a haircut three months ago.

Jett wiped the curls from his eyes. "You want to go first, Drew?"

Drew shook his head, lids drooping, the clock beneath the television pointing out the time of 10:32 p.m.

Jett turned to Dakota. "You want to go?"

"Me start." She pointed to herself, then to his chest. "Me, then you. Dear God."

"Oh, okay." Jett nodded to this new reversal. "Dear God."

"T'ank you for Uncle Jett."

He smiled. "Thank you for Uncle Jett."

"T'ank you for the Godfather."

"No." Jett shook his head. He had conceded enough to let them call him Godfather Sunny, but Sunny had also taken that inch and pushed it a mile, training the kids to drop the "Sunny" part altogether. "Thank you for Godfather Sunny."

Dakota nodded understandingly. "T'ank you for the Godfather."

"Thank you for Godfather Sunny."

"T'ank you for *the Godfather*."

Jett sighed. "Thank you for the Godfather."

"And t'ank you for Sarah. Amen."

His smile waned. Already she had forgotten to mention her own mother, replacing her with the neighbor who had visited a matter of weeks.

Still, Jett nudged. "And who else?"

Dakota nodded. "T'ank you for Buttons," she added, noting Sarah's dog. Then, at the top of her lungs she began, "Doe, a deer, a female deer. Ray, a drop of gold'n *sunnnnnnnn*—"

She went on for a solid minute, singing *The Sound of Music*, the movie that had been playing when he had gone to retrieve the kids from Sarah's apartment several days ago. Soon enough, Drew was jumping into the song as well, united in a perfect disharmony.

"Very good. Amen," Jett said loudly, squeezing Dakota's hand. "Your turn, Drew. You want to pray on your own?"

Drew opened both eyes. "T'ank you for cows and the floor."

He closed his eyes.

"Uh . . . Amen," Jett said, and clicked off the lamp. "Amen."

"Hold my hand." Dakota's hand balled up inside his while they sat in the dark living room. Moonlight peeked through the balcony blinds, creating slivers of silver beams on his stretched-out legs. Sunny had gone over to Sarah's, avoiding any responsibility for the bedtime madness, yes, but also leaving the place unusually serene.

No television, no lights intruding beneath the crack in his door. Just Jett, the twins pushed up against his side, and a little boy in the other room he had the feeling he would start calling Timothy. Timmy, maybe.

The small Christmas tree twirled like a slow-moving disco ball on the table, yet another fingerprint of Sarah's presence.

Jett reclined deeper into the couch pillow.

So, this was how it was going to be. He'd thought that exact thought a thousand times since entering that long stretch of highway between his aunt's house and his own. Every time, however, the blow lessened. At first it was like he had stood against a wall, and a truck had slammed into his body at seventy-five miles an hour. Then it felt like being strapped to a tree, an archer shooting an arrow into his chest. This morning it was a brass-knuckled punch to the face. Now, however, the hand giving the blow had softened, no more of a sting than if Sarah had slapped him on the cheek. He was getting used to the pain.

Could perhaps even acknowledge a part of him liked watching the two small heads huddled close together beside him, Dakota's little hand in his. Could acknowledge he was getting used to seeing a stack of diapers next to a stack of movies.

It wasn't as lonely.

It was even—he stroked the backside of Drew's boyish and babyish arm—sort of nice.

Sarah made sense. Sarah wanted kids. She didn't have to say it. Everything about her screamed this was her calling; she was born to raise a brood.

And the twins *loved* her. Oh, how they loved her. If she ever tried to move away, they'd hop in the car with her with hardly a good-bye-forever kiss to him.

Right now, he could go to Sarah's apartment. Ask her out. Have "The Godfather" babysit.

But he knew how a date like that would go. He'd see her smile try hard not to freeze as he brought her to the old gym. She would throw a playful ball or two for the sake of being a good sport, then let him take the floor, finding her comfort in complimenting him with every shot he made. She'd think he was a good player. She'd only say nice things.

They'd give up early, find a place to eat dinner. Take a stroll.

All a perfectly good plan, except he wanted to be with someone who made him sweat. Someone who knocked him over—not flirtatiously but as someone who cared less about him at that moment and more about the ball. Someone who didn't mercifully pretend not to see the coffee spilled all over his shirt but pointed directly to it, chortling loudly. Someone who ducked down with him in the middle of a crowd. Someone who wore Nutcracker Toms.

He wanted Cassie.

It was time to tell her the truth.

Tomorrow night he would explain it all.

Tomorrow night he would know what the future held.

19

Cassie

The ball rolled across the concrete court, landing at his sneakers.

"Forty-three, twenty-eight, hot shot. I'm gaining on you." Cassie slapped her hands together, breath clouding and swirling from her lips. She sniffed and rubbed her frostbitten nose with the back of her hand.

Jett bounced the ball once, the yellow light from an overhanging streetlamp lighting their small court. Headlights from a couple of oncoming cars lit up the road beside them. Otherwise, it was dark—so dark they'd lose the ball if it flew out of hands and into the grass. "Tell me again why you prefer playing in eighteen degrees when we could be playing in the luxury of a fifty-year-old high school gym?"

Cassie leapt forward, bouncing the ball out of his hands.

"Hey, hey, *hey*!" he called, watching her dribble the stolen ball and shoot it into the basket.

"Two-point penalty for small talk and two points for the shot. Forty-three, thirty-two." Cassie grinned wickedly as she threw the ball to his chest. "And to answer you, this is about home-court advantage."

"You mean hypothermia advantage."

Her grin widened as she put her hands out in false apology. "It's not my fault you forgot gloves."

"Because I didn't need them," he shot back, "seeing as I expected to be inside before you called *on the way here* with your 'great idea.'"

Despite the weather and the cold, sweat ran down the back of Jett's neck as he dribbled toward the basket.

Cassie lunged, her right thigh taut as she reached forward before he slipped past. Fingers gripped, then wrapped around his T-shirt. It was an illegal move, she knew. But they liked to play illegally.

Still, there was little resistance on the shirt. He could've planted another foot forward and been out of her grip easily.

And yet, Jett stopped. His feet stumbled back unnecessarily.

And now here he was in her face, her nose inches from his neck.

"Whoa, now. Am I going to have to call a foul on you, Miss Everson?" He gave a crooked smile.

She liked that look. She liked that look so much she found her mind forgetting how to answer, her already speeding heart rate raising another ten miles per hour. Where was her quick wit now? Her lips opened, searching for words to match his rhythm. Some vague idea of a referee was forming, but her scattered mind couldn't finish it. His blasted chest kept rising and falling in front of her, so close that at each peak, the ball at his side touched her waist.

She looked down at her feet, out of bravery or cowardice she couldn't tell.

She took a step back, and the magical, tenuous bubble popped.

Before going a second further, she had to tell him. Now.

There was a question in his eyes as he clearly saw the struggle she held with herself. "What?" He smiled lightly, though there was a seriousness about the brow. "You have a thing about fouls?"

"No, I, uh . . . I wanted to see . . . wanted to revisit that conversation about . . . kids."

She swallowed and felt as though she had ingested a golf ball. Three and a tenth dates in, and horror upon horrors, she was bringing up kids. In romantic comedies, this was the shot just before the guy's fork clattered loudly to the ground and he ran outside for a taxi.

But what else was she going to do?

She'd thought through the options.

First, there was The Door Wide Open Plan, where he'd drop her off at her house. He'd use this rusty, beckoning voice as he observed some mistletoe above them. He'd lean in, she'd move on her tiptoes, and . . . a flash would go off. They'd step back. Star would be there, standing on the stairs declaring she was texting a photo to everyone at the Haven. Kennedy and Deidre would grab onto his legs, screaming, "Dadddddyyyyyyyyyy!"

Then there was The Stealth Plan. Taking Edie's advice, Cass would hide the kids in the basement until their wedding day. As the minister declared them Mr. and Mrs., the girls would rush out of the pew, grab them in a tight hug, and jump up and down. Cassie would join in the jumping. The photographer would take a hundred shots of the moment. Edie and Donna Gene would clap in teary celebration.

Then there was The Middle Ground Plan, the plan she'd landed on. Dip his toes in the water first, ask in a general way about kids. Dig a little deeper to see if he could get on board in the future. Then, if that went well, knock him off the high dive: *Hey, so you know how you just said that maybe you could see yourself with kids one day? Well, guess what? I have three now. Yay!*

So, here she was, doing the unspeakable. Asking on a third-and-a-tenth date about kids.

And, to her slight surprise, he wasn't running desperately for his car. To her definite surprise, in fact, his expression lightened.

"Really? You know, I wanted to talk with you about that too." Headlights illuminated the grass around them, the Haven beside them, as another set of cars passed. He scratched his head. "Uh, so you go first. What did you want to say?"

"Well." Cassie took a breath. "You know, when I put down on my profile that I didn't want kids, I didn't mean that exactly. It's not that I don't want kids. It's more that I can't have kids."

"*Really*?"

She frowned. His face had lighted up like a house wrapped in five thousand feet of Christmas lights. He might as well have said, "Really? You're infertile? That's fantastic!"

His face mellowed. "And by 'really,' I mean I'm so sorry to hear that. Continue."

"But, despite that . . . hurdle . . . I'm not really opposed, per say, to kids. I even like them."

He shook his head. "I was wondering why on earth you hung out with kids for a living if you didn't."

"Yeah. Well, anyway, I think it's important that you be aware, that you know, that—" She straightened, dropping the bomb. "—I'm thinking about adoption. Like, seriously."

"You're kidding." The ball dropped to the cement.

He looked as though he was trying hard not to throw his head back and laugh. Then, suddenly, he *was* laughing. A laugh of such relief, of such joy, that her eyes drifted to the apartments behind the Haven, half expecting faces to peek out behind the blinds. "Me too."

"You too? Wait. You're thinking of adoption too?"

Jett wanted kids.

Jett was even considering *adoption.*

All the hurdles that had been ten feet high, that she had somehow been expected to jump over in her five-foot-nine-inch frame, were somehow behind her. She had crossed the finish line and stopped, amazed and surprised to see that the journey that was so impossible five minutes before was over before it had barely begun. He was *not* concerned about wanting kids after all. But even better, even harder to achieve, he was *not* concerned about her desire to adopt. If she had said that to a hundred other men with the same original stance, she doubted there would've been five who would've changed their tune so readily.

And it took so little convincing. In fact, it took *no* convincing.

It was exactly what she'd dreamed of.

Maybe crazy Edie could've snuck the kids into the relationship, but that was the last thing she wanted—for Jett's sake, of course, but even more so for the kids. Star, Deidre, and Kennedy were not tag-ons. They weren't one of those "Buy this kitchen set and we'll throw in a useless spatula" kind of deals.

They were equally part of the package, as essential as the stainless steel in a stainless-steel stockpot. She wanted nothing more than for a man, this man, to be as excited to get to know these girls as potential daughters as he was to get to know her as a potential wife. And yes, though this was only a possibility for the future, she needed that assurance now. She needed to know he would never "put up with the kids" for the sake of having her.

Suddenly, however, that needless worry was over. He wanted kids. He wanted to adopt. There was nothing left to fear.

"My story is going to be a little crazy, Cassie." He rolled the ball lightly beneath his tennis shoe, a sudden ease in his demeanor she hadn't noticed before. "Honestly, I didn't want kids. Not until three weeks ago—no, not even that long. Days. But now, I'm starting to get it. Starting to see just how amazing little people are. Of course, I still don't know how you do it with all those teens."

Glistening sweat beads fell off the tips of his short hair

as he raked a hand through it, smiling at what was supposed to be a compliment.

Cassie hesitated. "You . . . don't like teens?"

"Let's just say they're better off under your wing."

"Teens are pretty great, Jett. You just have to get to know them."

"Oh, yeah. Of course." His eyes widened, clearly realizing he was barking up the wrong tree. "But you gotta admit it takes a special person to be able to work with them. Me, I'd rather haul a hundred-and-thirty-five-pound hose into a burning building than spend ten minutes with one of them. But the little kids now. Toddlers. They're incredible."

Being "able" to work with them. Her focus narrowed in on that word, distinct as the crow soaring beneath a blanket of snow-white clouds. Her voice hitched. "Toddlers? Toddlers are the ones who throw temper tantrums in the middle of a grocery store. Whenever you see a parent who looks like they hate life, you can bet there's some little kid around."

"They can be exhausting, sure, but at least they're not having moody blowups every ten minutes," Jett said. He paused as though recalling a particular situation. "They can be so ungrateful."

Cassie laughed without humor. "And toddlers *aren't* moody?"

"Sure, but they're just a few years old. Teens are old enough to know how they should be acting, without doing it. But babies. When they snuggle up to you—"

"And poop in a diaper. It's disgusting. You won't ever

change a teen's diaper." She picked up the ball. Tossed it a little harder than she intended at his chest.

He caught it, his eyes narrowing. "Yeah, with teens all you have to worry about is them cussing you out and stealing your meds. Sure. Teens are a breeze."

His return throw bounced loudly on the concrete before she caught it. She bounced it back. "Babies spit up."

"Teens *throw* up after getting drunk at a party you didn't want them to go to in the first place." He bounced the ball back to her.

She caught it. A frustrated *huff* escaped her chest, and she didn't try to hide it. "At least you're not walking around like a zombie with three hours of sleep a night."

"At least you're not worrying about them getting *pregnant*."

They stared each other off, she with the basketball on her hip, he with sweat dripping down his forehead. A bead drifted into his brow, then eyelid, but he didn't move. He was too busy resisting her, ignoring the drop as though any movement whatsoever would have been a white flag.

Her gloved fingers wrapped around the ball. "So that's it, then. You hate teenagers."

He waved a hand in the air. "Sure. Yes. Forgive me, but I'm like every other person in the world who would rather dive into a shark tank than sit with them for ten minutes. And you are the one female in existence who doesn't look at a picture of a baby and think they are adorable."

"Oh, I'll look at the picture, alright," she said, her voice rising menacingly. "Then laugh at how miserable the parents are every single night of their lives."

He nodded once, twice, lips once so attractive now tightening into a firm, straight line. "I'm sorry to hear that."

"Likewise."

She stared at her ball for several long seconds, aware of just how badly things had turned in a span of a minute. "I guess I'll see ya."

She heard him clear his throat, all the while incapable of looking up. "I guess so."

A heavy moment passed in silence. Then she dropped the ball, and they both moved.

There was no sound but the slow, rhythmic bounce of the ball thudding against the concrete as they both walked swiftly across the grass to their cars.

20

Jett

His frozen knuckles gripped the wheel tight enough to unlock a bank vault.

A woman who hated toddlers. It was insane.

Sure, every point she had brought up had been verbally plagiarized from his own mouth. Sure, when Drew had torn open the shower curtain on him that morning, he'd declared he'd find the padded white walls of a mental hospital a welcome alternative to the chaos of his own apartment. Yes, Timothy had spit up on his shirt enough times to make him a walking advertisement on the benefits of stain remover. True, Drew had fallen flat on his face crying bloody murder in the middle of the cereal aisle because he wanted to hold the blue box instead of the brown one.

But there was nothing quite like holding a sleeping baby at 4:00 a.m. against his chest.

But no adult could make him laugh so authentically as the twins did over the silly things they said each day.

But no one could walk past those curly-headed three-year-olds without feeling the urge to rub their heads.

But—and here was the big one—he had no other choice.

So, if children were her archenemies, if that was her authentic opinion, far be it from him to chain her down just for his sake.

He swung into his parking spot and went up the stairs, his featherlight tennis shoes feeling more like tactical boots trudging through swampy waters. By the time he reached the top stair, he might as well have fought a mile against a river's waist-deep current. The string lights framing his neighbor's door looked dull to him. The large red bow on the wreath drooped as if it, too, wanted to give up on the holiday.

All right, he thought, *not give up. But still.*

He shuffled through his keys, trying to muster the energy to see the kids again. Because once that door opened, if any of them were awake, there would be no time for private thoughts, no moments to brood, no seconds to pity himself or complain. It was just 170-mile winds of twins; the only thing he'd be doing was hanging on tight and trying not to get tossed into the hurricane.

He waited, but a sudden burst of energy didn't come. Home hours early with nowhere to go, he had no choice but to turn the doorknob.

And walk straight into Trina.

"Trina?" He stepped back and looked down to the plastic bag at her feet. "How . . . how long have you been here?"

Thoughts whooshed in on him. Trina had returned. She'd come back. She was standing here. She was sorry for dumping the kids on him, of course, and was about to jump in with apologies. Admit her life was out of control—there was no way she could deny it now. She'd have to 'fess up to it, and then, *then* they could have a realistic talk about rehab. It wouldn't take that long, maybe a few months, but eventually she'd get out, get a job, take the kids . . .

Take the kids.

Freedom. He would be the fun uncle he was meant to be—

She put up her hand.

"Don't say anything, Jett. Don't. I'm just here to get them."

But whatever she had expected his response to be, he was certain it wasn't for him to kick the door shut behind him. "Over my dead body you are."

They stared each other down. Him with hands on hips, chest starting to pant, the same stance he tried on his own mother when he was fifteen. (It didn't work then, either.) Her with skinny jeans hanging loosely off her hips. Her dyed hair stripped at the roots, a thick coat of malnourished gray aging her beyond her mere twenty-eight years. She sucked in a deep breath, her collarbones rising from the thin layer of pale skin like a wishbone ready to be snapped.

It wasn't she who was snapping, though, but him.

"*Where the heck have you been*?" He was tired, so tired, of tiptoeing around her. "You scared your kids to death."

"I knew you were coming back." She said it as if concluding the conversation, moving past him and toward the hall.

He reached out and grabbed her wrist. "*Trina*. That is no excuse and you *know* it."

His last words emphasized the truth, the shared memories of an unsupervised childhood—particularly the fresh-colored scar along her jawline serving as the daily reminder of the two-story fall out the window when she was five years old. Guilt found him every time he looked at it, always aware that though only six, he had been there, had gotten her to sit on the sill with him, had experienced the horror of seeing her suddenly explode through a screen that, to his child eyes, looked like a concrete wall only moments before. He'd never forget the horror of thinking she'd died that day, seeing her body laid out on the grass below.

But instead of stilling her, of making her remember, she shook off his hand as though he'd tried to capture her instead. Her face grew indignant, her neck red. "Get out of my way, Jett. I can take *my* kids if I want."

"Take them where, exactly? Last time you were here you had no place to go."

"I found an apartment."

"Where?"

She lifted her chin. "Beaver Run."

Jett shook his head, knowing exactly the shoddy complex she was referring to. The very thought of Dakota skipping down the cracked sidewalk littered with cut glass, curls flying, made his stomach ball up. "If that's really where you want to go, fine. But you'd better go ahead and lease a one-bedroom."

Her eyes were starting to bulge, the explosion imminent.

"Well, what did you think was going to happen after you left them here, Trina?" He held out his hands. "That I was just going to turn them over to you as if nothing happened? Help you load up them up in their car seats? You aren't in a position to keep them safe right now. For their sakes, and your own, you *need* to take a good look at yourself and get clean."

Trina put a shaky hand behind her ear. Her voice was tense, tight. "I'm fine, Jett. I've taken care of them just fine for three years."

No. She wasn't fine. Nothing was.

"Are you high right now?" He took a step toward her, knowing the familiar scent on her breath, seeing the dilated blacks of her eyes trying to swallow the celery color whole.

This time she retreated, pulling on the sleeves of her jacket as though hiding her fingertips helped conceal the truth.

His chest felt like it was going to burst at that moment. The world was insane. Everything, *everything*, about it was broken, and he was utterly powerless to change any of it.

Except right now he could do one thing. And everything within him pointed to that one thing. He could keep them safe. Tonight.

Jett forced his voice to remain calm. He took a step toward her. "Stay here. Sleep it off. And, for the love of God, yourself, and your kids, let us get you help tomorrow. Please. Your kids *need* you, the Trina I know. They *need* their mom."

Jett held out a hand to her, prepared to usher her toward the bedroom. To the kitchen. To the shower. To wherever she needed to go.

And for a fleeting second he felt he saw the dilated pupils recede and the celery irises of her eyes fight to return.

His hand stretched out.

Dakota's giggle floated down the hall, and Trina's eyes flickered toward it. Her expression widened as though trying to peer down a hall that looked miles away. A single expression: longing. A single moment: contemplation.

He'd finally struck a nerve.

But then, quick as a wink, she was gone.

Jett stood in the open doorway and looked out for a long time on the parking lot below, the icy breeze billowing up the dark stairwell.

He heard Drew call out for Jett from the bedroom. He moved inside, shut the door.

Always love. Always try. But never, *ever*, raise your expectations.

21

Cassie

It's a . . . Grow Your Own Boyfriend," Cassie said, speaking to Bree through her smile and gritted teeth. "Just what I always wanted."

Frank Sinatra sang over the speaker on the fireplace mantel, trumpets interrupting conversations on couches and love seats, recliners and floor. Star, Deidre, Kennedy, and their soon-to-be cousins were huddled up beside the tree they had not so long ago called the fire department over, intently sorting through the presents for name tags they recognized, passing out—when prodded—ones meant for the adults.

Christmas morning at its finest. Well, technically two days after Christmas morning at its finest, given Cassie had learned the hard way why mothers everywhere dreaded winter and all its shower of germs. Even so, the family was all here at her house now. The stomach bug had finally been purged, and there were gallons of eggnog to go around. The sun couldn't have shone brighter on her happy little home.

"What did you get, dear?" Cassie's mother stood up from behind the couch, finding another shred of wrapping paper to squeeze into the overstuffed trash bag. "Show everyone. We want to see."

Cassie bit her bottom lip and held up the package that looked like it contained a Ken doll. Only instead of a Ken doll, it was a purple blob of a figure. Directions on the box proudly directed the user to just drop the thing in water and see it grow overnight.

Bree stepped in.

"A Grow Your Own Boyfriend," Bree declared loudly. "I got one for both of us." Bree whipped hers out of her purse and held it up, either ignorant to the vapid smiles of Cassie's family or, what was more likely, totally unconcerned about them. She wrapped an arm around Cassie. "I threw in a gift card. We'll take 'em out for a night on the town."

"That's hilarious." Star dropped her new burgundy jeggings in her lap and reached over Bree's knees for it.

"Oh, my turn. Robby, give Cassie her gift, please." Cassie's mother grabbed another piece of wadded-up paper with the superior-quality aluminum reacher she'd unwrapped this morning—known by her mother as "the claw thingy that picks up stuff like those nice people do when picking up trash from the side of the road." The reacher zoomed over several heads as she pointed it to the coffee table. "That one, with the big bow."

Cassie's brother-in-law grimaced as he pushed himself off the couch and handed her the book-sized gift. "Sorry," he said under his breath.

"You don't suppose this is a hammer to put me out of my misery?" Cassie whispered back, grinning as she took the present from his hands. The close-up of a woman in an overwhelming amount of pink winked on the cover titled: *The Magic of Singleness: Live Your Best Life Now.*

"Wow. Seems like this'll be the year of reading for me. Thank you, Mom." Cassie smiled politely to her mother, who was now reaching on top of the ceiling fan with her reacher. She set the book on top of the foot-and-a-half-high stack. At this point, she had enough titles to cover a shelf at Barnes & Nobles. *Raising Them Alone. Living a Month on One Hundred Dollars. Crockpot Cooking for Families.*

Waving hands caught her attention, and she looked above the crowd to see her uncle and father. They stood halfway down the stairs. Sweat matted her uncle's salt-and-pepper hair. Her father lifted the hem of his red cardigan and wiped his face. Both grinned with triumph. Her dad gave her a thumbs-up.

It was time. The present she'd been waiting to give all morning.

Cassie moved around the wasteland of presents and across the room to put her hands on the girls' shoulders. "Girls, I think we found one more present for you upstairs."

Kennedy dropped the doll in her hands like a hot potato. Together, the girls bounded up the stairs behind Cassie.

A slow procession up the stairs began, and when Cassie looked over her shoulder, she saw the family following behind. She could see the excitement on their faces. Her sister, one arm gripping the handrail, the other beneath her protruding, eight-month pregnant belly, beamed as she carefully dodged the hem of her long, striped skirt and mounted the stairs. Bree, squeezing the life out of Star's arm as she nudged her onto the top floor. Her mother, clipping off dust balls and stray lint with her reacher as she followed them up each step.

But as much as everyone had gathered together this morning acting as if it was like any other day, each and every one of them was acutely aware that it wasn't. The gathering place was new. The monkey bread Cassie and the girls had clumsily prepared replaced over twenty years of her father's eggs Benedict. It felt like at any given time someone's phone was upraised, snapping pictures. Seemed everyone wanted to know and remember this Christmas day as special, as the first of many.

Cassie's uncle pushed the door open, and Deidre and Kennedy ran beneath his arm.

Star stopped inside the door, and Cassie stood beside her. "I figured if you girls insisted on sleeping together, I might as well get something big enough for you all."

Star ran her fingers down the king-sized black-and-white comforter replicating a map of New York. She picked up the green pillow declaring in cursive "*morning sunshine*" and set it back next to the mustard-green one with a winking face. Photo frames lined the bookcase headboard, including the one of them standing arms-over-shoulders with the girls and surprise Santa at Girls Haven.

"You like it? We can still trade the comforter out for something different. I tried to think like you, but I may have missed it altogether."

Faces framed the door as everyone tried to get a good view of the room's makeover.

"Miss C—Cassie—I love it." Star hugged her tightly.

When Star started taking pictures and texting furiously, and the girls were bouncing on the bed, Bree stepped beside Cassie and whispered, "Now, I'm no parent, but I think that's the twenty-first-century way of knowing if something was a hit."

Deidre ran around to the other side of the bed, opened the waist-high, old-fashioned Coca-Cola fridge. All the snacks Cassie had been supplying before were set in neat rows inside.

Suddenly her nephew was tugging on her sister's skirt, the new skateboard forgotten as he begged for a fridge of his own.

The moment was perfect.

"Honey?"

Cassie heard people's voices drop off as she turned and saw her mother parting the doorway crowd. She held the reacher limp at her side.

She took a step forward, looking at no one but Cassie.

"Honey, a woman is here to see you."

It was her mother's eyes that frightened her.

"Who?"

"A woman from DCS. She says her name is Rachel."

As if on impulse, Cassie picked up Kennedy. Cassie's tone lifted. "Thanks. I'll just . . . be a minute."

Her mother reached her hands out for Kennedy, but as

if her instincts were on high alert as well, Kennedy's knees pressed tightly into Cassie's ribs.

Cassie's legs numbly took her down the stairs, chest pounding so hard her heart threatened to fall right out and tumble down. She shouldn't expect the worst. And yet, every detail in her surroundings right now was an immediate reminder of what today was for: celebrating Christmas. Family was welcome today. Yards of crinkled wrapping paper and the scent of cinnamon cloves from homemade eggnog—these were welcome. Case workers making house calls were not.

Rachel's legs came into view first, a parka still hanging loosely over her as she stood beside the piles of visitors' shoes. In the last seconds before she saw Rachel's face, Cassie wanted to be naïve, wanted to coax her fretful mind to believe there was nothing to worry about. But instead she found herself pressing her cheek against the cornrow braids of the child in her arms. Found herself kissing the top of Kennedy's head.

She would know when she saw Rachel's face what this meant.

Her knees weakened and she gripped the railing. She didn't think she had the heart to find out.

But there, she took one more step. And knew.

Rachel's voice came low as she fidgeted with her keys. "I'm sorry, Cassie. I've been trying to call all morning."

Cassie felt like she couldn't breathe. Slowly, she started to lower Kennedy to the ground. Kennedy only gripped tighter, however, the tulle of her velvety red dress covering both of Cassie's arms.

Her mouth felt numb, her throat numb, as though it belonged to somebody else. "Sure. Thanks for coming by. What's going on?"

An ocean of sympathy lay in Rachel's eyes. "I checked with all the relatives first. In our initial call he told me he couldn't take them on—"

"Who?"

"Their uncle." She wrapped the parka tighter around her chest. "Their uncle came back to claim the girls. Seems he had a conversation with their mother and decided. He's taking immediate custody."

"*He can't do that*!"

Though Cassie felt every word, it was Star who spoke, who was now tripping down the stairs two and three at a time. She looked down at Cassie. "I'm fourteen, right? I can stay here if I want. I'm fourteen."

Rachel took a breath, turning her eyes on Star. "Yes, legally you have the right to stay. But the younger ones . . ."

Cassie held Kennedy tighter, disbelief in her voice. "You would separate them?"

"No. The last thing DCS wants is sibling separation. But if Star chooses to stay here, with you . . ." She hesitated.

Star's eyes bulged. "I don't want to be separated from them. I choose *here*. We all want to stay together *here*."

"Sweetie, he is your uncle, your mother's brother—"

"*So*?" Star's voice cracked. "Miss C is a hundred times the family he's ever been. We don't even know him! We haven't ever even *met* him!"

"What you must remember is that he cares about your well-being—"

"If that were true, where has he been all my life?" Star's

voice was cracking as it rose higher and higher, her movements becoming jerky and sporadic. "Tell them, Miss C! Tell them you want to keep us!"

"I *know* she does, Star," Rachel said. "I know it. And I feel for you both. But legally, she has no right—"

Star flung her finger toward the upstairs. "Just now she got us a new bed! We're already settled here. You'll just have to tell him it's too late. Come see!"

But as Star tried to coerce Rachel up the stairs to her bedroom, all Cassie could hear was the pulse in her eardrums. Vision started to blur, her body reminding her at random intervals to breathe. She couldn't trust her arms to hold Kennedy, and yet she couldn't manage to let her go. She sank onto the steps, Kennedy's dress fanning around them.

Her mind was groggy, fighting and yet unable to keep up. She'd seen this situation before, watched the same thing happen to foster girls at the Haven. She'd known her heart could take a beating, that it was just the way the story played out sometimes. But this was different. Yesterday she'd been close enough in the system to be kin. She had kept her hopes tethered tightly while Rachel checked around for relatives, while she figured out the situation with Star's mother. Only when Rachel had called, giving her the news of the termination of rights, did she start to even let her imagination go.

"Where is he?" Waves of nausea threatened as Cassie spoke.

Rachel took a heavy breath. "Spartanburg, South Carolina."

"*This is ridiculous.*" Vaguely she heard her mother push around people and down the stairs, felt her hand squeezing against her shoulder. The words spat from her mother's lips with a tone as close to cussing as she had ever heard. "My daughter hasn't *once* wavered in her decision to protect and care for these youths. From moment *one*. If some man these girls don't even know can change his mind like flipping pancakes, you can just tell him he missed the boat. These girls deserve more than a wishy-washy—"

"Mom, please."

Awareness of Kennedy's trembling body alerted Cassie to speak up, gave her strength to stand. Kennedy, Deidre, and Star didn't need more drama to remember, another scene of raised, chaotic voices to replay from their childhood. Raising her voice, showing her weakness, wouldn't help.

Cassie tried to speak calmly. "What about their schools? I know the state recognizes the value in keeping children in the same community, with as many familiar faces as possible. Surely they would agree that moving states isn't in the best interest of the children."

"I know. Moving states isn't ideal, but it's best, always, to stick with family."

Cassie continued, undeterred. "What about Star's attendance at the Haven? The state itself funds the program. I have the statistics regarding the success rate of those who stay loyal through graduation."

Rachel nodded through it all, was still nodding when she finished. The tenderness in her voice, though she hadn't moved a muscle off the welcome mat, was clear. "I know, Cassie. Believe me. If there was any chance I could work around these regulations, I would. But as far as the facts go, you've provided emergency shelter for a number of weeks. Not months. Not years. This relative is stepping up in a comparatively short amount of time, stating he wants to take charge of his nieces. His background check clears. He and his wife have the appropriate housing and funds required to take on three children. This . . . as much as it pains me to say right now, is truly in their best interest." She glanced at the other children on the stairs. "Wouldn't you fight for the right to parent your siblings' children if something were to happen to them? Wouldn't you jump on a plane for your nieces if you could?"

Yes, but where was he three weeks ago? Cassie stopped herself from repeating the fruitless words.

Not a foot moved.

Not a voice spoke, except good ol' Frank Sinatra.

She closed her eyes, letting herself embrace every selfish thought one moment more. When she opened them again, dimly, as through a heavy rain, she tried to see things from the other side. He was their uncle. And Rachel was dead on: Cassie would fight tooth and nail to get her nephews and nieces back if the state tried to give them to a stranger.

She'd also heard the fact tagged on in Rachel's final plea—that the kids would be getting an uncle and an aunt. A father and a mother figure. Two people to split their duties and twice the amount of love to go around. Spartanburg was only a two-and-a-half-hour drive. If she played her cards right and didn't resist, maybe she could get on good enough terms to visit sometimes . . .

Still, she felt sick.

Cassie smoothed down Kennedy's dress. Kissed her temple. She didn't trust her voice as she spoke. "I suppose we ought to pack."

A scream raged behind her.

Cassie turned, seeing tears filling Star's eyes. "*You can't do this*!" Her voice was hysterical. "*You can't just give us up, Miss C!*"

Deidre started crying behind her, and Cassie's mother bent to pick her up.

The anger, the horror, on Star's face was unquenchable as she jerked her head around the group like they were complete strangers. Worse, like they were exactly what they were: bystanders watching as something she didn't understand happened to her—and not lifting a finger to defend.

Star bounded down the stairs, tripping on the bottom step. She pushed off Cassie when she reached out to help. "*I hate you! I hate all of you!*" came her hoarse voice, choking as tears streamed down her cheeks. The black, mascara-mixed drops splattered on her fresh red sweater. Cassie had let her borrow that mascara only hours ago.

Cassie pushed Kennedy into Bree's arms and ran.

The pastureland was frozen, slick to the touch. A cold wind ripped through Cassie's soft pink, billowed sleeves as she followed. Smoke curled from the neighbor's chimney as Star ran through their front yard, through the back of the carport.

"Star!" Cassie shouted, gravel driving into her bare feet. "Star! Stop!"

But Star climbed up the pasture gate and jumped over, running as though her life depended on it. The wind propelled her down the cow pasture like a kite about to take flight.

Cassie ran around the chicken gate, stumbling over stray corn. She pressed harder into her muscles. Ran faster.

The gap between them lessened with each step, with each stride Cassie took down the hill.

"Star! Please stop!" Cassie yelled again, close enough now to hear the breaths piping through the girl's lungs, to see white clouds forming at her lips.

Star's barefoot feet danced around a group of cows at the creek, her jeans splashing between rocks.

If Cassie stopped, if she slowed down, she knew what that would mean to Star.

The gate bordering the neighbor's land came into view, with nothing but the mass of shadowy, leafless woods beyond. Cassie watched as Star tripped and tumbled into the grass. She heaved herself up a foot, paused, then slumped back down.

Breathless, Cassie knelt beside her.

Wrapped her arms around her.

Above their heavy breathing the wind whistled through the grass, the creek bubbling as the cows lifted their heads on occasion then lowered for another drink. Smoke still curled from the neighbor's chimney, though the ranch itself, and the road, was some distance away. Frozen blades of grass were melting on Cassie's jeans, making the cold shiver down her spine. One toe bled from a sharp rock encountered sometime before.

Still, Cassie held on. And eventually she felt Star's breaths slow.

Then, suddenly, Star's breaths turned into sobs.

"Oh, Star." Cassie didn't let go, didn't move while Star released into the wind what sounded like the cry of a lifetime of pain. She clung tightly as the dampness soaked through her jeans, through her shirt, the cold settling somewhere far deeper, far further, than any physical thing could reach.

There were no words.

Three hours later, Cassie's heart poured all over the road as she stood, again barefoot, in the driveway. Deidre looked out the window as Rachel's car began to move. She held onto her doll with one hand and waved.

Cassie lifted her own hand. Waved back.

The living room was empty as her numb feet walked onto the tinsel-laden rug. Her mother and Bree stood beside the tree, waiting. Gifts and family members had swiftly gathered into their vehicles, giving space while the few who remained set about packing. The dining room table, once so full, lay empty, the mahogany glossed over with fresh polish while the fridge was stuffed with hastily Saran-wrapped plates. Everything had been put back in order. No trace left of the children.

No trace besides a long red streak of crayon across the couch.

22

Jett

If Sarah was any clearer about her interest, their names would've been written together in sky writing. Or in this case, knitted in a winter hat.

"It's just so cold out, and I was already making hats for the kids." Sarah shrugged. "The yarn was there so I kept going."

"These are awesome." Sunny checked his new look with the orange-and-white beanie in the mirror.

"Wow. Thank you." Jett didn't feel like mentioning that the yarn of the crocheted hat in his hands looked nothing like the pink of Dakota's or dinosaur green of Timothy's and Drew's.

He wasn't a crocheting expert, but he had a feeling the yarn couldn't have "kept going" from pink to orange. No, the fact that she had knit a total of three baby blankets, six pairs of toddler socks, and not one, not three, but five hats since the night Trina had come, unsuccessfully, to retrieve her kids six weeks ago was the writing on the wall.

Timothy rolled from his stomach to his back on the baby blanket, eyes widening as he surprised himself, as he did every time since the first one week ago. He started squeaking, and Dakota, seated at the dining room table, pointed with her pink marker, her cheeks stuffed with Cheerios.

"Timmy's fussin'," she declared, marker scribbled all over her hand. She went back to coloring her paper heart.

Sarah picked up the baby, placed him on her hip as though she'd done it a thousand times—which at this point, wasn't too far from the truth. She touched the back of Sunny's beanie, inspecting what appeared to be a loose yarn.

"I like the stripes. Nice touch." Sunny gave her a wink and she backed up immediately, turning to Jett.

Suddenly her perfume was washing up in his face. And as she tugged nervously on the skirt of the satin number she was wearing, Jett suddenly knew. It was time for a sit-down chat.

It didn't matter that he only had about five minutes to spare before having to jump into his truck for work. The woman—the poor, sweet woman—had made herself available too many times. Had twisted his arm with her baked goods and kid expertise and willingness to throw away her perfectly good evenings to watch the Bentley circus. It was time.

There was absolutely nothing wrong with Sarah. Just that, even after these two long months she'd helped him break in his new life, he still found he'd rather spend the evenings alone than muster up the energy to walk across the hall for a night of kabobs and wine.

Sarah deserved a man who'd walk across the hall for kabobs and wine.

Shoot. Sarah deserved a man who would *make* the kabobs and pour the wine.

She picked the hat up from his hands and reached for his head with a wry smile. "You, too, Jett. Don't scoot out the door before we get to see how it looks."

He gently took the hat from her hands and dropped his overnight bag to the ground. "Actually, can I talk with you for a second?" His eyes shifted to Sunny. "Privately?"

"Um." Her eyes skirted to Sunny and back to him, looking as awkward and uncomfortable as he was. "Sure."

Still hip-holding Timothy, she followed Jett into his bedroom.

"Don't worry, guys," Sunny called out, the twins now busy coloring the five o'clock shadow on Sunny's chin, their new canvas. "I'll hold the fort down here."

Jett quietly shut the door. Rubbed his hands.

"Sarah," he began slowly. This was going to be painful. There was no getting around the guilt he would inevitably feel after this. There was no getting around the hollow disappointment she'd feel after too. But he could try to minimize the damage. He just needed to cake on as many compliments as he could before throwing the knife. "You are just *so* special."

Sarah's soft blue eyes widened.

He hated that he was about to break her heart.

"These past months," he continued. "I don't know what I would've done without you. Honestly, you've been a lifesaver to all of us. Me especially."

She shuffled Timothy to the other hip. "Well, thank you, Jett. That means a lot to me."

Not enough. After this long of her sacrificial kindness, he needed to truly emphasize, deeply, how great of a human being she was.

He took a step closer. "Really. I've never met anyone like you. You're sweet. You're giving. You're the kids' favorite person by far." He laughed. "You beat me by a landslide." *C'mon, man. Don't limit the compliments to what she has done for you. She's more than a maid.* He threw out a hand. "And you look absolutely beautiful—stunning—in that dress."

She pressed her free hand against the waist of the fitted pink satin. "Oh. Well. Thank you."

"I can't thank you enough for everything. You've been like—" He paused, searching for the right words. "—like a mother to them. I only wish they could be so lucky."

Was it enough? Were those enough compliments to compensate for all the money she had spent, all the socks she'd knitted, all the evenings she had devoted her time?

Whether it was or not, she spoke. "Jett. I—I don't know what to say. You've never given me any indication you felt this way—"

"How could I possibly *not* feel this way? I admire you deeply. You're as good a human being as they come." He hung his head briefly. "I'm just so sorry that it can't go any further."

She looked uncertain, and he continued. "I sort of know . . . about your feelings."

The dresser rattled as she stepped back into it. Her voice held utter mortification. "You do?"

He hesitated. "Well . . . I'd have to be blind not to." Jett smiled, one side of his mouth lifting gently. "Who crochets a hat for a grown man? It's so thoughtful—and practical," he added swiftly. "But it does give a pretty big hint."

There was silence for a moment, and he kicked the floor. "Anyway, I understand if you don't want to watch the kids today—"

"No, of course I do." Her hand went protectively to Timothy, rubbing his bald head lying against her chest. She hesitated. "I mean, you are special to me, too, Jett. I'd do anything for you guys. But—" She looked to the door. "—I just felt like there was a connection between us all this time. It seemed obvious to you, too, right? This wasn't just one-sided?"

Poor thing. He thought she might have a hard time letting it sink in. Jett put his hand on her shoulder, squeezed softly. "I'm afraid in this case it was. But believe me, any guy who doesn't treat you like a queen isn't worth it. You are, truly, one in a million, and you deserve someone who recognizes that."

Sarah lowered her eyes. Huffed a little at the floor.

But just as his hand started to let go of her shoulder, she reached out and captured it in hers.

"You're right," she said. "I must admit I didn't feel this way toward you before, but if you can just give me some time, let me think all of this over . . ."

She paused again, her eyes darting back and forth from the door to him as if making a hasty decision. She shut her mouth. Lifted her chin, then squeezed his hand as she took a tiny, confident step closer. "Yes, Jett. I would absolutely love to go out with you sometime."

Jett's brows furrowed. "Wait. Uh."

She laughed, turning her head as Timothy suddenly cooed. "Seems Timmy approves."

In a flash he mentally thumbed back through their conversation, trying to find the missing link. He'd complimented her, told her that their relationship couldn't go further, that he knew of her feelings for him . . .

She ticked her head. "Really, though, I can't believe Sunny would do this to me. I feel like he's been leading me on for months."

Eureka.

"Sunnnnnny." He said the name entirely too long. He pulled his hand away and tapped his temple twice. Waggled his finger at her. "Sunnnny. You like Sunny. You thought he liked you."

"The man's been eating dinner over at my place for weeks. He always claimed he was avoiding you guys, but I thought, *surely*—" She shrugged, blinked twice, and smiled up at him with an expression that made him uneasy. "Never mind. It doesn't matter. What's important is what's happening now, between us . . ."

Now it was Jett's turn to step back, into the wall, the picture frame behind him pressing into his shoulder blades. "No, no. The thing is . . . you were right about the original plan. Sunny's a great plan. A terrific plan. Who am I to get in your way?"

"But you just said he's not interested—"

He shook his head, brain reeling like a wheel of fortune, waiting desperately for the ball to land on something worthwhile.

"My admiration." He closed his eyes and pinched the bridge of his nose. Then he slapped the wall. "My stupid, stupid admiration. I let it get in the way of two people I cared about most. Of course he's attracted to you, Sarah." Jett waved an arm out at her, circling her. "Who couldn't be? It's just . . . I knew, if I lied to you, told you he didn't care for you, maybe I'd have a chance."

He looked at her imploringly. "But I can't do that to you. To him. It's just not right to get in between two people so perfect for each other."

She took a step toward him, and with nowhere to go, he stood pinned to the wall as she rested a tender hand on his arm.

"That's so thoughtful," she whispered.

Jett nodded, uncomfortable by just how doe-like her eyes were as they gazed up at him.

"And yet," he whispered back, "not thoughtful enough. You deserve to be with the one who would never try to deceive you . . ." He paused before whispering the word momentously. "Sunny."

Frankly, he had no idea if Sunny was attracted to Sarah.

Frankly, he didn't care.

Before Sarah's affections could bounce back into his court he squeezed around her and opened the door. He held both hands up to her. "Please, don't follow me. Don't make this harder on me than it already is."

She bit her lip. Then nodded as though accepting his valiant offer to sacrifice his life for hers.

"Thank you," he said, and flew out of the apartment as fast as he could.

·♡·

Two hours into his shift, he was still vowing never to communicate with a woman ever, *ever* again.

"There we go, Donna Gene. Good as new." With Sunny at home either frying in Sarah's frying pan or melting in her crocheting arms, Jett tossed the tablet to the new guy and helped Donna to her recliner. As he did so, realization caught his eye. "Say. This place is looking pretty sharp."

Nick, the most recent member of the station, looked up from typing the medical details and glanced around the room as if he was not seeing the same thing Jett was.

The living room was still overcrowded with furniture. The house still smelled of old fried chicken. Several new cats lined the windowsill, rapping it with their tails.

But the number of soda cans on the table was down from pyramid-worthy piles to three. There were actually streaks in the carpet, as though it had been recently vacuumed. The sun shone nicely through their window.

Donna beamed. "I was wondering when you'd notice. Your sweetheart's girls have been coming up every couple of weeks, helping us spruce up the place." She lifted her gaze meaningfully. "You know, I haven't heard you talk about her in some time."

Some time. More like forty-four days, not that he was counting.

"Well, that's probably because I never spoke about her, Donna Gene."

"The girls tell me they are throwing a nice event for the

seniors on Valentine's Day." Donna crossed her hands across her lap. "Will you be saving me a dance?"

His smile widened as he shook his head, just imagining the woman who couldn't even pick herself up off the kitchen floor doing the Charleston. "Wish I could, but I believe I'll be working that day."

"Oh, just give us a little hint." Edie clasped her arthritic fingers together, her posture straight as a board on the couch. "Tell us you two's status, and we won't bother you anymore."

Jett smiled politely, but felt it fading despite himself as he opened the door. "Sorry, ladies. In the end, we realized we just didn't see eye to eye. Wish I had better news."

The women frowned.

"I'm sorry to hear that," Donna Gene said.

"And after all that hemming," Edie added mournfully.

Quietly he moved to the Medic 2–10 and turned on the ignition.

Forty-four days had passed since that terrible night when his hopes with Cassie were shattered and his future with the kids was made more or less certain. Something about defending his niece and nephews before Cassie's callous judgments, something about being forced to defend them when his sister wanted to take them back into a hazardous home, threw down the last shreds of his resistance and put him completely on board. Parenthood? He'd bought the ticket. Set sail.

He'd thought about calling Cassie that first week, when his nerves settled. Then after New Year's, when the holiday havoc had simmered down. But every time, he heard the tone in her voice when she'd so vehemently made her opinions on small children clear. Every time he lifted the phone he felt the guilt creep in, asking him why he would start a relationship with someone who wouldn't love his kids as much as they deserved. It was about them first, now.

That was when he knew, he guessed. He was really a parent.

"Bentley. You got a second?" Captain Ferraro pulled up beside him two days later, lunch plate in hand.

Up to his elbows in soapy water, Jett swiftly rinsed a sudsy cup and laid it in the drying rack. "Got nothing but time right now, sir. What's up?"

He took the captain's plate and dunked it in the sink half full of water. Captain Ferraro dropped his crumpled napkin in the trash can.

"I wanted to talk with you about the Skyline Drive situation. Again."

Jett started to shake his head. "I know, sir. I've tried talking to them—"

All conversations stopped at the alarm.

"Medic 2–10, Ladder 2–0–2, med 3 response . . . US 321 adjacent to Cliff Branch and Quality Inn Suites. Tractor trailer down. Multiple cars . . ."

The plate dropped out of Jett's hands, splashing into the tub of water.

"Move it, Loguercio!" Ferraro roared as he got caught behind Kevin and several chairs. Jett followed on the heels of the men, each running for the pole. Though they were fast every time, they were quieter now, more focused as they swung on their jackets and jumped into their boots. The garage door roared open as Jarod peeled the truck out of the station.

Multiple cars. Tractor trailer down.

A big one.

"Who's on jaws?" Ferraro said, casting a glance back, his grip firm on the roof while the engine swung around a set of cars.

"I will." Jett pulled on his gloves, hands still damp with soap water.

The pileup was considerable on both sides of the highway, cars jammed together as the engine made a slow turn onto 321. Brakes creaked on and off as the truck inched forward, the road so congested cars had but feet to turn.

"Come on," Jarod grumbled, laying his hand on the horn. He threw his head out the window. Laid on the horn again.

Smoke rose from the tractor trailer on its side, as giant and foreign on its side as a dead dinosaur. The bright-blue cab of the semi lay across another car, though too many vehicles blocked their way to see its condition.

Still, it didn't look good.

"*Come on*!" Jarod laid on the horn unceasingly now, while the crisscrossed maze of cars kept pulling forward and backward to get out of his way.

"Male in semi. Possible companion," the dispatcher updated as Jett's eyes searched the road for a way through. But wedged between the mountain on one side and the creek on the other, cars were pulling up onto what little sidewalk was available as they moved forward what felt like a foot a minute. "Honda Civic. Female. Multiple children."

"Honda Civic."

Jett squinted, trying to recognize what little of the car was visible. He jerked off his seatbelt. Pushed his head out the window.

"Multiple children."

Jett pushed himself higher out the window. Over a couple of SUVs he saw the top of the toppled blue cab of the semi. A battered, dust-ridden Honda as its pillow. Duct tape stretched across what was left of the bumper.

Jett jerked the door open and stumbled to the asphalt, breath caught in his throat.

"Jett!" Ferraro called. "What are you doing?"

"That's my family!"

They said you gave your all, every day, for this job. Until now, he had lain to rest easy every night, believing in all good conscience he had. But his legs didn't know the speed at which they could travel until this day, until this moment. His chest didn't know the capacity it could fill of car exhaust, smoke, and the crisp scent of creek, until this second.

He didn't feel his muscles throw his body forward, just felt the whip of wind in his face as he maneuvered through the maze of cars. He wedged himself through two cars spaced half a foot apart. Dodged around a driver stepping out of his car. The tractor loomed as he jumped over the front of the SUVs crushed against each other.

Suddenly the tractor let out a loud *creak*, and the cab dropped another few inches onto the car below.

Please, God. Please, oh, please.

Jett ran around to the side of the car. He took in the spiderwebbed windshield, glanced momentarily to the driver: the body leaning over the airbag, hair the color of Trina's splayed across the steering wheel. His stomach dropped as he turned to the mangled back door. Took in the leering cab directly overhead.

Bent down.

Stopped breathing.

One yank on the locked door and he whipped off his helmet. There was no choice. There was no time.

He smashed it once, twice into the window. Reached inside and unlocked the door, then yanked.

The mangled door resisted, and another deep *creak* ran through the cab overhead.

Jett reached through the window.

Sirens got louder as he bent inside, fumbled with a car-seat buckle. Face soaked in tears and blood, Drew wailed, reaching desperately for Jett. The buckles were flimsy but Jett reached the lock, pressed hard, and felt the release. Drew's head scraped against the quickly crumbling roof. His scream pierced inhumanely high as Jett pulled him through the window.

He started to set Drew on the ground, but suddenly there was Captain Ferraro, a firm hand on his shoulder. Kevin and Nick followed shortly behind.

"Give 'im over," Ferraro commanded, and Jett pushed Drew into his arms.

"Someone get Trina," Jett began to say, but Kevin was already taking off his helmet, was smashing her window.

Jett began to press his body through the small window

opening, but his coat pulled against him, his shoulders fighting to get through the rapidly declining hole. Swifter than he'd ever done in his life, he stripped off the coat. Shards of glass pressed against his waist as he levered half his body into the hole. Within the car's confines, everything felt eerily silent as he pressed his shaking hands against Dakota's buckles. Blood covered her blond curls, her head pressed forward against the weight of the crushing roof.

Another *creak* overhead as he pulled her limp body into him, the roof crackling like an empty plastic water bottle.

He fell to his knees with her in his arms, ripping one glove off with his teeth. He wiped away the blood-soaked curls. Wiped. Wiped. There was no movement.

Oh, God. Please.

The door pushed open in the cab overhead, and one arm of the truck driver reached over the edge.

"Don't move!" Ferraro yelled to the man above, now working with Nick to pull Trina out of the car. Kevin held tightly onto Drew while he screamed.

No time.

Jett's face turned to the crumpling inside of the vehicle, and he yanked Nick's ankles. "Help her," he said, his voice hoarse.

Nick immediately knelt down.

Ferraro yelled to Jett as they heard the roof crush several more inches. He grabbed at Jett's shirt. "It's not going to hold, Bentley. Wait for the jaws!"

But one glance over to the fire truck still five cars back was enough confirmation. Jett shook his head.

Ferraro gripped his shirt harder, watching the roof with

his calculating gaze. There was pain, but steadiness, in his words. "That's an order, son."

Jett blinked. Shifted his gaze. Saw the window and the crumbling roof and the menacing cab overheard. Saw it for a split second as Ferraro did.

And threw the arm of his captain off him.

"That's my *family*," he said and squeezed his upper body through the window.

His head pressed against the roof as he reached beyond the two car seats for Timothy. He reached blindly for the car-seat buckles.

Felt one click.

Then another.

A second later he tore Timothy's body out of the seat.

He felt his own waist bending under the weight of another deadly *creak*. There was no room left between his body and the door, not an inch, not a millimeter. It was now, with everything he had, or never.

Knifelike scrapes cut from his naval to his neck as he threw his body backward, not daring to stop, to slow down.

And then he was free. He stumbled back, cracked the back of his head against the pavement.

Silence.

His hands shook as he sat up. As he pulled Timothy up to eye level.

With relief beyond words, he watched Timothy open his mouth as the blood-curling screams began.

People pulled him up, but Jett just fell to his knees beside Dakota. He searched Nick's face for any clues, then dropped his head to Dakota's chest, his ear pressed to her heart.

He felt it.

The quiet rise.

The quiet fall.

Sirens closed in on them as the minutes passed. But he just sat there on the ground, one arm wrapped around Timothy, the other hand clasped around Dakota's small fingers.

Watched as two stretchers made snaking paths through the crowd.

As the boots of those in uniform circled Dakota and stopped.

As they lifted her.

The second stretcher passed carrying Trina. His eyes strained to take in his sister's injuries, then ripped away, unable to bear the pain of seeing them all. Another man in uniform walked beside the limping truck driver clutching his arm. Two more covered the body of another with a white sheet.

"Make way," a woman said, gripping the stretcher with one hand and waving as it began to move.

Holding tightly to Drew and Timothy, his own chest ripped and bleeding, he followed.

23

Cassie

It was the most incredible thing she'd experienced in her life.

Driving along the highway, mind halfway on the same muddled, melancholy thoughts she'd had the past month and a half since she'd walked away from Jett, since the girls had walked away from her, since everything she'd clung to collapsed. Brain suddenly snapping to attention as she noticed the car several vehicles ahead. The car swerving like an ice skater, gliding back and forth across white and yellow lines without regard. Swinging close, dangerously close, to the edge of the road. To the creek. Cassie had exhaled just about then, started to consider reaching for her phone to call the police.

Her foot eased on the gas, giving space between herself and the cars ahead.

She could recall holding the phone in her hand when she watched the car suddenly pass over the lines again, this time not stopping as it swerved into an oncoming truck.

An echo of screeches followed down the highway as she and everyone else slammed on their brakes. She heard the unmistakable collision of cars around her. But none of it matched the terror of seeing the looming semi swerve, tilt, and, almost as if in slow motion, topple across the highway. She could never erase the sound of what must have been eighty thousand pounds crashing, skidding until its mighty wheels dug into the side of the mountain.

Silence. Terrible silence followed.

Her legs had begun to quake so much she threw her car into Park, unable to trust her foot on the brake. She pressed her hand to her mouth, eyes widening as she saw the small car being crushed underneath.

She and everyone else, it seemed, waited. Motionless. Hearing the sirens growing in strength every moment.

And then, quite out of nowhere, there he was. His jacket whacked against her window as he ran past.

Without even realizing what she was doing, she gripped her steering wheel, watching him rip off his helmet. Saw the sweat of his forehead sparkle like crystal dewdrops. Heard the window cracking. And before her next breath he was pulling out a toddler, a little boy hardly more than two or three. The boy was thrown into the arms of another firefighter as Jett reached in again. She held her breath, eyes unblinking. The roof was crumbling before her very eyes as her grip on the steering wheel tightened like a python. The bloody little girl in her pajamas, her head against Jett's chest, limp legs. Barefoot toes. And then, one more time, unbelievably, he dove inside.

Her eyes jumped from the precariously perched cab to his legs, terrified, dreading every second he didn't move. There was a flurry of activity all around them, the fire truck at her ears now screaming at her to move, and she threw her car into Drive. As she pushed her way to the embankment, her eyes never left the scene, bated breath starting to make her head swim.

And then, with the shakiest intake of air, she saw Jett emerge. Watched feet so small they could fit in the palm of her hand kicking.

One minute later, the cab crushed the backside of the car entirely.

Jett was a hero.

She'd known that every day since their argument that she hadn't called him was a mistake, but the thing she didn't realize until watching him firsthand was that he was a hero. A bona fide hero.

And she couldn't let him go.

Pulling herself back to the present, Cassie shook out the pink tablecloth and threw it across the Ping-Pong table, shaking out her thoughts as she did so.

Meanwhile, Bree, with crossed arms, stared at her as though she'd watched every bit of Cassie's playback reel. "Listen, if you don't call him, I'm going to. I'll marry him myself, Cassandra Everson."

"You wouldn't."

"With the story you've told me three hundred times? Oh, indeed I would. And make you my maid of honor. So call him. Now." Bree turned back to the storage closet and threw the door open. When she emerged, she was carrying a stack of cups four feet high. "I'll get the ice and tea while you *call* him."

Oh, she planned to.

At the perfect moment.

Cassie split the cups and arranged them on the table. Then gave a look around the game room of the Haven, which the Leadership Club was transforming in a matter of hours into the Valentine's Dance venue of the century. Bailey and Keely were pushing the beanbags to the corner of the movie area. Savannah draped pink streamers across the line of computers. Caden stood in the corner, playing with Cassie's phone—or rather, playlist—where it was hooked up to one of the large, borrowed speakers.

Star, as she was always so keenly aware, was nowhere to be seen.

For the past seven years she'd watched for the magic minute when the girls left their schools and made their way to the Haven. At the window, at 2:15 p.m. every day, she'd waited for them to come. Like the rumblings of thunder before a heavy storm, she and her staff would feel the anticipation, the shake, before the magic minute struck. The sudden rush at the computer to finish that report, to send that e-mail, to put the finishing touches on that flyer. The dash to the coffee station for a refill, because it very well could be the last calm moment for the rest of the day.

Often Cassie couldn't stand it any longer and would step out the front door with her fresh mug, beckoned by the distant sound of the final school bell.

And oh, how they came. To passing cars, the steady stream of kids walking along the sidewalk from the schools meant nothing more than keeping an eye out for flying skateboards and mischievously tossed cans. But to Cassie it was seeing the march of forty-eight flames, each licking the air with its own spectacularly colored blaze.

Where was Star's blaze at that minute?

How bright was the light she was giving off somewhere in that town of Spartanburg, South Carolina?

Did whoever saw it appreciate it? Did they care?

Of everything that had happened that Christmas celebration morning, that was the most painful part of all.

She hadn't just lost the chance at being a mother. She'd lost a dear friend as well.

Bree and her mother had been understanding the past couple of months. Bree, specifically, had eventually realized the depth of her grieving and dialed down her snarky charm, letting Cassie embrace the time of mourning she had needed. Calmly taking the pink bow from her hand when Cassie found it beneath the recliner. Dragging her out to dinner when the house was so quiet it threatened to swallow her whole.

Cassie was grieving. Would grieve.

But what Bree didn't know was that Cassie was now ready. Not ready to move on from them, because she never would. But ready to make something else right in her life.

Everybody paused, hearing the tires turn into the parking lot. Cassie moved up to the window, watched one of her staff slide open the van door.

"It's time, everyone!" Cassie called over the room, cutting the overhead lights. The disco ball spun as can lights spotlighted it. "Hit the music, Caden. Let's go get them."

One by one, elderly men and women walked into the game room, each accompanied at the elbow by one of the girl leaders. Cassie stood at the door, greeting each one with a carnation corsage for the ladies and a boutonniere for the men. Meanwhile, she kept an eye on the parking lot.

When she saw Edie and Donna Gene through the window, abandoning walkers to steal into the arms of helpful gentlemen, Cassie's attention averted from the boutonniere she was pinning. A yelp brought her back.

"So sorry, sir." Cassie gave a distracted pat on the elderly gentleman's shoulder.

"What's going on?" Bree peered out the window.

Cassie's lips drew up in a sly grin.

Bree looked from her to the window to her again. Even with a pitcher of tea in her hand, she pumped the air. "*At last*! My scheming girl returns."

Donna Gene lifted the collar of a luxurious, plum-colored, floor-length evening coat, held onto the arm of her date, and winked at Cassie as she passed. Edie threw the head of one of the poor minks, strung together in a stole, over her shoulder.

"Ah. Bringing in the big guns," Bree said, watching them pass. "I already like this plan."

Music quieted while the teens gave a welcome speech, then came on again for the few willing to brave the pink glow of the dance floor.

And, then, while everyone mingled around tables, Donna Gene and Edie stole the floor.

Seniors bobbed their heads to "The Twist" while Donna Gene grabbed the hand of her date and twisted her way onto the floor. The girls especially cheered, several lifting their arms and clapping while Donna Gene swung her knees back and forth to the rock song. A moment later and she was unbuttoning her coat, dropping it beside her. One girl went to pick it up, but Donna Gene dropped a foot on it, continuing to twist.

And here we go . . .

Cassie felt herself clutching her hands together, hoping Donna could pull off her stunt as confidently as she claimed.

Suddenly, one knee buckled against another and she rocked sideways. Slowly, slowly, slowly, she toppled to her side on the floor. And, most conveniently, onto a very comfortable coat.

Everybody gasped. Caden cut the music.

Cassie threw her hands into the air as she strode forward. "Oh no," she said loudly and, to her own ears, a bit theatrically. "We're going to have to call somebody."

"We can help her up," someone said, and several teens and men gathered around.

"No, I don't think you're supposed to touch her," Cassie added swiftly, standing in front of the crowd. "I'm pretty sure there's something about that in first aid . . . leave it to the medical professionals . . ."

"Nonsense," an elderly man replied, his smile friendly and dentures pearly white as he reached down for Donna's elbow. "The things classes teach these days. You'd think they wanted us to believe we were as smart as a sack of potatoes. You're alright, aren't you, ma'am?"

Donna looked into his eyes and faltered momentarily, a dazed smile spreading across her face. "Oh, yes . . ." Suddenly she was placing her elbow on the ground and resting her head on her hand like she was posing for some beach magazine. The woman practically started batting her eyelashes.

Cassie coughed loudly.

"You can always try with those *nice* strong arms of yours . . ." Donna was saying.

Cassie coughed again, and Donna snapped back to attention.

Several hands grabbed onto her arms and shoulders, simultaneously working to raise her up. She lifted several inches.

"*Oooh*. It's no use." Donna fell back to her side.

"No problem. Let's try again," the man soothed.

They grabbed her again and began to lift. Cassie watched as Donna's body tightened, her face puckering.

"It feels almost like—you're pulling against us," someone commented between grunts.

"*Oooh*." Donna pulled her arm back and let herself fall to the ground. "Oh dear. I'm really, really stuck."

Cassie began pulling the hands off. "I think it's time we call the professionals."

"Are you sure?" the man said. "I think if we just—"

"No, it's no use," Cassie snapped back quickly. "No use at all. Isn't that right, Ms. Donna?"

"Absolutely." Donna Gene turned deeper onto her side, hiding one of her arms beneath her while flailing the other like a shored-up fish.

"Ma'am, if you could just—give us your arm . . ."

Swiftly, Cassie dialed 911.

"Nine-one-one operator. What is your emergency?"

"Hi. We have an elderly woman here who has fallen down."

"We got her up, Miss C! We got her—" Caden called out. The floor shook. "Oh . . . no, wait."

"State your address, please."

"Girls Haven. 109 East Cedar Street."

Cassie rattled off the rest of the answers to the operator's questions while Donna did everything she could to push the unruly, helpful citizens off and to stay down. By the time Cassie saw the fire station's response vehicle slow to a stop on the side of the road, Edie was beating people off with the heads of her mink stole.

"Go get 'em." Bree slapped Cassie on the backside. Cassie stumbled in the pink stilettos that, in any other circumstance, she wouldn't be caught dead wearing.

Well, well, well. How the tide had turned. Cassie worked to walk smoothly as she moved onto the same sidewalk Jett had met her on those months ago. Back then she had been the unknowing one, his offer of a night on the town received with as much gusto as if he was offering to pull a tooth. Tonight, Jett was the uninformed one. Tonight, it was her turn to ask for that chance.

In a very convenient, roundabout way.

Was she sweating?

As inconspicuously as possible, she began flapping her pink cardigan.

She closed in on the ambulance, the engine still humming. Rapped twice on the glass. Took a breath.

She had this moment memorized. A startled look as she told him how surprised she was to see him. A light joke about how she guessed he couldn't escape Donna Gene. It was good to see him. How had he been?

Wait. Pray. Hope he turned the conversation into a tread upon fresh waters.

Through the darkness of the interior cab she watched two people separate. A woman brushed quickly at her bangs as the window went down.

Cassie's mouth opened. Shut. "I'm sorry. I didn't mean to interrupt—"

The man, most definitely *not* Jett, waved her off quickly. "Oh, no, no, no. We were just . . . training." He threw an arm back. "And you see, Sarah, in situations like this, you may need to use the head-immobilization device, for stabilizing the head—" He motioned to his own. "—and keeping the neck secure." His hands went up and down his own neck as though she needed the visual. "We also might need an Entonox Analgesic Apparatus, or what I like to term *happy gas*."

Two seconds in she recognized his voice as the Haven's very own Santa visitor. Sunny, Jett's roommate. And just one of her many failed dates.

"I think some of your trainee's lip gloss got on your face there. Somehow. Accidentally." Cassie rubbed at her own cheek.

Sunny grinned, rubbing the shimmering red spot from his cheek.

"So . . . Where's Jett?"

But Sunny just shrugged, a meaningful smile—of what,

she didn't know—rising. "It's Valentine's Day. Like everybody else around here, he's got a date."

"Oh." Cassie shifted her weight, suddenly very uncomfortable in her heels. "Okay, then. Thanks."

Sunny called after her. "Wait. You guys need me in there?"

She waved him off. "No, we got it."

She turned her face back swiftly, unable to bear the pity in the other woman's eyes.

"Happy Valentine's Day, Cassie," Sunny called.

So he remembered her after all.

"You . . . too."

Crossing her arms tightly over her chest, she strode as quickly as she could across the sidewalk, averting her gaze from the sneaky, shadowy figures of Bree and several teens at her office window.

Jett had moved on.

Of course. What should she have expected?

The helium in her balloon of enthusiasm had depleted almost entirely by the time she yanked open the front doors and let herself back inside.

She shook her head to Donna Gene across the room.

Donna Gene frowned. Gave a single, white-flag sort of nod.

Then, to everyone's amazement, she rolled onto her side and stood with the agility of a yoga instructor.

"It's a Valentine's Day miracle!" she cried, gazing down at her perfectly smooth dress. A moment later she latched on to the man's elbow. "Now, how about we see if those strong arms can dance?"

Cassie watched the rear lights of the ambulance as it made its way down the quiet road.

Across the dance floor, beneath the slowly rotating disco ball, several couples began shuffling across the room. A few elderly men braved swinging hands side to side while their Tabor Cap Toes pivoted left and right by degrees.

"So?" Bree pushed a cup of sweet tea in Cassie's hands. Several of the teens surrounded them at the window.

"It wasn't him." Cassie's attempt at a smile was fading before she even finished her sentence. "Evidently Jett went on a date. You know, Valentine's Day." She gave a humorless laugh. "I shouldn't be surprised, of course. I'm not surprised. If I was being totally honest, I don't see why he wouldn't have jumped on the dating train right after me anyway."

The girls nodded uncomfortably.

Bree opened her mouth. "Cass—"

"Right now he's probably cozying up to her at some restaurant, and she'll be telling him all about the time she spends saving elephants from inhumane treatment in Thailand when she's not curing cancer. He'll say he wants to have babies one day, and she'll say, 'Oh, that's so convenient, because I'm unusually fertile.' Slip the ring on, they'll swing through *Drive-Thru We Do* on the way back to his place, and by the end of the night he'll have himself a perfect little Mrs. Bentley."

Bree shook her head. "That's not going to happen, Cass."

"Why not? Our town is loaded down with drive-thru wedding chapels. I almost got married last week when I mistook one for Arby's."

Several of the girls started grinning.

Cassie continued miserably. "But you know what really kills me, though? Now I'm going to spend the rest of my life avoiding calling the fire department. I'll have to rely on you guys from now on." She took a sip, her throat dry in her self-depreciating speech. "Cooking one day and my cabinets catch on fire? Nope. Can't call. My fuse box blows in a house that hasn't been inspected in fifty years? Can't call. I'm going to have to count on you guys as my bucket brigade for the rest of my life, just so I can avoid seeing him and that handsome face of his—

"If that's true, I'm going to need to take a look at this fuse box you're talking about."

Cassie's sweet tea sloshed over her hand as her stiletto wobbled. She felt her hand releasing the cup as Bree reached out to take it.

She turned.

There, standing before her very eyes, was Jett. Tall and handsome in a blue blazer, grey pants, tan leather shoes. Face clean-shaven. As stunning as she'd ever seen him, with his short hair gelled back.

And with him, three kids.

24

Jett

Dakota's Mary Janes dug uncomfortably against the bandages covering the wounds from his neck down, but he didn't dare move her from his side.

He'd taken pains getting them all dressed up, including a bath—which, given that those came about once a week, emphasized the importance of this moment. Even Dakota's neck brace couldn't diminish how beautiful she looked in her frilly pink dress with a bow that looked more appropriately sized for a sailboat.

He felt the tug of Drew in his right hand. Before Sarah had ducked off with Sunny she'd dressed him in a tiny gray vest with lime-green bowtie. Jett had reminded him only thirty times not to take it off on the car ride here.

From the stroller, even Timothy's small fingers played with the button on his own matching vest.

"Jett . . ." Hesitation and hope filled Cassie's eyes as she stepped forward. Her voice was soft, unsure, as though afraid he was an illusion. "I thought you had a date?"

Drew began to pull Jett's arm toward the candy table, but he didn't move. Jett's lips turned upward slowly, eyes flashing with a hint of mischief. "I do. I just thought you might like to join us."

Dakota lifted her head from Jett's chest, and he let go of Drew's hand long enough to swipe the curl blocking her view behind her ear. Even with several large unicorn bandages covering her cheek, she was beautiful. "I'd like you to meet Dakota. My niece."

Cassie lifted her hand, a look of recognition dawning. "It's a pleasure to meet you, Dakota."

"And Drew. Her twin brother." Jett tugged on Drew's arm, and Drew paused long enough to give a toothy smile.

Jett turned the stroller by degrees. "And this here is Timothy. Their little brother." He paused significantly. "And they're the children of whom I have legal custody."

Cassie paused as she bent over the stroller. She stood upright slowly. "In your custody, you said?"

He nodded. It wasn't easy to make that motion. For Trina, whom he and the kids had visited in the hospital every day since Dakota had been released, it wasn't easy. In the hours they had sat beside her, trying to comfort her—their mother. Through the grief of facing broken bones and charges of vehicular homicide for the death of an innocent forty-one-year-old man, it sure wasn't easy.

"Three kids."

Jett nodded again.

And Cassie's smile broke out like the rainbow after the flood. She looked down at all three. "Well, I must say I'm very, *very* happy to make your acquaintances."

She shook each of their hands, even the youngest, who continued staring at his button.

"May I?" she said, pausing with both hands on little Timothy's sides.

He paused, his tone holding the steadiness of the deeper question. "If you want to."

Nobody could've nodded faster than she had. "I do, Jett. More than you know."

She cupped Timothy's legs beneath the crook of her elbow, pressing his small body to her. "Is he hurt anywhere?" she asked, touching his back lightly.

"You heard?"

Out of the corner of his eye Jett saw Donna Gene and Edie gliding by, holding on to the arms of two elderly gentlemen. Edie lifted her maroon-feathered hat and waved.

"More than heard. I was just a few cars back."

Jett nodded solemnly. Even mention of that incident brought storm clouds overhead. "The boys had a few cuts. Dakota here gave us a scare for a few days but—" His voice sounded unsteady. He cleared his throat. "Forensics called it a true miracle. For her to come out with a neck fracture as minor as it is. For the roof not to have been crushed completely right away. Well, I was in that car, I know what an inch lower would've meant."

He wrapped his arm tighter around her dress, hating

even the memory of that awful day. For five days he'd sat in the intensive care unit of Monroe Carell Jr. Children's Hospital in Nashville, watching Dakota breathe. Waiting. Hoping. Praying. His life had been turned upside down the moment he heard the description of the accident over the radio, taking the stack of priorities in his life and throwing them in the air, over and over and over again, until they came down newly ordered and filed. And one of the top things on the list was being here. Now.

He bent down and whispered in Drew's ear. Drew, with several gleeful, Tigger-like bounces, hopped for the covered pool table full of candy jars.

A couple of girls followed him.

Jett resumed. "She was quite the snuggler before, weren't you, Dakota? But now I have a feeling I'm going to be wearing one of those kid carriers for the next eight weeks. Between Timothy and Dakota, I'll never see my arms again."

"Oh, I don't know." Cassie turned her head toward Bree and the others and gave them a look that screamed *Beat it*.

Bree just stood there, however, taking a long, slow sip of Cassie's tea, grinning like she'd landed the best front-row seat in the house.

Ignoring her, Cassie slid a heel his way. "You'd look pretty dashing in one of those twin carriers that straps one kid to the front and one to the back. Would make you a real winner with the ladies."

His brows rose, interest sparking his eyes. "Is that so? And here I was wasting my energy on pull-ups."

"Well, nobody's saying you should quit that." With

Timothy pressed closely to her side, Cassie's free hand drifted upward and grabbed his tie.

He grinned as she began to tug him down to her level, his smile dropping slightly as his focus moved to her lips.

But just as his face was an inch from hers, the flapping, tooting music of the jazz era stopped, replaced by an obnoxious ringing coming over the speakers and throughout the room. Everyone stopped dancing.

Cassie lifted her voice, her eyes still steady on his. "Cancel it, Caden. Press the red button."

The teen nodded and pressed the button, the beat of "Blue Suede Shoes" erupting once again through the room.

Cassie shrugged with a smile, her breath on his face. "Work. What are you gonna do?"

Dakota reached out from him just as he closed in again, grabbed for the string pearls around Cassie's neck. Jett swiftly grabbed her hand, stilled it as he leaned down.

He was close enough to feel the tip of her petite nose against his.

The music stopped again. The infernal ringing blasted the room.

He felt his tie slacken. Felt her hang her head momentarily on his shoulder. Then, she lifted her finger.

"Just one second. *One.*" Her grin was bright enough to light the whole room. "Stay right there. Don't move a muscle."

She moved quickly to the teen, who was now mouthing apologies, and took the phone, making as though to cancel it again. But as Jett watched her face, she stilled. Her lips parted. She yanked the USB cord connecting the phone to the speaker, and the room went silent as she turned her back to the crowd and pressed the phone to her ear.

"I kiss you, Uncle Jett." Dakota gingerly moved her neck up toward him and pecked his cheek.

Jett grinned and kissed her cheek back. "Thanks, baby girl. How about some candy?"

He moved slowly toward the candy table, sending furtive glances to Cassie while he loaded down a plate. She appeared very intent on whatever conversation she was having.

Food in hand, he moved over to Drew's table, where his feet swung merrily between a flock of teen girls. His fingers and mouth were covered in chocolate.

Cassie's head tilted down and, still clinging to Timothy on one hip, she began to nod rapidly.

"Sit here a bit?" Jett sat Dakota in front of a plate loaded with chocolate. "I'm going just over there for one minute."

Dakota barely registered him as she stared at the plate then shoveled a handful of M&M's as though they were jewels.

Jett swiftly went up to Cassie's side. She was nodding to the floor. "Well, I'm very glad she told you to call me." She spoke rapidly, the soft husk of the former moment long gone. "No, I don't need a night to think on it."

She paused, listening.

"I understand, and I'm prepared for that, sir."

Again, pause.

"Right now. I'll be there in three minutes."

And before he knew it, the phone dropped to her side, where she began sliding it against the hip of her dress as if expecting a pocket. When none magically appeared, she pressed the phone to his chest, followed a second later by Timothy. "I'll be right back."

She danced around him, then began to sprint across the room.

"Where are you going?" he called back. "Don't you want your phone?"

"Consider it collateral," she shouted back.

Suddenly she stopped and plucked the heels off her feet, then bent down, lifted Bree's legs one by one, and yanked Bree's flats right off her.

Five seconds later, she was streaking across the yard.

Jett sidled up to Bree, who was holding the heels in her hands like they were jellyfish. "What's happening?"

But Bree just shook her head. "I don't know. The klepto took my shoes and left."

They both looked out the window. "You know, I prepared myself for the possibility of her running away after seeing these kids. I just didn't expect it so literally."

For fifteen endless minutes he sat at the table beside Dakota, taking intermittent sips of tea, keeping his eyes on the door. Where could she have gone? What phone call could be so important she would, quite literally, drop everything and go? Not only deserting him midkiss, but the very program, the whole building she oversaw.

Just as his tea was at the dregs, the doors opened. His eyes lifted. He set his cup down and rose.

Light from the hallway shone upon her. Her biceps were taut as she gripped two young girls against her sides. Her formerly polished hair now sputtered out in different directions. Black smears just beneath the eyes hinted that she had shed tears. But while many in the room didn't notice all of these details, he knew one thing they all did see: she was positively radiant.

Cassie caught Jett's eye and walked through the gazing crowd, glancing often to the teen walking beside her. "Jett," she said when they arrived in front of him. She took a breath. Then another. "Allow me to introduce you to Kennedy."

The little girl peeked her eyes out from beneath Cassie's neck.

Jett nodded, unsure of what was happening. "Nice to meet you, Kennedy."

"And Deidre."

The girl outstretched her hand silently, and he shook it.

"And Star, one of my most wonderful Haven teens."

As he began to shake her hand, Cassie added, "And one of the three in *my* custody. Permanently."

His grip tightened on Star's fingers as his face jolted Cassie's way. "Three?"

Cassie nodded, the spark in her eyes just daring him to question her.

Couples swirled around the stuffy room, the scent of chocolate heavy in the air. Slowly, Jett took in the faces around him, from the syrup dripping off Drew's chin to the baby in his arms. From Dakota sitting so sweetly in her chair to the two young girls on Cassie's hips. Finally, to the teen standing, beaming, beside Cassie.

"So, what'll it be, Mr. Don't-Want-Kids?" Cassie said. "The ball's in your court."

Without waiting one second more, he bent down and met her lips.

There are moments in life when time stops and the objects in the world around you quiet into hovering silence. Important moments. Critical moments.

This was theirs. And he could practically taste the hay barrels, the porch swings, the summer's-eve sunsets in it.

Gently he moved his hand to her face, feeling the soft curls of her hair on his fingertips as he slowly stepped back. When he did, he saw the unmistakable twinkle in her eye.

"I'd say it's about time we joined the same team."

Epilogue

One Year Later

Timmy squirmed on Cassie's lap as she unbuckled her seat belt and looked at the menu board. Flurries dusted the windshield, blades methodically reaching up to slide them out of the way.

More dashing than ever in his black tuxedo, Jett cast a glance to Cassie, his voice rich with anticipation. "Ready?"

She took a deep breath then looked to the back two rows of the minivan. Car seats covered every available space, barring Star's seat in the captain's chair, where the green taffeta of her dress overflowed. "Ready, guys?"

The explosion of cheers was enough for Cassie to nod her head.

Jett rolled down the window, where a woman waited at the drive-thru. "One order of your Let's Just Do It, please," he said to her.

The woman smiled to the group, her eyes falling particularly on the infant wrapping his hands around the lace of Cassie's dress. Deidre rolled down the back window, and the woman saw the rest of the kids. She gaped. "My, aren't you all just the Brady bunch?"

"We're not the Brady bunch. We're the Bentleys," Deidre corrected, her grin a mile wide.

Cassie grinned back to her middle daughter, adopted legally a mere two weeks ago.

"Oh, then," the woman trilled. "My mistake. Well, for ten dollars more you can have the ceremony and a high-quality five-by-seven photograph to memorialize this special occasion."

"No, thanks," Jett said. "We have photography covered. And witnesses."

Jett jutted his thumb back. Her gaze followed and eyes widened. Sunny and several others were already spilling out of the rumbling fire truck behind them, car paint and string in hand. A trail of cars that looked a mile long led from the *Drive-Thru We Do* on the side of the parkway. Bree, her red hair high and polished in a bun, was already snapping away with her camera. Edie and Donna Gene, the kids' adopted grandparents, stood three feet off blubbering into handkerchiefs. In between sprays of hand sanitizer, Edie threw rice at the van.

The woman chuckled as she tapped on the register. "You know, I've worked in this business twenty-two years. And

I've seen a lot of unique people come my way. But now? Now, I've seen everything."

Three minutes and twenty-three seconds later, aluminum cans scraped along merrily behind the van, *The Bentley Bunch* in foam paint across the window.

Acknowledgments

Oh dear. I fear this is going to be like my wedding day again. Leave me to my own volition and I'm going to end up with ten bridesmaids, five quasi-bridesmaids, one twenty-two-year-old flower girl who rejected bridesmaid status in order to toss flowers, and several invited friends who really should've been bridesmaids and I've regretted not asking ever since. In other words, *how on earth can I squeeze all the wonderful people in my life onto two pages?*

For starters, thank you to my terrific family who has supported me all the way. My husband, who patiently encouraged me all the way back to the twelve-hour days I'd spent holed up in a room writing somewhere, not having a clue what I was doing but finding myself exclaiming, "I think I've stumbled into something, and I think I won't ever be able to stop." Well, Ben, sure enough I couldn't stop, and by your endless support, I never had to try.

My children, who lived out the real-life story of nearly every comedic scene involving a very adventurous set of twins and baby sibling. To every member of my extended family, especially my mother-in-law, who enthusiastically read my manuscripts *well* before they were ready. Multiple times. To my mother, who has spent my entire life believing in me.

To my agent, Jim Hart, who has been nothing but communicative, kind, and encouraging from the start. Thank you for taking me and my stories with you!

To the ACFW community at large, especially those author friends who eventually just became friends, especially *especially* my dear Betsy Haddox, Megan Gonzalez, Lauren Brandenburg, Annaliese Flautt, and Bethany Turner. This is a wild jungle we're bushwhacking through together, and I'm so blessed to be dodging quicksand and hopping rocks with you. To the multitude of friends and mentors who've walked beside me and encouraged me on this journey, both far and close, both online and through a pat on the back, thank you!

To Christine Berg, bosom buddy since those college days of listening to *Comptine d'un autre été: L'après-midi* on repeat, dreaming on the oval, my spontaneous dance partner, convertible-top-down, hands-in-the-air adventurer, and now friend in our greatest journey of all—motherhood—thank you for all the times you dropped life to read and edit and cheer me on.

To Cassie, who answered random texts for months about the ins and outs of Ripley's scuba-diving world. To Jarod, whose hilarious life inspires hilarious stories—keep on helping up those elderly ladies. To Linda Parham, who so kindly guided me through the DCS-related regulations. To Katie, Paige, and Laura, who read my first, very atrocious manuscript with smiles years ago—your collective ability to lie was both uplifting and disturbing.

To every YMCA teen I had the blessing of laughing to death with (especially the teen leaders!), and who gave me *such joy* every single afternoon you walked through those doors, thank you for being "my teens" for such a special season. Obviously there are many differences between Girls Haven and the Y program, but all the wonderful parts are inspired by you.

To God, for ignoring my life plans to so blatantly push me into something far greater.

And, of course, to the Thomas Nelson team. Jocelyn Bailey, you are incredibly talented, shrewd, and scary clever. My days would be utterly incomplete without your memes. Leslie Peterson, I'm proud to have you for my line editor, and neighbor! Thank you for being so gentle, professional, and insightful with my book. Kristen Andrews, you gave me the most wonderful book cover in the world! Paul Fisher, Allison Carter, Kerri Potts, Laura Wheeler, Amanda Bostic, Becky Monds, Savannah Summers, Matt Bray, Kim Carlton, and the incredible sales team—I once saw some of you walking down the hall together at ACFW, and time slowed, and everyone was smiling, and somebody flicked her shiny hair. You were The Plastics, yet in the very best way. And after a year with you all, all I can say is that you are even more organized, effective, kind, generous, thoughtful, *wonderful* human beings than I ever imagined—I'm just so glad to wear pink on Wednesdays with you.

Discussion Questions

1. Just when all of Jett's dreams seem to fall into place, he is forced to take on the responsibility of his niece and two nephews. Have you ever had to carry a friend's or family member's burdens? How did you react? What gave you the strength to carry on?
2. Some of life's biggest gifts come in the smallest of packages. What is a blessing in your life that initially came as an unwanted surprise? Why?
3. Both Cassie and Jett were affected by the foster care system, and statistics show that on any given day, over 443,000 children live in foster care in the United States.[1] There are many ways to help in this crisis. What is one way to care for someone affected by abuse or neglect today?
4. Both Jett and Cassie hold off talking about the kids in their care for fear of overwhelming the other person. Have you ever purposefully

....

1 "Foster Care," Children's Rights, accessed April 24, 2019, https://www.childrensrights.org/newsroom/fact-sheets/foster-care/.

miscommunicated about something to another friend, spouse, or employer in hopes of avoiding conflict? Has it ever backfired, and if so, how?

5. Star's reaction to the news that she could be adopted isn't cut and dry. What emotions might she be feeling? Why do you think she'd feel each one?
6. This book demonstrates the power of family, however they come to be. Sometimes family includes friends, neighbors, and other people patchworked into our lives. Who do you consider family? Why?
7. At the start of the book, we see Cassie struggling with unfulfilled dreams. Do you have a battle you find yourself fighting day after day, week after week? What encourages you to persevere? Whom do you seek for support?
8. Both Cassie and Jett make sacrifices for the sake of the children in their care. When have you ever sacrificed your dreams for someone else? Why? What was the consequence?
9. The support of Sarah and Sunny was imperative to Jett as he started wading into the waters of parenthood. Likewise, Cassie relied on her mother and best friend. Who do you turn to for support? Who turns to you when they need an extra hand?
10. Jett struggled with a roller coaster of emotions as he helplessly watched his sister battle drug addiction—something over thirty-one million

people around the world deal with every day.[2] What are some practical things you can do when you see a friend or family member dealing with an addiction?

11. In the first half of the book, Donna Gene and Edie keep the television on loudly throughout the day. Have you ever used technology to keep yourself distracted from unwanted feelings like loneliness or isolation? Why? What are healthier ways to pull those problems up at the roots?
12. Why do you think Cassie and Jett waited a year to get married? What sorts of things do you imagine they learned about each other in that time?

2 "Facts and Figures," World Health Organization, accessed April 24, 2019, https://www.who.int/substance_abuse/facts/en/.

Hey there!

Snag my free e-book when you sign up for my newsletter (full of extra content and fun insider news) at www.melissaferguson.com!

Hope you can join me!

Love, Melissa

About the Author

Melissa Ferguson lives in Bristol, Tennessee, where she is an assistant professor at King University and pens books that make her laugh and grow. She used to have hobbies like running and backpacking the Appalachian Trail outside her door. Now she and her husband are outnumbered, and her hobbies include diaper changes, chasing toddlers in parking lots, and admiring the Appalachian Trail out her minivan window while singing "Winnie the Pooh." She survives by Jesus, rom coms, and roughly two espresso shots a day. *The Dating Charade* is her first novel.

Join her monthly newsletter at melissaferguson.com
Instagram: melissafergusonwrites
Facebook: AuthorMelissaFerguson